THE HEALER'S LEGACY

by M MacKinnon

For permission requests please contact DartFrog Books.
This book is a work of fiction. Names, characters, places and
incidents either are the product of the author's imagination or
are used fictitiously, and any resemblance to actual persons,
living or dead, events, or locales is entirely coincidental.

Published 2020

Printed in the United States of America
Print ISBN: 978-1-951490-54-6

Library of Congress Control Number: 2020905855

Publisher Information:
DartFrog Books
4697 Main Street
Manchester, VT 05255

www.DartFrogBooks.com

This book is dedicated to Scotland, land of my Pictish ancestors and home to my heart. The Highland Spirits series was made possible through your history, beauty, and the generosity of your people. Thank you.

OTHER BOOKS IN THE HIGHLAND SPIRITS SERIES:

CONTENTS

ACKNOWLEDGEMENTS

Carl Dannenberger, my tireless husband and agent extraordinaire, who kept the business side of this series afloat and let me concentrate on writing. Love you, mo ghráidh!

Kathleen Kiel, my esteemed personal assistant, who has traveled with me to Scotland through the books and by plane more times than I can mention. My gratitude is endless.

Máiri MacKinnon, my Inverness language connection, who put the Scots in Scotland and was always ready and willing to share her heritage. You made the books sing.

Victor Cameron, guide and friend, who opened my eyes to the hidden wonders of his native land and gave life to the tours in the books. Thanks so much.

Steve and Mary Maclennon, my Highlanders for Hire, who shared the wonders of The Waterfront and the secrets of a real Scottish wedding. You truly enriched Colleen's adventure!

Kenny Tomasso, who helped me finesse my police investigations and murder scenes with the usual knowledge and enthusiasm—we did it!

GLOSSARY OF SCOTTISH AND SCOTS GAELIC TERMS

AGA – an iconic heat storage stove made of cast iron

Arasaid – a draped garment worn as part of traditional Highland dress for women

Blether – chat idly, chew the fat

Bogle – an ugly or terrifying ghost or phantom

Canty – happy

Dinna, Didna – don't, didn't

Dreich – dreary, miserable (weather)

Dour – relentlessly stern or gloomy

Feckin' jobs-worth – a person of power who is a nuisance or hindrance (in this case, the police)

Greeting – crying

Ghruamachd – in Gaelic, means 'grimness', or 'ghost'

Heid – head

Ken, kent – know, knew

Leery - odd, suspicious

Midgie - midge, a small biting insect that is the bane of Scotland

Radge - insane with anger

Skelped - beat, spanked

Targe – round wooden battle shield, covered in leather

It is hard to let go, to imagine alternatives, but you are bold with unknowing, you are ready to explore.

Terra Elan McVoy,

SCOTLAND, 1918

She sat alone in the dark room, arms wrapped around her knees, and wondered how it had come to this. Only a week ago life had been perfect. They had such plans... When he was well they would leave this place of sadness and death, go to the island of his youth and make a home far away from the blood and violence of war. They would have a life, a family. They would wrap themselves in the surety of their love, and they would live in peace.

But life is often cruel. It sweeps the innocent away like so much detritus on the shores of the North Sea, caring not for the grief of those left behind. It laughs at love, at the pitiful attempts of puny humans to make sense of its horrors. It rips at the edges of sanity until there is nothing left but tears.

They called it the Great War, but there was nothing great about it. Nothing noble to be found in the shattered bodies of a generation of young men who had set out with such high hopes of making the world a better place, only to return torn and battered, eyes empty and hearts crying for release. For so many, death was a welcome respite from what they had seen, what they had done, and what had been done to them.

But he was one of the lucky ones. His infection was clearing, he was on the way to a full recovery, at least of the body. Of the spirit, time would tell. Some never recovered from the horrors they had seen. But they had never met a healer with such an implacable will, and in this place of loss and pain he had found a love that healed his body and cleansed his mind. She was his soulmate, he told her, and it made all the difference,

And she, who had wanted only to help, to heal, had found her heart's meaning. In him she had discovered solace amidst the horror of broken bodies and dying men. She had talked to him in his darkest hours, had held him when he begged to be let go, and refused to allow him to give in. And their love had grown with his returning strength: their love, and their hope for the future.

And then he was gone. Like the winter wind that swept out of the Highland passes to freeze the traveler's blood and take away his hope for spring, he was carried away from her. He had looked at her with sudden terror as his throat closed and his breath stopped. He reached for her and she held him as his eyes widened and glazed when the life drained from them, leaving her clutching an empty vessel that used to hold her heart.

And the whispers had begun.

She gave him his medications, the whispers said, she had been alone with him. Something was wrong here, and she, his nurse, had to have known.

Poison! the voices whispered.

They came for her while she was weak and unshielded in her grief, asking questions she could not answer. They locked her in this room to wait for the law to come and judge her. And here she sat, dry-eyed, no longer caring what happened to her. He was gone, and there was nothing left for her in this life.

The door opened and a dark figure slid into the room. She hardly looked up as it approached, cloaked in black and gliding silently toward her.

"I don't want pity," she managed. "Please, just leave me alone."

"Pity!" a furious voice snarled. "You fool, it is not pity I have for you. You thought he was yours," the voice hissed in her ear, "but he was not. He was meant to be mine. He was helpless against your treachery and you turned his heart away from me. Now you will join him in hell, and the world will never forgive you!"

She gasped as a rope looped around her neck and pulled tight. This was how he must have felt in his last moments, unable to draw breath, fighting for his life. The difference was that she was not fighting. The pain was unbearable, but only for a moment. She drifted in a twilight world. As the room went red, then black, she knew only that she would have her wish. As she went into the darkness, her last feeling was one of joy. The voice spoke the truth. Now, she would be with him.

9

CHAPTER 1
THE ONE

"He's perfect, Kate! He's the one, I know it!"

"Fitz—" Colleen Fitzgerald's best friend's voice came down the line from Edinburgh, sounding as if she were sitting right here in Harrington, New Jersey, judging.

Colleen understood, but it still hurt. Why couldn't her friends trust her, just this once? How could she make them understand? She had caught the brass ring with this one, won the lottery, found her soulmate. All those trite clichés were true with John. If you wait long enough, true love will find you. He was proof.

"Kate, won't you just be happy for me for once? You found the man of your dreams, not once but twice! Can't you allow me my chance at happiness? Jeez!" Colleen wanted to reach through the ethernet and shake her friend. Still, she understood her hesitation and knew it came from love and concern.

Kate and Aubrey had been through countless phone calls like this one. Every man she fell for was the one. Every guy had been perfect, until he wasn't. Colleen was a complete disaster at love—there was no other way to put it. Like a defective cruise missile, she invariably honed in on the wrong guy, and her heart had been broken more times than either of them could count. They had decided that her love meter had to be broken. But she never gave up.

Colleen huffed in frustration. Love wasn't supposed to be easy; it was a tricky emotion for anybody. Not everyone could be like Kate, who seemed to find love without trying. The worst possible thing had happened to her, but did Kate give up? No, she'd gone to Scotland and found love again, and now she was married and living in a cloud of happiness in Edinburgh. Proof that second chances did exist.

Aubrey had known heartbreak, too. When Colleen and Kate met her only four years ago, she had been engaged to Harrington's resident heartthrob, Marco Russo. Even Colleen knew *that* was a disaster in the making, and when he'd broken up with her in a text message, neither she nor Kate had been surprised. But Aubrey had pulled up her big girl pants and recovered. She was the first of them to go to Scotland, and whadya know? She'd found Mr. MacRight and married him.

Colleen, left alone in New Jersey, had been wondering if maybe there was something about the air in Scotland that produced amazing men. Maybe she should quit her job as a nurse at Nesbitt General Hospital and caper over to the Highlands to test her luck.

Then she'd met John Clayton. Dr. John Clayton, to be precise. He was a resident at Nesbitt, and the moment their eyes had met over Mrs. Fenelli's bedpan, she'd known.

She shook herself back to the conversation. "Kate, trust me. I know I've been a screwup at picking men, and I know you and Aubrey laugh at me behind my back, but this time you have nothing to worry about. It's real. He's just my type."

"Okay, okay." Kate's voice held defeat. "I just love you and I want you to be happy. And you're right, I do worry. Your history with men hasn't exactly set the world on fire, you know. And I kind of wish you hadn't said he was your type. I mean, they're all your type, and how has that worked out for you?"

Colleen laughed. "I do know, and I love you for caring. I just wish you were here to meet him, then you'd understand how I feel. He loves me, Kate. And he's due any minute for dinner, so I have to go. Bye, sweetie, and give my love to Jack."

She put the phone down on the side table. *I can't help it if they don't trust me. When they meet John, they'll get it. Maybe we'll go to Scotland for our honeymoon, and I can prove it. You can't lose at love forever, can you?*

John. He *was* just her type: tall, blond, with those gorgeous blue eyes that melted her resolve when he took her in his arms. A part of her wondered why he hadn't been snapped up by now, but when she'd told him that he'd laughed and told her the life of a resident didn't give him much time for women.

"Until I met you, sweetheart." He'd kissed her and whispered in her ear, making her shiver and go weak in the knees. "When I first saw you I thought you looked like an adorable little doll playing dress-up. Nobody ever looked so cute in a nurse's uniform, and I've seen my share, believe me." He'd grinned at her and ruffled her curls. "Kind of like a miniature Barbie, you know? That lovely red hair, perfect figure, tiny waist and those big boobs—ouch!" He'd rubbed his arm with a mockingly reproachful look that turned into a smolder. Colleen couldn't remember much after that, except that it had ended in her bed and no clothing was involved.

Colleen smoothed her militant red curls. John loved her natural color. She'd been a hair dye addict throughout college, changing the color every time a new man came into her life. Blond for a while, and there was that horrible time with Doug, who'd told her he liked brunettes—best forgotten. Kate had rolled her eyes every time the color changed, warning her that a man who truly loved her would never insist that she change anything for him. As usual, she'd been right. So annoying.

The doorbell rang, and Colleen jumped to her feet, heart racing. She ran to the door and tried to regain a modicum of dignity before opening it to admit John. She took a moment to study him, wondering if she'd ever get tired of that face. He stood on her doorstep, a pot of flowers in his hand. Six months, and he was still bringing her flowers. *Oh, Kate, I wish you could see what I'm looking at right now!*

She took the arrangement from him and put it on the hall table, admiring the pink roses that he knew were her favorites. Always in pots, never a bouquet after the first time, when she'd asked him not to bring her any more cut flowers.

"They die," she'd told him honestly. "I love them, I do, but we work in a world where sometimes we lose a patient no matter what we do, no matter how hard we work to stop it from happening. It makes the idea of life that much more precious. So the idea of cutting beautiful flowers, knowing they'll die just so we can enjoy them for a few days... Well, somehow it just hurts. Do you understand?"

He'd enveloped her in his strong arms and held her, placing his chin on the top of her head.

"It's one of the things I love about you," he told her, his voice husky. "You care so much about life. You're so little, and yet so ferocious about healing. I think you'd march into the jaws of hell to keep one of your patients from losing the fight. You're amazing."

Now Colleen turned to John. "Thank you, honey, they're wonderful."

"No, *you're* wonderful." He moved toward her, a glint in those blue eyes, and she pushed him away laughing.

"Whoa, dude, stop right there. I know what that look means, and this time I'm going to be strong. I don't think we've actually eaten a meal on time yet, and tonight I'm making chateaubriand. It doesn't taste good cold, so back off!"

John put his hands up in surrender. "I don't know how I got so lucky. Sexy as hell, and the best cook in Harrington. Okay, I can wait. But not too long, please? I'm only human!" He gave her another one of those looks that registered somewhere between lustful and pitiful, but Colleen shook her head. Right now she didn't want the damn chateaubriand herself, but it had been a lot of work and they were going to eat it. Besides, it didn't hurt to make a man wait for dessert. She stole another look at him, and that was her mistake.

Later, as they munched on cold chateaubriand, Colleen's mind wandered back to the phone call with Kate and the thoughts it had generated. A honeymoon in Scotland. She was getting a little ahead of herself there, of course. They'd only been together for six months, and much of that was spent apart. The life of a resident was chaotic, and time off was sporadic. On top of that, he volunteered at a clinic back home in New York, so he was gone on the weekends.

"I wish I hadn't taken the clinic on, love," he'd told her shortly after they met. "But I owed my roommate from medical school a favor, and at the time it seemed like a good chance to visit family and take in the city life. I never suspected I'd have a reason to want to stay in Harrington all the time. But it won't be forever. Trust me. There's no place I'd rather be than right here, with my little Fitz."

She loved it when he called her that. Only her closest friends called her Fitz—it was a stupid nickname—but he had taken it up almost immediately, and from him it sounded romantic. His little Fitz. Colleen had always hated her diminutive stature, but he said it with such love that it sounded just right. She could put up with not seeing him as often as she wanted, because when he was there life was perfect. *He* was perfect.

So Colleen took on extra hours and spent her weekends reading, cleaning, and studying the bridal magazines she kept hidden in her closet. Never hurt to be prepared. And the nights they had together were all the more precious for their scarcity. He was a fantastic lover, and she felt like a queen the way he wined and dined her. Well, more wined than dined, to be honest; neither of them seemed hungry for food when they were together. They made love, and they talked.

He had shared the details of his childhood and his upbringing with her, telling her of his struggles as a young boy on the streets of Brooklyn. He came from a large family, four sisters and two brothers, most of whom still lived in New York City. He was the youngest and the first of them to go to college. Hard work and scholarships had given him this chance at his dream, and a letter from his mentor at Columbia had garnered him the residency at Nesbitt. Colleen was proud of his drive, and of the way he'd caught the attention of Richard Burbank, the hospital CEO, to become something of a protege. Probably why a resident was allowed to spend his weekends away from the hospital, she reasoned.

Burbank wasn't one to have favorites. He was a taskmaster, unapproachable and stern, but for some reason he had taken John under his wing. Colleen was secretly terrified of the great man. She hadn't spoken more than ten words to him, which was just fine with her. Nesbitt was a huge regional hospital. A mere nurse was unlikely to cross paths with someone on his level. Besides, she wouldn't find herself in his orbit because John insisted on keeping their relationship a secret.

"Burbank doesn't like fraternization between doctors and nurses, sweetheart. I don't care, but I'd hate to get you into trouble. For now I think we should keep what we have a secret—just between ourselves. Safer that way." He'd hugged her and winked. "After my residency is done, we can shout it to the heavens! Then the old man can go to hell!"

Colleen hated subterfuge. She wore her heart on her sleeve, and she could see no earthly reason to keep her love for John a secret. Who the hell cared if doctors and nurses fell in love, or got married and had ten children? There was life outside the hospital, after all, and what adults got up to in the privacy of their own homes should be their business! Besides, she'd never actually seen that rule written down, and she knew of at least two couples on staff who were married. John was just being paranoid, but since he was protecting her she didn't mind so much. She envisioned the day when they could announce their love to everyone.

A foot covered her own under the table, the toes running up and down her bare instep. She looked over to see a pair of blue eyes glinting at her. His gaze moved down her face and rested on the cleavage that was barely covered by the turquoise silk robe he'd bought her last month, and she felt her pulse start to race.

"Stop it! You have early rounds!"

"Rounds? What rounds?" The voice was a purr. He was her tawny lion, all muscles and grace and wild beauty, and she was lost. John stood up, rounded the table and swept her up in his arms. As he carried her back into the bedroom she thought, *Take that, Kate! I told you!*

Later she watched him get dressed. She never got enough of watching him—the long, lean legs, the golden hair curling over his chest. Funny, she'd never been a fan of body hair on a man until John. Love changed everything. She lay on her bed and studied every line of his physique as if there was going to be a test and she had to pass. Flat abs—check. Round butt—double check. Muscular arms—oh, yeah.

He turned and grinned at her. "I'll be back Sunday night, little Fitz. What's for dinner?"

"Me," she told him. It was their joke. Lame, but love made you delirious. Every time he left for the weekend, he asked her what was for dinner on Sunday night, and she answered the same way. And then she would pore over recipe books looking for a dinner they would eat cold.

He paused in her doorway. "Love you," he said.

"Love you more," And she watched him stride away into the night.

Colleen walked back into the bedroom and turned on the TV, flicking through the guide. Oh, good, they were doing a marathon of *Downton Abbey*. She'd seen every episode twice, but it didn't matter. She settled back to enjoy a binge-a-thon of one of her favorite programs. It would get her through to Sunday.

She thought of Aubrey and Kate over in Scotland. In the old days, the three of them had watched this show and their other favorite, *Outlander*, countless times. It had gotten them through innumerable breakups and heartaches—mostly hers, if she were being honest—and it was almost as if her friends were there with her, laughing and making fun of each other.

She missed them. The nights without John made her long for the days when they had mended broken hearts—mostly hers—with TV and Rocky Road ice cream, the best medicine of all. They were closer than family, and if it hadn't been for John, she'd have given in to loneliness and moved over there long ago. A nurse can get a job anywhere. But now her life was here, with her doctor.

Colleen sat up suddenly and muted the TV. Had that been the doorbell? What had John forgotten? The idea of seeing him again, even for a minute, had her racing to the door. Without checking the peephole, she threw it open.

"Did you miss m—?" She stopped.

It wasn't John. A woman stood on her doorstep. Tall and elegant, she fixed Colleen with a frosty glare.

"May I come in?" The words were polite, but they sliced through the air between the two women like knives.

"Who are you?" Colleen asked, confused. She'd never seen this woman before; she'd have remembered her. She was gorgeous.

Model thin, she was dressed in a suit that had to have cost the equivalent of Colleen's annual salary. Her hair was swept into a chignon that should have looked severe, but somehow didn't. She was beautiful from her smooth, dark hair to the narrow feet encased in Ferragamo pumps that probably cost more than a nurse made in a week. Cold blue eyes pinned Colleen where she stood as if she were a bug.

"Oh, I'm sorry," the woman said. "I am Veronica Burbank Clayton, and you must be the whore who is screwing my husband."

CHAPTER 2
DOWN THE RABBIT HOLE

Colleen stood as if paralyzed. Her mind was a miasma of images and sounds, none of them connecting. Nothing made sense. John, his blue eyes lit with love. His touch, his voice. Her body's response to the wonder between them. Kate's face swirled into her memory, asking if she was sure. Aubrey's soft words, already taking on a Scottish lilt, telling her to be careful.

And the woman who stood in front of her, patrician nostrils flared and eyes glinting maliciously. Saying she was John's *wife*. It wasn't possible.

She backed away from the hatred in those eyes, and the woman brushed past her and into the apartment, slamming the door behind her.

"Sit down." The woman spat out the words and took a seat in Colleen's favorite chair, back ramrod straight. As if propelled by an unseen force that had taken command of her body, Colleen stumbled to the sofa and fell into its plush cushions. She felt bone-less, held up by invisible strings: a marionette with no will of her own.

"I knew something was going on." Veronica leaned back and crossed her legs, her posture relaxed and elegant. "I suspected he was seeing someone. But I must say, I never expected *this*." She sat up again and her eyes raked over Colleen's body. "I never thought he'd fall for a Little Orphan Annie with tits."

Colleen couldn't process the words—her focus was in shards. Then her world righted itself and relief flooded her mind. Of course, this was all a mistake. The woman had gotten the wrong apartment.

Her next words dispelled that notion.

"Where did you think he was, all those weekends in New York?" she asked. "It was a condition of our marriage, you know. Weekends in our Manhattan apartment, social engagements where we could be seen by those who matter. Keeping up appearances. Taking care of...business."

Colleen struggled to remember how to speak. "Th-that can't be...I didn't..."

"Oh, come now, of course you knew. Although for the life of me, I can't imagine what you thought you'd get out of it. A man like John would never settle for some little...*nurse*. My father is grooming him for bigger things. He's going to be a surgeon—we haven't decided what specialty yet, probably cardiology or neurosurgery. He has the brains, and I have the money. We're a team." She sat for a minute as if waiting for Colleen to say something. "That was it, wasn't it? You thought he had money." At Colleen's gasp of outrage, she held up a hand. "Of course you did. Well, the joke is on you. He has nothing. The money is mine." She shrugged and went on. "Harrington is just a way station, a chance for John to learn under the guidance of my father."

"Your-your father?"

"Yes, didn't I make that clear? My father is Richard Burbank. the CEO of the hospital you work in." She paused, and when she spoke again her voice was a low hiss, filled with venom. "The hospital you *used* to work in, I should have said." She smiled, a beautiful smile that didn't come close to reaching her eyes. "When I'm finished, you'll have no job, no license, no reputation. Maybe you didn't know what you were getting into when you tried to snare my husband, but you are going to find out. No one takes what is mine. I am going to ruin you."

The walls were closing in. Colleen had no words to offer this horrible woman who was taking her life away from her. All she could think of was John. *He's the one*, she had told Kate. *You're perfect*, he had whispered. *My little Fitz*. It was all a lie. She closed her eyes. It didn't matter what this woman said or did, she just wanted to curl up and die. *All a lie.*

The door opened and closed softly, and Colleen was alone. After an eternity, she walked stiffly, like an elderly woman, into the bathroom and threw up. Then she crawled into her bed, the bed that had held such love just an hour before, and cried until she was empty. She stared at the dark ceiling until daylight crept through the curtains, then she discovered that she did have more tears, after all. Was it possible for that much pain to exist in one body, or was she making more as she went along? She knew she hadn't dreamt it, because she hadn't slept. She might never sleep again.

Saturday inched by, and she didn't get up. At four in the afternoon, her phone rang. The display read *Mr. Right.* She didn't answer—couldn't answer. Twice more it rang, and then silence.

By Sunday morning she had decided that she was never getting up. She was never going back to work. She was most definitely never calling Kate or Aubrey and telling them that she'd done it again. It was too much to bear.

By afternoon the pendulum had swung back and she was sure it had all been in her mind, just a horrible nightmare. John would be here soon. She'd better get up and get dinner started. But first just a few minutes of rest, to get herself back to normal.

Colleen came out of a dark swamp of half-sleep at the sound of the doorbell. She felt sluggish and sick. Without thinking, she stumbled to the door and opened it. John stood on the step, and at the sight of his ravaged face, the truth hit home. It was true. All of it. Fresh tears welled and ran down her cheeks.

"Don't!" His voice reached through her grief as he stepped through the doorway and reached for her. "Please, just let me explain!"

Her head snapped up, and rage replaced grief. She backed away from his outstretched arms and crossed hers over her chest.

"Explain? Explain what? That you forgot to tell me you were married? Get out!" She turned her back on him and threw herself down on the couch, face in her hands. She couldn't look at him. She wanted him to leave before she lost the last shred of dignity she had left. She wanted him to stay and tell her it was all a silly mistake.

She felt him sit beside her, fold her shaking body into his chest. A distant part of her, the part that was eternally optimistic, wanted to believe that he could make it all right again, and for a moment she allowed herself to melt into his embrace. And then she remembered the hateful look of that woman who had called herself—what was it? Veronica. Veronica Burbank *Clayton*. John's wife. Colleen wrenched herself out of his arms and backed away.

"I love you, Fitz. I do. I never thought I'd find anyone like you." He spoke rapidly, as if afraid she would disappear if he didn't get the words out fast enough. "We're not together, Veronica and I. No matter what she told you. We live apart, and we barely see each other. I don't love her." His clear blue eyes, those eyes she loved so much, pleaded with her to believe him.

Colleen heard herself speaking in a voice she barely recognized. "Are you getting a divorce?"

His head dipped. When he looked up again, she already knew what he'd say.

"I—I can't. She won't give me a divorce. She says she needs me. Window dressing, she calls it." His voice was bitter. "She has all the money. If I divorce her, she'll ruin me. Her father will ruin me. I won't finish my residency, I'll never be able to practice medicine. It's all I ever wanted, Colleen!"

Colleen. Not *little Fitz*. His words pounded into

27

her like lead weights, each one gouging a new hole in her heart. *All I ever wanted.*

I thought I was all you ever wanted.

She'd lost him, and he didn't even know it.

"And what do you expect me to do about all of this?"

He blinked. *Ah, you haven't thought about that, have you?*

"Don't say it." Her voice was soft. "Don't you dare suggest I become the whore she thinks I am." Colleen stood up, wrapping her arms around herself to keep the cold at bay. For the first time, she realized she was still wearing the skimpy turquoise silk robe she'd had on since Friday night. The one he'd given her. "I think you should go now."

John stared at her, and then he stood up. He moved toward her, and she backed away. His arms dropped to his sides. Head low, he turned and walked away from her, out of her apartment and out of her life.

Early Monday morning, Colleen made herself presentable and went to the hospital, reporting to the third floor geriatric care wing. Just because her life had fallen apart, there was no excuse to take it out on her patients. Mrs. Abernathy waited for her each day, and would take her medication from no one else. Mr. Carbone looked for her with hope in his tired eyes, knowing that she would tell him again who he was without making him ask. She was responsible for these people. Nursing was more than a job; it was a calling.

"Are you all right, Nurse Colleen?" Mrs. Abernathy's voice was kind. Her old eyes saw everything, despite her age and failing body.

"No, not really." Colleen was always honest with Mrs. A. Just because she was old didn't mean she deserved to be patronized or placated. Most of the staff used the royal *we* with the patients in geriatrics. *How are we feeling today? Are we taking our meds, dear?* But Colleen knew they hated it, because they'd told her so.

"What's the matter?" The faded blue eyes held hers, and it was all she could do not to throw herself into the old woman's arms and let it all out.

"Oh, just a romantic problem," she said, over the lump in her throat. "I'll be all right." *I'll never be all right. Never.*

"Oh, sweetie, I'm so sorry. Any man who could hurt you deserves to be drawn and quartered." She nodded her white head, her expression fierce. "And then hung." Despite her pain, Colleen smiled. Mrs. Abernathy was a Scot, and under her feeble shell was a warrior as stout as any of her Pictish ancestors.

The smile vanished as quickly as it had come. Scotland. The new home of Aubrey and Kate, whom she hadn't called yet. She knew she'd have to sometime, she owed it to them. They'd never kept secrets from each other, never allowed bad news to come between them. And her situation was no worse than anything that had happened to them before.

She was the one who'd had to call Kate to tell her that her husband had been killed in a construction accident. She had supplied the wine and the Rocky

Road ice cream when Aubrey's ass of a fiancé had dumped her in a text message to go back to his high school sweetheart. And she herself had been through innumerable breakups. They had always been there for each other. She knew they wouldn't judge.

But this was different. Colleen had been so sure John was her knight in shining armor. He did love her; she believed him when he said it. Just not enough. Not enough to fight for her, not enough to get that armor rusty.

Mr. Carbone's anxious smile waited for Colleen. He was suffering from dementia, and some days he struggled to remember who she was. But his biggest fear was not remembering his own name, so she always began their conversations with it.

"So, Mr. Carbone, are you up for a walk?" His gratitude was a balm to her soul. This was where she was meant to be, with these people. Who the hell cared if romantic love swept away from her like the tide at the shore? These people loved her, needed her. It would have to do.

"Nurse...C-Colleen." She grinned at him and his face relaxed into the sweet smile that reminded her of Aubrey's old Scot, Angus. Nothing wrong with *that* one's brain, but he was just as loveable as her wonderful Italian gentleman here.

A lot of the nurses were impatient with the elderly patients, and many asked for assignments in maternity, pediatrics, or even the emergency room, where life was more exciting.

"I don't mind the accidents, even though they're scary and sometimes sad," one nurse had told her.

"But those old people! Just waiting to die, most of them. And they smell. It's depressing."

It wasn't depressing to Colleen. Her patients had so much history in their minds, and so much joy in sharing it. Even Mr. Carbone, who couldn't remember his own name, could recite the names of every soldier in his platoon in the Korean War. He had been a history teacher, and he knew all the major battles and the reasons for their success or failure. And Colleen listened. It was something she did well, and her patients loved her for it.

She was gratified to realize, as she took her break in the staff lounge, that she hadn't thought about John more than fifty times during the day. Maybe tomorrow it would be only thirty-five, and the next day only twenty. As long as she didn't see him, she'd get through. If only she weren't so tired! She rested her head on her arms.

"Nurse Fitzgerald?" The voice came from far away, floating into her consciousness like a cloud. She brushed it away until the voice grew louder, more impatient. "Nurse Fitzgerald? Colleen!"

Her head came up and she fixed bleary eyes on the face frowning before her. The head nurse on duty. "I-I'm sorry! I guess I was really tired. What time is it? Am I late?"

"Never mind that—you're wanted in Dr. Burbank's office." Her voice held a question. No one was summoned to Burbank's office, unless there was trouble. Colleen felt an icy finger of dread run down her spine.

I am going to ruin you.

The journey to Burbank's fifth floor office took

forever. Arriving outside the door with *Richard Burbank, CEO* etched in filigreed letters on frosted glass, she stopped, unable to take another step. There *was* something worse than heartache. It was fear, and it was holding her immobile in its grip. She felt suddenly nauseous. Colleen took a deep breath, forced her stiff fingers to turn the knob, and entered.

"He's waiting," the secretary said, her voice impersonal. "Go on in."

Burbank looked up as she entered, her footsteps silent on the deep red plush carpeting that looked so much like blood covering the floor.

"Sit down, please, Miss Fitzgerald." Burbank watched her, his face impassive, as she sank into the chair in front of his desk. He consulted some papers on his desk.

Could he hear her heart pounding? Surely he wouldn't be so petty as to punish her for a romantic mistake. Even if John's wife complained to her father, he was much too busy to involve himself in gossip—wasn't he? John would stand up for her and take the blame, she knew that much about him. It had to be something else, but for the life of her she couldn't figure out what.

And then he told her.

"You have an exemplary record here, Miss Fitzgerald. Not a single disciplinary infraction, almost perfect attendance, and your coworkers speak highly of you." He stopped and stared at her, his eyes dark and bottomless. Cold, like a snake's eyes. "Which is why I cannot understand why you would steal medication from your own patients."

Colleen jerked in the chair. "W-what? I never—I wouldn't—"

"You were seen!" he snapped. "I don't have time to listen to excuses and lies. Someone saw you taking medications and secreting them in your bag. You are a thief, Miss Fitzgerald, and maybe worse. I can't have such a person working around helpless patients."

"B-but—"

"You will leave the hospital at once. Someone will escort you. If you go without a fuss, I will not press charges. You'll be able to keep your license. But know this—your reference will reflect your...activities. I hardly think you will ever work as a nurse again, not in any accredited hospital. I strongly urge you to think about a different career, Miss Fitzgerald. And get yourself some help." His dark eyes glinted as he pressed a button and an orderly came in. "Please escort Miss Fitzgerald to her car, and make sure she leaves. She will not be returning."

Without another look at her, he focused back on his papers. In a daze, Colleen stood up and stumbled down the hall to the elevator. An orderly led her through the lobby and out to the parking lot.

She had been wrong. Losing John was not the worst thing that could happen to her. Not even close.

Colleen had no idea how she got home. In the kitchen, she got out the bottle of wine and poured. She drank the first glass in two gulps and poured another. Somewhere between the third and fourth glass, she fumbled for her phone and dialed Kate's number.

CHAPTER 3
I SEE DEAD PEOPLE

A thin moon hung over the Highlands, creating long shadows on the lawn. Misshapen and menacing, they seemed to slink ever nearer to the castle like phantoms. A mist left over from the day's rain rose from the grass to form wraiths—slender, undulating forms that seeped into the watcher's soul and turned it to ice.

Simon Reid pulled himself out of his trance and turned away from the window. God, this place gave him the willies. Balfinnan House, a hall castle with its very own ghost! Whatever had possessed him to accept a job here, of all places? Skulking around at night? Well, in his defense he had been hired as the janitor, but a lot of people did more than one job here and nobody seemed to mind. Still, night watchman? He was the worst possible person to take on that job. Afraid of his own shadow, his ma had told everyone. Maybe "a little light in the heid," his uncle Martin had said, holding his finger to his temple while the others nodded. As if Simon wasn't right there in the room.

Well, there was nothing wrong with his head. Ghosts were nothing to mess with. There was a reason they had stayed behind after they were dead, instead of going on to heaven like good Christian folk. Something bothered them, and a bothered ghost was never a good thing. He knew that better than most.

Simon saw ghosts. No one believed him, of course, but he did. Like in that American movie, where the kid said, "I see dead people," and the man he was talking to turned out to be dead and didn't know it. Simon had rented that one and watched it loads of times. It wasn't just a movie to him. It was so like his life that he'd checked the credits to make sure he wasn't in them.

He'd seen ghosts ever since he was a little kid, when his uncle had appeared to him after the funeral and asked him to tell his aunt he loved her. He'd told her all right, and that was when the jokes about his mental capacity had started. *Poor Simon, off again. The lad just can't help it. Afraid of his own shadow, he is. Thinks he sees bogles.*

Well, just because he was afraid didn't make it untrue, did it? Being afraid helped you survive in a world with things like criminals and spiders and creatures that only came out at night. And now somehow he'd wound up here, in this ancient castle with secrets that were all too real. Maybe he *was* touched in the head, after all.

He'd seen Balfinnan's ghost the first week he was there. The Grey Lady, they called her. A young woman in a grey dress like nurses used to wear. Simon knew that Balfinnan House had been used as a hospital in World War I—maybe she had worked here then. She hadn't raised the hackles on his neck like ghosts sometimes did, but maybe that was because she was busy and didn't see him watching her.

She had been standing beside old Mrs. Muir's bed, just watching the old lady as she struggled to breathe. Reaching out, as if she wanted to help her. He would never forget the look on her pretty face—yes, she was pretty, even all wispy and faded and everything. The only color was in her eyes, bright blue eyes that seemed to hold all the sorrow in the world. Huge and sad in a face whiter than the doilies in the great room of the castle. As if something awful had happened to her to ruin her belief in heaven. And maybe it had; she was dead, after all, and still here.

Mrs. Muir was dying; everybody at Balfinnan House knew that. She was ninety-four and her heart had been failing for a long time. Flora Kemp, the nurse on duty, had confided to Simon in a whisper that Mrs. Muir was "going to a better place, she was, and soon." So it wasn't that surprising to see a ghost standing by her bed, really. And sure enough, the next morning Mr. Anderson had gathered the staff together and told them in a solemn voice that Mrs. Muir had died in the night. No one was surprised.

What was surprising, Simon thought, was that he had seen the ghost twice more since, standing at the bedside of someone who was near death. He told no one—Simon had learned to keep his thoughts to himself lest someone laugh at him, or worse, give him the sack.

Simon loved this job. It was a huge surprise to him that he did, since every shadow scared the living shite out of him and he spent a lot of his time looking back, sure something was following him. It was weird that, in spite of the spiders and shadows and ghosts, he felt at home here more than he'd ever felt anywhere before.

The nurses liked him and told him things they felt embarrassed to share with anyone else. Mr. Anderson treated him with respect and once had actually spoken to him personally. Yes, the head of the whole castle had asked *him* what he thought about the lights in the hallways at night. And when Simon had said he thought the patients felt comfortable with the low lights, Mr. Anderson had nodded and *thanked* him for his opinion.

Simon would have done just about anything for Mr. Anderson. He was tall and handsome, with dark blond hair and calm eyes that shone a clear blue. He was kind to everyone, treated the visiting doctor and nurses with the same level of respect as the lowliest staff worker—which was probably him. The residents loved Mr. Anderson, too, and looked forward to his visits like children waiting for chocolate.

Mr. Anderson wasn't a doctor. He owned the castle; it had been in his family for generations and it was he who had opened it up again as a nursing home. He was the CEO; it was etched on his office door. Simon didn't care about all that, and certainly no one would discuss such things with him, but anyway it wasn't the boss's credentials that drew the young janitor to him.

It was the way Mr. Anderson seemed to know just what every elderly patient needed to feel alive and cared for. He knew they just wanted to matter. Many of them had been placed here and forgotten by their families, as if being old was a disease or an embarrassment. No one seemed to want to listen to them anymore, to hear the wonderful stories they could tell. Except for Mr. Anderson and Simon. And the Grey Lady.

As he walked along the hallways of Balfinnan House, Simon checked for anything that might be out of place. Nurses passed him without speaking, sometimes looking right through him as if he weren't even there. Simon didn't mind, he was used to it.

It was his gift, if you could call it that. He had known for a long time that he had the ability to blend into his surroundings, to *disappear*. His thin frame, limp brown hair and hazel eyes, his pale face, everything about him projected silence. He didn't do it on purpose, it just happened. Unless he spoke, people had the tendency to forget he was in the room...and that was fine with him. It had always been that way.

Simon turned onto the second floor hallway, and there she was. The Grey Lady. She stood beside of Mr. Burns's bed, her white face etched in sorrow, startling blue eyes focused on the old man's face. As he watched, she reached out a hand as if in benediction and placed it on the older man's forehead. Mr. Burns's eyes were open, his raspy breathing loud in the silence of the ward. Simon saw his features relax and a soft smile cross his wizened old face. After a while, Simon realized that the sounds of breathing had stopped. Mr. Burns's eyes remained open and staring, but the ghost was gone.

No...the *Grey Ghost* was gone, but there was still something in the air. He couldn't see anything, but he felt it. Blacker than the shadows it was, floating just out of reach of his senses. It radiated cold and something so vile that Simon was pinned, frozen in the doorway.

He was more frightened than he had ever been in his life, and that was saying something. This was a feeling he'd never encountered before, something beyond his experience. He had never been afraid of the dead; the living gave him enough trouble. But this—this thing—was different. He knew, without understanding why, that it was pure evil, and that it meant harm to someone at Balfinnan.

And then, as quickly as it had appeared the sensation was gone, leaving a feeling of utter dread in its wake. Simon remained paralyzed for long minutes. Instinctively, he knew that this *thing* was different. He also somehow understood that it thought no one knew of its presence. It didn't know about Simon. He would never be able to explain how he realized that his life depended on things staying that way.

But he would keep watch, and he would stay invisible. It was, after all, what he did best.

CHAPTER 4

BALFINNAN HOUSE

hat the hell am I doing here?

Colleen looked around the sitting room of Nessie's boarding house, taking in the old-fashioned velvet couch, the tartan pillows, the ancient television set in the corner—and the Owls.

Aubrey had been on point with her description of the four people staring at her. They sat in their customary places around the room—Gladys Chesher held court in the center of the large couch, her corkscrew white curls bouncing and her taciturn son Ronald seated next to her as always, former dancer Maxine Deyeaux ensconced in her throne-like chair next to the fireplace, tapping her foot to the invisible music in her head, and Old Harry Campbell peering from behind his ever-present newspaper.

She'd met them all before, when she'd stayed here for short visits. But now they were *her* housemates.

This was the first time their attention was focused on her. They were all staring at her like birds of prey, waiting for a tasty morsel to appear so that they could swoop down on it and devour it whole.

And she was that morsel.

If she hadn't known from Aubrey and Kate that their nosiness belied a genuine, sympathetic nature, Colleen might have cut and run from the sitting room, out of the house, down the path...to where?

She sighed. There was nowhere to go. Not for her. In the six months since her dismissal from Nesbitt General, she had tried without success to find employment as a nurse. She'd applied to every hospital in New Jersey, Delaware, Philadelphia, and beyond, but none had given her so much as a return call until finally someone from human resources at Colfax Regional Hospital in Maryland sent her an email. It was imprinted on her memory like a scar.

> *Dear Ms. Fitzpatrick,*
> *We are unable to offer you an interview at this time, due to matters arising from your employment at Nesbitt General Hospital. While your resume is more than acceptable, these other factors deem you an unsuitable candidate for our hospital. Might we suggest that you attempt to find employment outside the medical field? Such a move might be best.*
> *Sincerely...*

True to her word, Veronica Burbank Clayton had ruined her. Her career was in tatters; her calling had been ripped from her as surely as if they had operated on her and removed her heart while it was still beating.

Kate had suggested that she come to Scotland, apply at Raighmore Hospital in Inverness or the many hospitals in Edinburgh. And she had come, hoping that an ocean, thousands of miles and five hours of flight time would be enough to outrun her shame.

But even letters of recommendation from Kate, Jack, Aubrey and Finn failed to achieve success. Richard Burbank had meant what he said. Hospitals, no matter where they were, required references. Colleen had worked at Nesbitt since she'd graduated from nursing school; she had no other job history. And Burbank had done his work well. No accredited hospital would accept someone suspected of stealing medication, no matter that nothing had ever been proven and she had never had her day in court. She wished now that she'd fought harder, but that was water under the bridge. She was blackballed. She had to face the likelihood that she would never work as a nurse again.

She sat staring back at the Owls, her throat too choked for conversation, wondering what they wanted now. She didn't have time for this; she needed to get to her job at Poundland and put in another boring day as a salesclerk. Why had they summoned her? To give her that stifling sympathy they'd offered Aubrey when she had arrived more than two years ago? Or Kate, when she had fled Harrington after Eddie was killed?

Well, there was nothing they could do this time, nothing that would make this horror that was her new existence go away. She just wanted to crawl back into her shell and hide, try once again to forget that her life might as well be over if she couldn't be a nurse. She opened her mouth to tell them that their sympathy was lovely, but they could not help. No one could help.

"Darling Colleen, Old Harry's found you a job!"

It was Gladys, of course. Gladys Chesher was the spokesperson for the group, eternally hopeful and always cheerful. Also beyond intrusive on behalf of those she deemed worthy. Colleen felt a tide of irritation wash through her.

"Thank you, but Poundland is fine for now. I don't have a lot of hours yet, but—"

"Not a sales job." Gladys was positively beaming now. Maxine Deyeaux tapped her foot a bit faster, the only sign that the Frenchwoman was excited. And suddenly Colleen noticed that the television was blank and silent. Ronald never turned it off.

"A *real* job, dear. As a healer." The old-fashioned word rolled off Gladys' tongue like honey.

"What?" Colleen stared at her. "I'm sorry, but that's impossible. I've tried all the hospitals, but my references—"

"Ach, lassie, will ye quit yer whingin' an' listen?" Old Harry slammed the paper into his lap and glared at her.

Colleen gaped at him, transfixed by his gimlet blue-eyed stare and the frustration on his wrinkled face. It was beyond rare for Old Harry to enter the conversation.

"Oh...okay," she said, in a small voice.

"Ah foond ye a wee job at Balfinnan, doin' whit ye like t' do." The paper went back up—Old Harry was finished. Colleen turned a helpless look to Gladys.

"He means, dear, that he's found you a job. A *nursing* job." Gladys beamed at her.

"What?" she said again. "How? Where? What is Balfinnan?"

A snort came from behind the newspaper, but Old Harry didn't reappear.

"Balfinnan House is a lovely place," said Gladys. "Just outside Inverness, so you can stay here."

Colleen's eyes narrowed. "*What* is Balfinnan House?" she said again. "Why would they hire me?"

"Well..." Gladys paused and looked uncertain.

Here it comes. The other shoe. Colleen waited for it to fall.

"Well," Gladys began again. "Balfinnan is a nursing home. Used to be a hospital in the Great War, and for a long while after that it was left to itself...that is, no one lived there and it became a bit run-down. But now the family's become interested, and five years ago they opened it up again as a care facility. They're fixing it up, too, hired a builder—preservation architect, I believe it's called—to bring the place back to its former glory."

"That sounds lovely, Gladys," Colleen said, "but what's the catch?"

Another snort from behind the newspaper. "Ach!"

Maxine spoke up for the first time. "And what is a—how do you say—catch?"

"What's the problem with the place?" Colleen said, with exaggerated patience.

"And why, I ask of you," Maxine said in her soft French accent, "must there be a—catch?"

"Because it sounds perfect. I worked in the geriatric department at Nesbitt, and I loved it! I think it's what I was meant to do. But geriatrics is still nursing, and no one will hire me as a nurse. So what's the deal with this place?"

Gladys had rallied and now took back the reins. "There's nothing wrong with Balfinnan House. It's just that they seem to have difficulty keeping staff. They hire people, and they don't seem to last very long. So they're a bit more *accepting*, you see?"

Colleen could feel the tension in the room. "And why can't they keep staff?" she asked, her voice soft.

"Well," Gladys said, "because..."

"Coz th' place is hoonted!" The paper crashed down again and Old Harry's face reappeared, a challenge written in the wrinkles. "It has ghosties. Ur ye afraid a' ghosties, lass?"

Colleen heard the other shoe as it dropped with a thud.

The rental car crept north on the A9 toward North Kessock. Drivers glared at Colleen as they blew by on the right-hand side of the road, oblivious to her terror as she gripped the wheel with whitened knuckles.

I'll never get there. I'm going to get stuck in one of these roundabouts and go around forever because I'll never have the nerve to get out. I'm going to hit a sheep and they'll put me in prison for life. I'm going to die.

But she didn't die, and the sheep remained safe. By the time she crossed the Moray Firth at the Kessock Bridge it felt as if the car had decided it had had enough of her nonsense and had taken over. She was getting the hang of this. She was still in the left lane, there were no sheep on the bridge, and the scenery was breathtaking. She was a boss!

She exited the motorway at a modern sign that said *Balfinnan House, 2 miles*. The road became single lane, then gravel, and then a hump of grass appeared in the middle and she had to slow to a crawl or risk bottoming out. Just when she began to wonder if she'd taken a wrong turn, the track opened up into a parking lot with a small gatehouse at its entrance.

There was no one in the gatehouse, so Colleen continued on into the lot, parked between a Porsche and a Volkswagen, and turned the key in the ignition to the off position. She sat for a minute just enjoying the sound of no motor running. Then she shook her head, took a deep breath, and opened the car door, stepping out onto the gravel. A sign directly in front of her indicated that Balfinnan House was just ahead at the end of a paved pathway that disappeared into the trees. She felt her spirits rise.

Colleen Fitzgerald had never been very good at worrying. No matter what life threw at her, she always managed to keep her glass half full. It was what had allowed her to rebound from a myriad of disastrous love affairs with her *carpe diem* philosophy intact. Until now, at least. This latest swipe at her happiness had brought her to her knees, made her wonder if karma had it in for her. Flattened her.

But there was always hope.

Well, here we go. My life can't get any worse, can it? So let's go. She sent a stern message to her feet. *Move!*

The pathway continued for some two hundred yards or so into the trees, and then suddenly opened into a vast meadow. An attempt had been made to turn some of the meadow into a lawn, with haphazard results. Colleen reflected that the whole enterprise gave the impression that it was trying to be civilized, but had miscalculated the immensity of the task. For some reason the thought cheered her.

I'm not the only one here in need of a makeover, she thought, and grinned. This place was growing on her, and she hadn't even seen it yet. And at the end of the path was a job, *in nursing.* With renewed energy she moved forward with a new bounce in her step.

She turned a corner, the trees opened, and there it was. Balfinnan House: a castle, not a house at all. Three stories high, with turrets on two corners and a huge arched wooden door set in the center of an expanse of grey stone, it looked like a medieval fortress. All it needed was a drawbridge and a moat, and any self-respecting knight would find the place perfectly livable.

Colleen let out a long sigh of delight. She was going to work here! She was going to work in a Scottish castle, and she was going to be a nurse again. No...a *healer.* Somehow Gladys' archaic term suited the place much better than its modern counterpart.

As she approached, she became aware of a pervasive quiet. No bird calls, no insect noises: the entire area seemed to exist in a cocoon of silence. As if the castle knew its place in the world and understood that it would be here long after everything else had crumbled to dust. It was like an old woman of a fine family who, though the money was gone, still commanded the respect her lineage deserved—a bit frayed around the edges, but possessing an eternal beauty. Colleen loved it.

She approached the huge wooden door and studied it. There was a modern doorbell that seemed out of place in these surroundings, and a huge ornate knocker in the shape of a snarling lion. She and the lion eyed each other, and then she pressed the button for the bell. No one came, and there was no sound within. She tried it again, with the same result.

What now? Old Harry said they knew I was coming.

After a third fruitless try at the doorbell, Colleen stepped back. It was unseasonably warm for early September; maybe they were all out in the back. She turned to the right and walked the length of the castle's facade, rounding the corner to find more miles of stone, more empty windows staring back at her.

Somebody had been at work here though. The castle was ringed with flowerbeds that showed artful planning. Bushes with red berries lined the base of the walls, and peeking between them were bluebells and anemones, heather and thistles. Natural flowers, Colleen guessed, but planted here on purpose and cultivated to make the most of the season. Wild, like the castle and the lawn and the meadow. A stone patio with five or six iron chairs faced a single door. Locked, like the one in front.

She resumed her walk, turned another corner—and stopped in shock. Much of the back of the castle was in ruins. The windows had been broken out, probably long ago. Black charred flooring gaped through gashes in the stone, weeds and vines choked the walls.

"Quite the spectacle, aye?" came a cheerful voice from behind her, and Colleen spun to face a young man with wild dark hair, dressed in worn jeans and a dark red sweatshirt with faded blue letters that read *Arsenal.* "Even the strongest castle can't stand against fire. The family wants to fix it up, though, bring it back to its original state. Going to be quite a job." He looked her up and down with calm grey eyes. His clothing suggested some kind of laborer—the gardener, perhaps?

"I'm Aidan," he offered. "I work here." He waited.

"Oh," she exclaimed after a moment. "I'm Colleen. I work here, too. Or at least I think I do."

"You're not sure if you work here?" The grey eyes sparkled with amusement.

"Well, I think I have a job as a nurse, but there doesn't seem to be anybody around to tell me for sure," she responded with an answering grin. "No one answered the door."

"Oh, I think the bell's broken again." He sighed. "Didn't you try the knocker?"

"I was afraid it might bite me, and losing a finger on my first day didn't seem like the best idea."

"Ach, lass, you'll have to be braver than that if you want to work at Balfinnan," he said, thickening his brogue. "There's worse than door knockers about, ye ken?" Then he burst out laughing at the look on her face. "Come on then, I'll see you in and get you sent to the right folk."

He turned and led her back around to the front door, lifted the huge ring in the snarling lion's head, and let it crash to the metal plaque underneath. A ringing sound filled the quiet air before footsteps pounded behind the door, and it opened to reveal a large, formidable woman in a black dress with a starched white collar. The woman stood there, glowering.

"Hullo, Mrs. Murtaugh," Aidan said. He seemed impervious to her dark mood. "I've brought you a new employee."

Colleen watched with growing trepidation as the woman took her measure for long minutes. Then she gave a snort and stood back.

"I s'pose you might as well come in," she said in a terse voice.

Colleen stepped through into a dark foyer, feeling like the world was closing in around her.

"I'll see you then," Aidan told her, as the door began to close.

No! Don't leave me here with her! A voice in Colleen's head protested, and then the door closed with a bang and she was alone with the black-clad woman.

"Well, you don't look like much." Mrs. Murtaugh sniffed. "You have the look of the Irish," she added, her tone dismissive, "and you're awfully small."

She sighed, turned, and led Colleen down the dark hallway toward a door at the back, muttering under her breath.

"Wonder how long *this* one will last, once she sees what Balfinnan has to offer."

CHAPTER 5

THE GREY LADY

"He's as handsome as a Hollywood star! And so nice!"

Colleen sat across from Aubrey and Kate at the Little Italy restaurant on High Street, her eyes shining. Aubrey glanced at Kate and rolled her own eyes. Kate shook her head.

There was just something so irrepressible about Fitz, Kate thought. Her life could be falling apart—hell, this time it had been *ripped* apart—and she just picked herself up and forged ahead, ready for the next challenge. Or mistake. All it took was wine, some Rocky Road ice cream and a shoulder or two to cry on, and she was ready to take on the world again.

Colleen was like a bantam hen or a tiny prize-fighter. Knock her down, and the next second she was dancing on her toes, ready for the next battle. No matter what life threw at her, she refused to stay down or give up. It almost seemed as if she'd forgotten that a week ago she'd been looking at a future without nursing—a dismal existence tied to a cash register, selling candy bars and laundry detergent at Scotland's equivalent of a dollar store.

And all because she'd dived into the love pool without her swimmies and chosen a shark for a lover once again. The problem was, Kate thought as she watched her friend, Fitz had the world's absolute worst luck when it came to men. She had a *type* that she always seemed to fall for—tall, blond, muscular—and she fell headfirst every time.

"He actually owns the whole castle!"

Kate jerked her attention back to the conversation. "What's this guy's name again?"

"Graham. Graham Anderson." Fitz waved her fork in the air. "His family has owned Balfinnan since the late 1800s. It's awfully expensive to keep up, and no one was living there for a long time. But now Graham's opened it back up. He's hired an architect to restore it and everything. And he's not just another entitled aristocrat; he's giving back. It was a hospital once, and now he's set it up as a nursing home. He's just so *passionate* about it!"

"Mmm, passionate," murmured Kate. She sent a helpless look toward Aubrey. *Do something*, the look said. Aubrey was the one with the imagination. Surely she could come up with something.

"Fitz—"

"I wish you two wouldn't call me Fitz," Colleen said, her brow creasing. "I know you always have, but that's what John called me, and I can't stand hearing it now. His *little* Fitz—the bastard." Her voice was tinged with bitterness.

"Well, too bad. You've been Fitz to me since first grade, and I'm not going to start calling you something else now." Kate's voice was brisk. "You can tell everybody else to call you Colleen, and we'll bear up, but you'll always be Fitz to us. And you *are* little. That didn't take much imagination from your married creep, now did it?"

Aubrey tried again.

"Fitz—I mean Ms. Fitzpatrick," she said in the poshest voice she could muster. "Oughtn't you to take some time to get to know this paragon before deciding he's the next Mr. Right? I mean, your love affairs just keep getting worse and worse. The last one almost put you in prison! I don't think my heart can stand another one."

"Tell us, *Colleen*, what does your Mr. Anderson look like?" Kate asked in an innocent voice. She shared a look with Aubrey. *Wait for it...*

"He's tall, and has lovely blond hair that falls into his eyes when he's talking, and blue eyes, and..."

"Da dumm," Kate said, beating the table in a drumroll.

"Shut it, Kate!" Colleen gave her a cross look. "So I have a type. Is it against the law to be attracted to a nice-looking man?"

"In your case, it should be," Kate said in a weary voice. "Don't you see that you have a pattern of destruction going on here? When will you—"

"So tell us about the other people at your castle," Aubrey interrupted. "Surely there *are* other people there?"

"Yes, of course there are," Colleen said in a relieved voice. "Quite a few, although not as many as

Graham—Mr. Anderson—would like. There's a doctor who comes in several times a week. Two other nurses and a nurse's aide, and a gardener—I met him the first day but haven't seen much of him since—he's cute and seemed nice. And there's an absolutely frightful housekeeper who looks like she escaped from the Addams Family.

"Let's see," she went on, "there's a cook named Mrs. Morton—she's friendly, but she's like Nessie and always trying to push haggis or some other Scottish mystery food on me," Colleen shuddered. "There's a janitor who kind of blends into the woodwork and looks as if he's afraid of everyone. He's not much older than a kid, really, and kind of sweet. I think I might make him my project. Oh, and the architect. *Preservation architect*, thank you very much. I haven't met him yet: probably some stuffy old university type with a bow tie and pens in his pocket.

"And of course there are the residents." Colleen's voice gentled as it always did when she talked about her charges. "Fifteen of them right now. They're sweet and so appreciative of any company, but they're old, and some of them are sick, and there've been a couple of deaths recently—very sad. Balfinnan has a waiting list, so there's never an empty bed."

"Aren't you forgetting someone?" Aubrey asked her. "I was talking to the Owls, and they said—"

"What? Oh, you mean the ghost." Colleen rolled her eyes. "That's what Old Harry says, and you never argue with Old Harry, but I haven't seen anything. She's supposed to be the ghost of a nurse who worked there during World War I, when Balfinnan was a military hospital. I don't know why she's haunting the place, but Simon—that's the janitor—says she shows up now and then when someone is going to die. She's called the Grey Lady, because of her uniform. Maybe you should come and see if you can strike up an acquaintance, Kate," she added in a wry voice. "After all, you met a ghost yourself, so you should know how to talk to them. Bring Jack, since he supposedly saw your ghost, too. And Aubrey, you and Finn should come and we can have a seance. You're all such ghostbusters!"

Aubrey laughed, ignoring the sarcasm. "Finn would love it, he's a maniac for ghosts. But he's a little busy now, what with the term starting at the college and his work on the book. And other things..." she stopped and gave the other two women a secretive look, her hazel eyes brimming with excitement.

"What?" Kate eyed her with suspicion.

"He's sort of been practicing some new skills. Like painting, carpentry—you know...new dad stuff."

Kate and Colleen stared for a minute, and then the tiny restaurant exploded with their shrieks.

"You're *pregnant*?"

"Oh my God! Really? Oh, awesome, Bree! When are you due?"

"We've known for a little while. The doctor says probably the first week of April."

"Did Finn buy a tiny set of bagpipes yet?"

"I'm going baby kilt shopping tomorrow!"

"We need some champagne for this!"

"Does Angus know? Oh lord, what about the Owls? I can't wait to see how many little outfits Gladys can knit in seven months!"

The owner of Little Italy swooped down on them with flutes of champagne on a tray as if he'd been waiting for a signal, and the next hour was spent toasting the advent of the new little Cameron. Aubrey passed on the champagne but accepted a glass of ginger ale, presiding over the babble with a self-satisfied smile.

Suddenly Kate choked on her champagne.

"What's the matter with you?" Colleen said, pounding her on the back.

"I just realized—now we finally know what *one* Scotsman wears under his kilt!"

Colleen was still thinking about the lunch as she walked up the front steps of Balfinnan House on Monday morning. She was so happy for Aubrey, and for Kate and her policeman, too. She'd only met Jack a couple of times, but he seemed like a great guy, dashing in his kilt at the wedding and so obviously gaga over his new bride. Still, there was a little feeling of something ugly niggling at the back of her mind. She tried to push it away, but it refused to dislodge itself, and as she raised her hand to grasp the ring of the great knocker she acknowledged it for what it was. *Jealousy.*

Why couldn't she find that perfect someone, a man to treasure her for what and who she was, a man unencumbered by baggage? What was wrong with her that her compass kept pointing at "wrong'uns," as Aubrey's friend Angus would say?

Well, she was going to change all that. Scotland

had given her a chance—maybe a last chance—to clean up her act, and she wasn't going to throw it away. She'd get to know the next man before she fell for him. Really know him. She'd be ruthless, ask questions, do a damn background check if necessary. Maybe Jack could find her a private detective who would follow her around with his laptop.

She giggled. With her luck, the detective would be tall, blond and blue-eyed. She was a hopeless case. Colleen glared back at the snarling lion and let the ring fall.

"You just mind your own business!" she told it, and swept into the dark hall of Balfinnan House, giving the glowering Mrs. Murtaugh her biggest, sunniest smile.

There was one person at the sign-in desk. Flora Kemp, one of the two other nurses, was just signing out from the night shift. Middle-aged and motherly, she wiped a chubby hand over her brow and sighed.

"Morning, Colleen! Glad you're here—Dolly's out again, and Mr. MacNabb had a bad night in one of his states. He's been asking for you. Can you go work your magic on him? Please?"

"Sure, Flora. I'll get right up there. I'm a bit worried about him; he's been having some pain and it's affecting his normally sunny disposition."

She winked at her colleague, and Flora laughed. Gordon MacNabb had probably never had a sunny day in his life, and old age was just making him more dour, as the Scots would say. But for some reason he had taken to Colleen. She suspected it had something to do with Old Harry.

MacNabb had told her how he'd met a "young" Harry Campbell five years before on a fishing expedition given for the residents, and despite a fifteen-year age difference they had become fast friends. The old man regaled his favorite nurse with tales of the exploits "that young dunderheid" had gotten up to on the trip, and how he probably would have been thrown overboard were it not for the intercession of one Gordon MacNabb, fisherman extraordinaire.

Colleen suspected that the stories were wildly exaggerated, but maybe that was because she just couldn't imagine Old Harry anywhere else than behind his newspaper at Nessie's. And Gordon MacNabb was approaching the grand old age of one hundred now, so perhaps his memory was slipping just a bit.

Unlikely, she thought with a snort. Underneath the crabby exterior, Colleen had found a sharp mind and a wicked sense of humor. But that all went out the window when he was in one of his "states." She sighed and turned toward the massive staircase that led to the upper floors. It was shaping up to be a long day already.

"Weel, whit took ye s' long? Ah doonae hae much time left, ye ken, An' ah'd like t' make it to a hunnerd!"

Colleen stifled a giggle. "Like to make it to a hundred" was the biggest understatement of the year. Gordon MacNabb was fierce in his determination to see his centennial birthday, and he was prepared to face down his doctors, time, and the devil himself to make it happen. He talked about it to anyone who would listen, stating that as soon as it happened he'd "be glad t' git outta yer hair an' gie ye some peace."

She doubted that, too. Never had she seen a man so proud to be alive.

"Oh, Mr. MacNabb," she said, "you don't need me to make that happen. You're fit as a sixty-year-old. You just need to keep calm and let the people who care about you help get you there!"

The old man snorted. "Ach! Nobody cares abit me aroond here except fur ye an' mebbe 'at Anderson lad, but he jist wants t' keep me alive fur th' munny Ah gie heem tae bide in this ...*palace*." He gestured to the ancient walls of his room with disgust.

Colleen had no answer to that, but she knew there was no truth in his assertion that Graham Anderson only worried about his patients for the money he could get out of them. He truly cared about them, and she knew it. During her interview with him on her first day he had told her that it was the people under his care, these old souls nearing the end of their lives, that made him want to restore his castle and make it a special refuge from the indignities of aging.

"So many of these people are frightened of the future, knowing that they don't have a lot of time left and worried because their once reliable bodies are breaking down," he'd told her, his blue eyes earnest. "I feel as if I've been called to make it easier for them, to help them understand and accept what's happening."

It had so mirrored her own feelings about geriatric nursing that she had immediately been drawn to this man. No, it did *not* have a damn thing to do with the handsome face, the lovely hair that she'd wanted to brush off his forehead, the intense blue of his eyes. She was over all that—smarter now. Everyone had a type, it didn't mean there was something wrong with h—

"—an' Ah felt it starin' at me. It was standin' in the shadows, all dressed in black, but it stared at me, an' it had nae face!"

Colleen jerked out of her memory of Graham Anderson's finer qualities to find MacNabb gesticulating with gnarled hands, an anxious look on his wizened old face.

"Ah kent it was tryin' t' tell me it was mah time tae die, and it'd be helpin' me git on wi' it. Ain ye cannae let 'it happen! Ah'm nae goin til mah birthday! It cannae make me!"

Colleen reached for MacNabb's hand, running her fingers over the papery skin with a practiced, gentle motion. She'd never seen him like this, so distraught and agitated. He was *frightened.*

"Who did you think you saw?" Her voice was soft.

"Arenae ye listenin'? 'Th' ghost! It's waitin' fer me t'die!"

"But you're not dying, Gordon." Colleen used his first name and held his rheumy blue eyes with her own. "You must believe me. You're old, but you're not sick. Everything works just fine, as long as you make sure to take your heart medicine. You're going to make it to one hundred, probably a hundred and five if you're careful." Her mind fastened on something he'd said. "Do you mean the Grey Lady? The nurse in World War I who killed her lover and then hanged herself? I've heard the story, Gordon, but that's all it is. Old castles have creaks and groans, and stories that come down through the years to explain odd disturbances. But they're not real. There's no such thing as ghosts."

The old man sat up straight in his bed and glared at her.

"Ye yoong folk think ye ken everythin', don' ye?" MacNabb snatched his hand back and crossed his spindly arms over his chest in exasperation, fright fading as his frustration mounted. "Fer yer information, lassie, Ah wasnae talkin' abit '*at* ghost. Ah didna see '*er*." He pulled at her hand with a strength that belied his age, forcing her face close to his. "Th' ghost 'at stood lookin' at me was th' other 'un. Th' *bad* 'un!"

We're all ghosts. We all carry, inside us, people who came before us.

Liam Callanan

FRANCE, 1916

I t was supposed to be easy, thought Alexander as
he huddled in the trench with members of the 16th
Highland Infantry.

After seven days of unceasing bombardment, the
Scottish solders were confident that the enemy in the
opposing trenches only yards away had been elimi-
nated. The barbed wire had been cut and the trenches
were theirs for the taking.

It was supposed to be easy.

Alexander listened to the silence with growing dread. It was ominous and deceptive, and every
nerve in his body told him to stay in the trench, to
wait. The crushing loneliness he had felt since leaving
Scotland for the Somme sat on his shoulders, weigh-
ing him down. These men who were supposed to be
his comrades were strangers to him. They had grown
up together in the streets of Glasgow and looked with
barely concealed disdain at Alexander, a MacLeod
from the Isle of Skye. A teuchter, they called him: their
derisive name for a Highlander.

Alexander had signed up and embarked on a path that took him to Glasgow and eventually here, to this rotten corner of hell in the north of France. The violence was a part of his existence now, filling his soul and reverberating in his head.

What he would never get used to were the gifts of war—the shell shock, rats, and the ever-present danger of cholera or trench foot. Most of the men were exhausted beyond the point of emotion, mere machines digging incessantly to keep up with an enemy hunched only two hundred yards away and digging just as fast. In between the digging was the firing, the never-ending cacophony of war and death and destruction. The only thing that kept them going was the promise that what they did here today would surely end this war soon.

The order was given and the men surged up and over, covering the short distance easily...until they reached the barbed wire.

It had not been cut.

And the Germans were not all dead. As the helpless Scots pressed against the unforgiving wire, machine guns roared to life and cut them down like stalks of wheat. Alexander and a few others had made it through the barbed wire and were running at the trench ahead, knowing that it was all they could do.

They fell into the trench on top of the German soldiers manning the guns, flattening some and knocking the weapons from the hands of others, but lost more men in the effort.

Alexander scrambled to his feet and found himself staring at the frightened face of a boy, and at shaking *arms that held a machine gun pointed straight at his heart. So, this was it. The end of his road.*

A shot rang out and the boy's eyes widened. Almost gracefully, his knees folded and he slumped to the mud floor of the trench. Alexander pulled his gaze from the empty eyes to look at the grinning face of Lewis Walker, one of the Glasgow boys.

"Ach, ye wee teuchter," he said. "Thought you'd bought it, didn't ye?"

A sharp crack. Lewis jerked and the smile was wiped from his face, replaced by a look of profound surprise as he toppled over the embankment and landed on top of Alexander, pinning him to the muddy ground.

Bridget Halloran swiped damp red curls off her forehead with the sleeve of her uniform and gazed at the carnage arrayed before her bleary eyes. Impossible numbers of men lay in excruciating pain, their bodies mangled by machine gun fire and their limbs torn and bleeding. So many injured and dying—how was she supposed to help them all?

As if she could sew arms back onto shredded bodies, or replace organs that had been torn apart by the unforgiving artillery. She was only one nurse. Many of the men had succumbed before she could reach their cots, and many more were going to die despite her best efforts. And for what? This stupid war was robbing the world of its future, no matter who won in the end. The best of its young men were dying...and she was so tired.

A bedraggled figure stumbled into the hospital tent carrying a limp body over his shoulder. He was covered in blood and looked close to collapsing. Bridget called for an orderly, who gently removed the unconscious man from the soldier's back and carried him away. Relieved of his burden, the young man swayed and would have fallen if not for Bridget's strong grip around his shoulders. She guided him to a cot and helped him sit down.

"It'll be all right," she told him in a soft voice. "I'm going to have to remove your jacket so I can find out where you're injured. Can you understand me?"

"No, no," the man choked out. "I'm fine, I'm not hurt. It—it's my friend. He saved my life and got shot. He's the one who needs you."

Bridget looked across at the cot where they had laid the unconscious soldier and caught the eye of the orderly. He shook his head, looking drained and sick. She turned back to the young man on the cot.

"Your friend is being taken care of," she said, her voice gentle.

He searched her steady gaze with astonishing blue eyes, and in hers he read the truth. Spent and consumed by the horror and waste of war, Alexander MacLeod broke down and sobbed, horrible wrenching sounds that sounded almost inhuman in their grief. He clutched the young nurse as if she were a lifeline, his only grip on sanity.

Bridget rocked him like a baby, crooning meaningless phrases until exhaustion claimed him and he relaxed and closed those lovely eyes, long lashes wet and sticking to his mud-streaked cheeks. She laid him back on the cot and covered him with a blanket, then stood and looked down on him for a moment. He was one of the lucky ones—at least this time. She had no business lingering with an uninjured man, though something she couldn't identify drew her to him and whispered that this was where she was meant to be.

She sighed. No time for fantasy. There were men here who needed her if they were to have even a chance of surviving this day's butchery. Bridget wiped her hands on her apron and moved to her next patient, pushing the young man on the cot out of her mind. After all, it wasn't as if she'd ever see him again.

CHAPTER 6
GHRUAMACHD

olleen gaped at Gordon MacNabb. "The other one? There's more than one?"

The old man sat back, triumphant. "Aye. 'Ere's two. An' I saw th' other 'un." His faded blue eyes speared into hers.

"Th' Ghruamachd."

"What's a grew-muck?"

The old man sat straight up in his bed, his thin body vibrating with exasperation.

"The Ghruamachd! Th' one that killed th' sodger! It was 'at one whit did it. It's puure evil, 'at one!"

Colleen felt a shiver go through her at his words. She had no idea what he was talking about, but for some reason it seemed important. More to the point, Gordon MacNabb thought it was important, and he was her charge. He was ninety-nine years old and had a weak heart. It wouldn't do to let him get so upset.

"It's all just a story, Gordon." She pitched her voice low, trying to sound calm and comforting. "One of those old legends that get passed down. Whatever people say—ghosts can't hurt you because they aren't real."

A flash of unease speared her when she thought about Aubrey's ghosts, and Kate's story about a ghost saving Finn last year. It would have been understandable for Aubrey, with her runaway imagination, to see spooky apparitions, but Kate? She was the most practical person Colleen had ever known, and she'd been the first to pooh-pooh Aubrey's story. But then last year she'd sworn she met the ghost of a woman who had lived almost four hundred years ago, and the spirit's lover had saved her and Jack from a maniac drug dealer! Even Aubrey couldn't make this stuff up!

So who was she to be making fun of things that happened in this ancient country? She looked at Gordon MacNabb, a Scot's Scot, and flinched from his beseeching eyes. He *needed* her to believe. Maybe if she went along with his fantasies he'd calm down, and that was what *she* needed. She was a nurse, and her job was to keep him alive. She sighed.

"How do you know it's real?" she asked him, and was rewarded with an exhale of relief from the old man.

"Ah ken it's real coz mah mam told me," he said, his voice strong and sure. MacNabb might be losing more recent memories these days, Colleen thought, but he never forgot the past.

"Your mother?"

"Aye. She was here back in th' Great Wahr. She kent th' Grey Lady when she were alive. She tauld me when Ah was a wee lad."

"Really? Your mother was here? During World War I?"

The old man gave her a look of impatience.

"Dint Ah jist tell ye so? She waur a nurse—like ye. An' jist as bonnie."

He was beaming now, his frustration and fear forgotten. Colleen relaxed. The color was returning to his dried-apple face, and his breathing had slowed to a reasonable rate. She wondered if it would be safe to press him for more information.

Colleen had never cared much before about the past and people who lived long ago. History was Aubrey's territory. From the time she was a little girl with a stethoscope pressed to her doll's chest, all she had ever wanted was to make people well. Now that she had almost lost her calling, nursing was even more precious to her.

And yet, Scotland was changing her. Its incredible ancientness was stimulating her curiosity about the past, teasing her mind with questions about the people who had walked this land long ago. She gave the old man a fond look. Here, right in front of her, was a living encyclopedia!

"Gordon, will you tell me what your mom told you?"

He gave her a sly eye and beckoned her closer.

"It's nae guid t' be gabbin' too free in these walls," he whispered, "In case th' bad ghost be listenin'."

Colleen put her finger to her lips in agreement, but the sincerity with which he spoke gave her a chill. She leaned closer.

"Mah mam was a nurse here, like Ah said," McNabb spoke in a whisper, "an' she said th' lass loov'd th' sodger—Alexander 'is name was— an' ne'er wood hae killed him. But somebody else wanted him, too, an' 'at one was jealoos. An' 'at one killed him."

"Being jealous doesn't make you a murderer, Gordon," said Colleen. "It just makes you sad. Believe me, I know."

Gordon MacNabb's voice rose. "Wood ye jist listen? Mah mam, she said th' lass didna do whit they said!"

"Why did she think that?" Colleen was immersed in the story now, forgetting that it had no chance of being true.

"Awright. So thaur was a nurse; 'er name was Bridget an' she was Irish. She was in loove wi' a sodger, a Scot." The old man looked into Colleen's eyes, challenging her to interrupt again. "He loov'd 'er too. Mah mam said she ne'er saw sich' loove 'atween two people. It was as if they were meant t' be together."

"And what happened?" Colleen was a sucker for a love story—nothing was going to stop her from hearing this one.

"Thaur was anuther nurse. She had th' eye fur th' sodger, an' she was jealoos."

"But what happened?" Colleen's voice was breathless.

"He died." MacNabb stopped and dipped his head.

Colleen thought for a moment. Then she gently asked, "Well, wasn't it a hospital? Presumably he was wounded, or he wouldn't have been there. I mean, it's very sad, but World War I was one of the worst in history—a lot of men died. Medicine wasn't as advanced then, either."

"Aye, mah mam said he was verra sick, an' almost died efter he got t' th' castle."

"So?" Colleen prompted.

"He was gettin' better!" The old man's voice rose in triumph. "Bridget hardly ever left his side, an' he was healin'. Mah mam said everybody was verra canty fur them, 'cause it waur so romantic."

"So how did he die?"

"Nobody kent. Bridget wouldna talk t' anyone, bit she was th' only one t' gie him his medicine, so folk started talkin' abit how it wasna natural."

"But why would she do it? She was in love with him!"

Colleen felt herself responding to this tragic tale, her natural compassion rising to the defense of this poor nurse who had lost her lover despite all her efforts to save him. She wanted to shout at the accusers, to tell them they were wrong.

"Weel," he said, "th' nurse 'at wanted heem fer herself put it aboot 'at Bridget had done somethin' tae him. 'A coorse nobody believd 'er. But then they found poison in his medicine, so they locked Bridget in a room an' called fur th' polis. But afore they got there, she hanged herself!"

"So...she did do it." Colleen felt deflated. She had been transported into this tragic story, back to wartime Scotland, so sure that this Bridget was innocent. It was like having cold water thrown into her face. It wasn't fair!

MacNabb eyed her, a glint in his sharp beady eyes.

"Noo keep yer heid!" he barked. "Ah'm nae done! 'At's th' thing. Not many ken it, bit mah mam said th' owner o' th' castle thooght th' whole thing was leery, an' he didna believe it. He was anuther Anderson, this 'un's great-great granfather, an' he ne'er believed Bridget cood hae done it. Mah mam thoght mebbe he was a wee bit in loove wi' 'er himself."

"Oh, Gordon, that's such a lovely story, and so sad. So who did it?"

MacNabb snorted, but he looked pleased at her reaction.

"Weel it isnae a *story*, lass, it's real life. Sae nobody knows th' truth 'o it. But mah mam always wunnered aboot it."

"But why?" Colleen found herself pleading for an end to the story. "Why did your mom wonder?"

"Coz after 'at folk began t' see Bridget's ghost aboot th' castle, always when some'un was gon t' die, an' she seemed t' be tryin' t' save them, like she couldna save 'er loover. Would a guilty lass bide behind like 'at? Mah mam thoght she had t' do somethin' afore she could move on t' be wi' 'er sodger. Mah mam had a bit o' th' sight, ye ken?"

"So..." Colleen was reeling with the effort of trying to keep up with Gordon MacNabb's thickening accent. "Bridget is the ghost you saw? And you think that means you're dying?"

"Havena ye been listenin', lass?" He wrung his hands in frustration. "It wasna Bridget! The Grey Lady tries t' help folk." He took a deep shuddering breath. "It was th' other un. 'T'was th' Ghruamachd. An' 'at one isna here t' help!" His voice had risen again and he shuddered. "Ah saw 'it! All in black wi' no face. An' seein' 'at un canna be guid."

Colleen took his hand again. "Shhh, everything will be all right."

Gordon MacNabb gave her a beseeching look that broke her heart. It didn't matter if she believed the story—he did. And worrying about it wasn't good for him.

So she put on her nurse face. "Look, Gordon, I want you to calm down. I'm not going to let anybody hurt you! As long as you take your medication, you'll stay fit as a horse!" Inspiration hit her. "Listen—I'll talk to Simon about it. You know how he is about ghosts and such. He'll keep an eye out and warn us if he sees any ghosts—grey or black—and we'll make sure they keep their distance."

She was babbling now, just spewing nonsense to make him feel better. She didn't believe for a minute that Simon Reid could really see ghosts, but he said he could and Gordon MacNabb believed he could. She'd do anything in her power to keep her old man safe and calm. She patted his frail hand and turned to leave.

"Miss Colleen?"

She turned back. He was staring at her, tears in his bloodshot blue eyes.

"Yoo're a special 'un. Thank ye."

Back home, Colleen cornered Nessie in the kitchen.

"So I'm afraid he's going to work himself up into a state over this, and it isn't good for his heart."

Nessie took a tray of scones out of the AGA and

answered without pausing in her work. "Gordon MacNabb is auld, Colleen, but from what Old Harry says, he's a fighter. He hasn't lived this long jist t' up and die from fright."

"But you should have seen him," Colleen told her. "He was really upset. He says that there's a good ghost. She's called the Grey Lady, but her name's Bridget and she loved a soldier named Alexander. She's been haunting the castle since 1918, but she comforts people and tries to help. Supposedly she killed her lover and hanged herself in remorse, but Gordon's mother didn't believe it and neither did the owner of the castle, who was the ancestor of the current owner. And Simon Reid, the janitor, says he's seen the Grey Lady many times, and she's not dangerous. He's a bit odd, but I don't think he's a liar: rather sweet and very shy, actually. I don't think he'd make it up to get attention. In fact, I had to pry it out of him when I asked him to keep an eye on Gordon."

Nessie said nothing. She continued to arrange scones and cakes on trays for tea, as if this kind of discussion went on every day in her house.

Colleen took a deep breath and continued.

"Gordon said the bad ghost—the Ghruamachd, he calls it—has only been haunting Balfinnan recently, which is odd. He said it was never seen until Graham Anderson reopened the castle as a nursing home. It picks the people who are old and weak and sick and fills them with thoughts of death and misery. Gordon thinks it's the spirit of the nurse who killed Alexander, and it's come back and taken a new body.

"Simon says he felt an evil spirit once," Colleen

went on, trailing after Nessie as she bustled around the small kitchen. "He said he knew it was there because the air changed. It was in the room where one of the patients had just died. The room seemed to darken, as if someone—some*thing*— was angry that the poor old man had died peacefully. But of course it's all superstition and nonsense. Isn't it?"

Nessie put the scones on a tray and added a small bowl of jam. She turned and eyed Colleen. "There's folks that can see things others canna." She waggled a finger. "Scotland is a verra old country, with a lot o' mysteries. In the Highlands, the veil between life an' death is thinner than in other places—dinna look at me like that, Colleen!" She snorted in disgust. "Havena ye learnt anything yet? What about Aubrey? And Kate? Those girls surely told ye about ghosts! Dinna ye believe yer friends?"

Colleen sighed and put her hands up in surrender. "Of course they told me, Nessie. I'm trying, believe me. I believe in goodness, and kindness, and I don't think those things change much over the years. People fall in love, and others are jealous. It's always the same. The problem I have is believing that someone could love someone so much that they would stay behind after they died." She shook her head. "I've never been loved that way, Nessie. And now I realize that I've never loved someone like that, either. Maybe the Grey Lady and her lover had it right. Their love ended in tragedy, but for the time they were together it was the way it should be. Someday I want a love like that."

Nessie came over and put her hand on Colleen's arm. "Ye'll have it, lass. Ye have a guid heart, an' there's someone out there who's achin' to give ye his. Trust me." She took the tray and headed for the dining room, tossing orders over her shoulder. "Bring th' teapot in, would ye dear? And grab some o' those napkins too. 'At's a good lass."

Colleen sighed and followed Nessie. As the other housemates filtered in for tea, she looked at each of them. What an eclectic bunch they were, she thought. Nessie was so down-to-earth and reasonable while she talked of ghosts as if they were friends of hers. Gladys seemed like any elderly Englishwoman as she stuffed her knitting into her bottomless bag, but Colleen knew differently. She looked at Ronald and Maxine, who looked back at her as if they knew exactly what she was thinking.

Not for the first time, she thought that there was something uncanny about these people. For one thing, hadn't Aubrey said that they came to visit for a month every year? But she'd been here herself in the summer, and the fall, and last spring for Kate's wedding, and every time the Owls had been here, too, almost as if they'd never been anywhere else. How could that be? And that wasn't the only odd thing about them. They all seemed to be able to read her mind, which was decidedly unsettling.

Old Harry came in and sat down at the head of the table. He looked at Colleen, his dark eyes shrewd.

"Ye'll nae find th' right one til ye ken whit ye need, lass."

He grabbed a scone and gave it his full attention.

CHAPTER 7
KISSING SEASON

olleen peeled back the top slice of bread from the sandwich Nessie had packed for her lunch today and peered intently at the contents. No haggis, no black pudding, no innards of any kind: just good old Scottish ham and cheddar. She took a bite and sighed, allowing the rich taste to linger on her tongue before swallowing it down.

Nessie was a fabulous cook. She had insisted on packing lunch every day with such enthusiasm that Colleen was sure there must be an ulterior motive, like foisting sheep's guts in some form on her unwilling victim in the guise of edible sandwich filling. She just hadn't been able to make Nessie understand that some people absolutely *hated* the insides of animals and couldn't be trained otherwise. But so far her lunches had been haggis free and delicious. It didn't mean Colleen would quit checking, though.

She finished the sandwich and leaned back in the wicker chair on the back lawn of Balfinnan, closing her eyes and enjoying the rare sunny day. The weather was unusually warm—or at least, warm for Scotland—and since it wasn't raining, a trip outside was in order. Her thoughts drifted. The last few days had been exhausting in the extreme. They were shorthanded because Flora was on vacation, and she and Liz Dunnet had to do everything without help from Dolly. As usual.

Dolly Gilles was the laziest human being Colleen had ever met. At least one day in every week the girl was "poorly," or there was an emergency at home in North Kessock where she lived with her ailing mother. When she was at Balfinnan, she shirked duty as much as possible, disappearing like Houdini when one of the more difficult residents was acting out. Her excuse was usually that she had been out in the forest, foraging.

"I know exactly where she is," Liz had confided one day after she and Colleen wrestled Mrs. Buchanan's three-hundred-pound body back into her bed while the woman showered them with complaints. "She's hanging around Mr. Anderson's office, hoping he'll notice her made-up cow eyes and fall madly in love with her."

Colleen's radar went on alert. "She's stalking our boss?"

"With every weapon in her arsenal," Liz said. "Fortunately for him, she hasn't got much subtlety, and she was hired as a nurse's aide, not a concubine. Frustrating thing is, she *could* be useful. She's a very good herbalist—knows every natural plant around here and the medicinal uses of all of them. I think that's the only reason she's been kept on. But if she's not careful, Mr. Anderson'll get tired of the unwanted attention and send her back to her mother." Liz snorted and wiped a hand over her forehead. "Who, by the way, is as strong as an ox and probably has no idea her daughter's using her as an excuse to miss work!"

Colleen grinned at the memory of Liz's tart word choice.

"Care to share what's making you so happy?" A voice broke into Colleen's thoughts. Startled, she looked up to find a pair of laughing grey eyes staring down at her.

"Aidan! How did you sneak up on me like that?"

"Your eyes were closed, lass. It wasn't too difficult." His lips curled into a smile and he plunked himself down on the chair next to hers. "Hard morning?"

"You could say that—Dolly went missing again, Mr. Allen fell in the shower and bruised his hip, Mrs. MacNally rang her bell at least fifty times because she was sure she was having a heart attack—indigestion, as usual, because she sneaks down to the kitchen when Mrs. Morton steps out and steals whatever isn't nailed down. Then Miss Curry tried to climb into bed with old Mr. Montgomery, and—"

"Whoa, I get it!" Aidan put his hands up in a warding gesture, laughing. "I'm glad I get to spend so much of my time *outside* those walls."

Colleen felt the fatigue of the morning drain away. There was something so joyous about Aidan Shaw, it was impossible to stay tired or depressed around him.

Two weeks ago he had joined her for lunch on the patio, and since then she found herself looking for him and disappointed if he didn't show. Next to Liz, he was the closest thing to a real friend she'd found at Balfinnan.

She studied him out of the corner of her eye. He really was very handsome, even if he wasn't her type at all. Dark hair in curls that rioted all over his head like an untamed mane, those grey eyes like a Scottish sky just before it rains, a full mouth that seemed made for laughter. Not tall enough for her taste—he was probably just under six feet—and lean rather than muscular. She preferred muscles, and a frame that towered over her by about a mile, and blue eyes and smooth blond hair—she jerked herself out of dangerous waters to find Aidan staring at her with a quizzical expression, and realized she'd been daydreaming again. She jumped to her feet.

"Show me the ruin?" she said, and watched as he peeled himself out of the chair with far more grace than she had.

"Sure." He put his hands in his jeans pockets and walked beside her along the side of the house and around the corner. As it had on her first day at the castle, the sight of the ruined part of Balfinnan House stole her breath, and Colleen stopped and stared at the three stories of devastation before her.

"Shocking, isn't it?" Aidan spoke quietly, although they were the only ones there. "It's going to take a lot of work if it's ever to come back from the dead, but that's what Anderson wants."

Colleen felt a shiver work its way up her spine at his words. *Back from the dead?* She was reminded of her conversation with old Gordon MacNabb last week. She shook herself out of the morbid feeling. Balfinnan had certainly seen its share of death and sadness, but she supposed that was to be expected when a house had so much history.

"When did it happen?" she asked him.

"Back at the end of the war—the first World War—though I'm not sure exactly when, and the castle was closed up not too long after. It only reopened a few years ago by the latest Anderson."

She stared up through the vines and tree branches that crowded against the walls as if to shield the stone from pitying eyes. Some of the windows were gone on the top floors, and blackened beams could be seen where parts of the ceiling had burned away in some of the rooms.

The ground floor looked in better shape; through an unbroken window she could see some furniture: bookshelves, mostly empty, and what appeared to be a drafting table with a leather swivel chair. Likely the architect's office. What a lonely place to work! No wonder she'd never met him. If it meant coming out here to this sad remnant of the past, she'd pass.

She caught the movement of branches near one of the third floor windows—no, it would be the second floor here in Scotland, she remembered—and her eyes were immediately drawn in that direction. There was nothing there, of course, but without warning a sudden feeling of dejà vu gripped her, and she shivered.

I swear, I'm turning into Simon! It was almost as if she recognized this place, and she felt the urge to get as far away from it as she could, without the faintest notion why. Then the feeling passed as if it had never come.

"It's sad here, but beautiful, too," she said, looking around her. "What're those yellow bushes? They're everywhere!"

"Oh, that's gorse, but we call it whin here. It grows all over in Scotland, and is very pretty...but especially in kissing season."

Colleen looked at him and saw that his eyes were shining with mirth. She put her hands on her hips. "Okay, what's kissing season?"

Well, the old-timers say that when the whin is in bloom, it's kissing season..."

"And..." Colleen prompted.

"Well, whin blooms all year round."

She laughed and punched him on the arm. "Funny. You're a comedian as well as a gardener."

Aidan looked startled, and then smiled. "If you say so. Do you have to get back right away?"

"In a few. Why?"

"I want to introduce you to some friends of mine." He grabbed her hand and pulled her away from the ruin, using the path that had been cut through the yellow bushes. At the end of the path, the trees opened onto a moor of wildflowers, thistle, and the purple bloom of heather.

Something touched her leg. Colleen gasped and whirled around to find a close-set pair of black eyes staring up at her from a long, serious face. The sheep opened its mouth and let out a happy, welcoming bleat, and Colleen turned to find Aidan grinning at her.

"That's Artemis," he said with a solemn air. "Artemis, meet my friend Colleen."

"Um, hello, Artemis." Colleen regarded her new acquaintance. "Can I pet her?"

As if in answer, the sheep butted her leg with a wooly head. Colleen ran her hand over the animal's fleecy forehead and then scratched her tentatively behind the ears. She knew that cats and dogs enjoyed that, but this was new territory.

Apparently Artemis thought it was just fine. She gave another soft bleat, then leaned into Colleen. She raised her head and let out a louder bleat, and suddenly they were surrounded by woolly bodies, each pushing to get close to the human visitors. Colleen was entranced.

"I've never been this close to a sheep, not even at a petting zoo!" she said. "Why are they so friendly?"

"Well, sheep are domestic animals; they're used to humans. They're handled all the time, so they expect it."

"How many are there? Do they belong to Balfinnan?"

"About fifty—it's a small flock, more of a hobby than anything else. And yes, they're Anderson's, although he doesn't have much to do with them. He gets in a local lad to do the shearing. And there's Archie, of course."

"Archie?" Colleen hadn't heard the name. "Who's he?"

"We'd better get back," Aidan said, and turned away from the sheep. As they walked back to the castle, he told her a little of the wonder known as Archibald Ferguson. "Archie is a man of mystery. No one knows what his job was before coming here, but he was a wanderer for a while. Do you know what a wanderer is, lass?"

"Why yes I do," Colleen told him with pride. "One of Aubrey's friends, an old man named Alastair MacGregor, is one. He was at her wedding, and Kate's. She says he's eccentric and brilliant, and quite wonderful."

"Aye, everyone in the Highlands knows Alastair MacGregor. Made a fortune with his photography, though to look at him you'd never guess. If you catch him out while he's on a wander, you might smell him first." Colleen wrinkled her nose and he laughed. "Well, if you met him at a wedding he was probably cleaned up and smelling quite different. He thinks Yardley's English Lavender perfume is bath soap."

"Oh, I get that," she said, thinking of Gladys. "One of my housemates labors under the same misconception."

"Anyway," Aidan continued, "Archie was a wanderer, too, sometimes hung around with Alastair, though he's pretty solitary. Shy, but not unfriendly. Just prefers his own company. Old Harry sent him to Balfinnan. He wouldn't set foot in the castle, so Anderson put him to work outside, where he's happiest."

They skirted the ruined section and walked around the side of the castle to the patio. Colleen knew it was time to get back inside to the bedlam that was nursing at Balfinnan House, but she wished she had more time to stay and talk with Aidan. There was just something so comforting about him. She waved goodbye and walked reluctantly into the kitchen and through to the hall.

"Nurse Fitzgerald?"

All thoughts of Aidan Shaw fled her mind as she found herself staring up into the brilliant blue eyes of Graham Anderson. Her heart began to pound. *God, he's gorgeous.*

"Can you come to my office for a minute?" His expression gave nothing away, but Colleen's senses went on alert. What was this about? Had she done something wrong?

Stop it, Fitzgerald! Just because he's your boss doesn't mean you're in trouble. What a scaredy-cat you've become!

Anderson indicated a chair in front of his desk, the same chair she'd sat in for her interview on her first day at Balfinnan. He rounded the desk and sat down, hands steepled under his chin. The gesture chilled her with its familiarity.

"I feel very uncomfortable with what I have to say," he began, and her heart sank. "I've received a communication from a colleague at Raighmore that is disturbing, to say the least." He paused and looked at Colleen for a long moment. Did he look sad? She was frozen in time, transported back to Nesbitt General in New Jersey, sitting in front of another CEO as he ripped her life away from her. "I want to hear your side of the story, because frankly, I don't believe it."

Colleen stared at Anderson in shock. She opened her mouth, but nothing came out. *Words! Where are my words? He's giving me a chance! What can I say that will make him understand what really happened?* But she sat like an animal at bay and stared at him.

"Miss Fitzgerald?" He studied her face, and sighed.

"All right. I'm going to ask you one question. Did you do what they said you did? That's all I need to know."

She forced her numb body to move, to make her head shake, just a little. It was all she had.

His posture relaxed. "I didn't think so. I admit that I haven't been as thorough in checking references as I should be. For some reason I can't figure out, our staff turnover is unusually high. I'll be honest—if I'd had this information before you began here I would not have hired you, in spite of Harry Campbell's recommendation. But I'm a pretty good judge of character, and I've had the chance to see how you feel about your patients, how much you care for them. I can't in my wildest imagination see you being capable of jeopardizing that." He leaned forward in the chair, his eyes intense. "But I will have the story from you, Miss Fitzgerald. I need to understand why a fine nurse like you was implicated in such a serious matter. Do you understand?"

Like a wind-up toy, Colleen nodded, tears of relief welling in her eyes. He believed her. He wasn't firing her! The rope around her heart loosened, and suddenly the words poured out as if a dam inside her had broken.

She told him everything—everything except how much John had meant to her. She felt a panicked need to get it all out on the table, to justify this man's willingness to take a chance on her despite her disgrace. And when she was finished, she sat looking down into her lap, unable to say another word, barely able to breathe. Tears poured unbidden down her cheeks.

Colleen heard the sound of a chair scraping back from the desk, and then suddenly arms were around her, strong arms that held comfort and trust and empathy. He sat still, his chin resting on top of her head, and said nothing as she cried herself out, too drained to think about the fact that Graham Anderson was holding her in a way that under normal circumstances would be quite intimate and inappropriate.

The moment passed and he dropped his arms, standing and returning to his position behind the desk. She looked at him with watery eyes, and he gave her a slight smile.

"Now, I think those patients you love so much will be needing you. But I want you to know that I have faith in you...Colleen." There was a new look in the blue eyes—something beyond the kindness. Or maybe she was imagining it. It didn't matter; she still had a job. She was a nurse.

The rest of the day was a blur.

CHAPTER 8
DIG TWO GRAVES

Everyone should keep a journal. I read that somewhere, and it's true. My journal has been my best friend in this venture—my only friend, really—the only one I trust. I don't know if I would have had the courage to put my plans into action without it.

Of course, I have to keep my journal secret. It's hidden in a safe place, one that no one will ever find. If they did, if my secret were exposed... Well, let's just say that would be the end of everything. Because people don't take kindly to murder.

What is it they say about revenge? If you plan revenge, dig two graves? Maybe so. But it's not revenge I want—it's vengeance. And it's not two graves I'm thinking of. No, my plan calls for more than two. Some will hold the innocent, necessary sacrifices. But only one of those graves will matter. And I'll stand over that one and know that I've won. Then it won't matter what becomes of me. I won't care.

"If you poison us do we not die? And if you wrong us shall we not revenge?" Shakespeare got it. It's all about poison. That is what started the whole thing, so many years ago. And now I'm going to finish it, and I think I'll choose poison again. It's only fair.

I have to be careful. It's a dangerous game, killing. I must wear this mask, lie and smile and pretend all the time. I can't be seen for what I am. These people here are old and frail and weak. But some of them are canny, and they talk. No one listens, at least not yet. But someone will. Not that it matters if they chatter away about ghosts and witches. They're old, and their minds are going. I rather enjoy the terror I can inspire in them, these useless feeble things.

But there are watchers, and I have to be very cunning. *She* is here—the one who started it all. She was a thief, so she had to go. Everything she had was taken from her—life, honor and reputation. Poetic justice. She's still here, watching. I don't know why, but I'm glad. If she's here, she can't be happy. It makes me feel good to know they were separated forever. She deserves to suffer.

I wonder about her, though. The Grey Lady, they call her now, because of the uniform. I haven't seen her, but I feel her presence. It's why they keep losing staff. Some people see her once and turn in their notice the next day. She doesn't frighten me, but I'm bothered. I can't figure out why she's here.

Why did she stay behind? She wasn't guilty, at least not of that crime. I know that better than most. So she could have moved on. She should have. She would have been with her lover, wherever murdered people go, but instead she's hanging around Balfinnan. Something's keeping her here, and I wish I knew what. I'll never understand ghosts.

She was Irish. They're all trouble, the Irish. Can't be trusted. She was from Dublin, and she came here as a nurse in the Great War. That's how she met him, and he fell in love with her. Then she killed him, and hanged herself in the east wing, and justice was served. So they said, and some of the story was true—but not all of it. I know better.

But no matter—she's not important, she can do nothing. She is nothing. Just a sad shade who once thought she had the world in her hand, when in truth she had it only for a while, and through theft. She paid dearly for her arrogance.

No, she's not the one I want. It's the one whose ancestor ruined my family, stole our future, our rightful place in the world. That one killed us, or as good as, and left us with nothing. And now I'll return the favor. I'll get vengeance for the harm they did us.

There are others here that I have to watch, though. That young janitor, for one. There's something odd about him; I haven't figured it out yet, but it's almost as if he can sense things others can't. I thought he'd caught me the other night. He stopped his skulking and just stared at the place where I stood, out of sight in the shadows. I would have made an excuse, of course; I had every right to be there, but dressed this way it would have raised questions. And he's nosy, like a little rat. He sees too much.

If he had seen me I would have had to do something about it, and I don't really want to. I can't go around just killing anyone—too many deaths would raise eyebrows. He's young and healthy; there would be questions. And I don't want an investigation, not until it's too late to matter.

When it comes right down to it, all this talk of not caring if I live or die as long as I get my vengeance? It's a load of rubbish, really. Of course I care. I can't die, but I can fail, and that's worse. I want to win. And that's why I have to be careful, and plan so that no one suspects. So that when it comes time for my enemy to die, there can be no suspicious fingers pointing at me.

There have been deaths already. There are always deaths in a nursing home, that's what makes it so perfect. Old people take lots of medications, and no one checks too carefully when they die to see if maybe they had too much, or the wrong thing. There is only one doctor here and he's too busy to wonder.

Call it practice. The old people are so grateful when I spend time with them, listen to them prattle on about their aches and pains or their families who don't visit them. And I listen, shake my head, and commiserate with them as if I really care. I'm good. Should've been on the stage.

I watched one of them die. She was past her time, but for some reason she was hanging on to life as if that shriveled up shell was worth keeping. People are funny. They complain about their aches and pains, cry that they should just die and save everyone the trouble, but then they fight so hard to stay in this world. And that one gave it a good go, in the end. I guess no one really wants to die no matter how old or sick they are, do they?

I have to admit I rather enjoyed watching the light go out of those old eyes. It amused me to watch her weak useless body try in vain to fight off death. But she was no one; she didn't matter.

I'm a bit worried about the old man in room ten. He's a talker, and he knows too much. He's so old that he can remember things about that time, and he talks as if he was there. He's becoming forgetful, and most people put his ramblings down to dementia like so many of the others, but I don't think he's demented at all. I think he is remembering things, and that means he's dangerous.

I think he saw me once, in my night form. He couldn't have known who I was, of course. But he called out in Gaelic and pointed right at me, and I thought for sure I was done. Then he told that new young nurse that he'd seen a ghost. Well, he was right enough.

That nurse spends a lot of time with him, and pretends to listen to his nonsense. She doesn't believe him, of course. I heard her talking to one of the other nurses about it. They were acting as if they were worried about his mind, and talking about his heart medication. And I find that very interesting. It could come in handy in the future.

I'm getting tired, and I think I'll put my journal away for now. But wait—a last thought just came to me, and it's perfect. That nurse—the new one? She's a redhead, and the coloring is right... Well, she's from America, but I think she's Irish. Just like the other one. Which would make it the perfect irony. I don't know enough about her yet, but I will. And maybe I'll figure out a way to use what I find out to bring the story full circle. When I'm done, I'll have to burn my journal. Too bad I'll never be able to share it, but it's enough that I'll know.

Another thing they say is, "Revenge is sweet." And that girl might just be the icing on my cake.

CHAPTER 9

SOMETHING WICKED THIS WAY COMES

Colleen arrived for work, rejuvenated by the first full night's sleep she'd had in weeks, to find the staff gathered around the sign-in sheet talking in low tones. Even Dolly was there, for a change.

"She was fine last night," whispered Flora. She had her coat on but showed no signs of leaving. "I gave her the tea and shortbread she always has and settled her in, and for once she wasn't complaining." Flora's eyes were damp. "The old witch was actually nice to me."

"What happened?" asked Colleen.

"Mrs. Buchanan died last night," Liz told her.

"What? Mrs. Buchanan? But she wasn't sick! Overweight, but her heart was as strong as mine!"

"Dr. Carnegie's up there now," Liz offered. "Of course, we're not to be told anything, as usual. But," she looked around the little group, "am I the only one who thinks something odd is going on around here? There seems to be a lot of turnover for a place with only fifteen residents. Most of them aren't sick, they're just old. Mr. Burns last month—that was right before you got here, Colleen—and a few weeks before that Mrs. Drummond...and now this."

"I don't know, Liz." Flora shook her head. "Mr. Burns was ninety-two and had kidney issues, and Mrs. Drummond had cancer." The color drained from her face. "Wait—what do you mean by odd? Do you think...the rumors...?" The nurse's watery blue eyes behind her wire-rimmed glasses were frightened.

"I knew it!" Dolly's voice was a whimper. "It's the ghost! The Grey Lady! My mam ain't gonna be pleased about ghosts hanging around where I work—she's not well, and she'll make me quit!"

Liz snorted. "I thought you'd already quit, as much as you take off. And you, Flora, you've been here longer than any of us. You should know better than to suggest that kind of nonsense! We have enough trouble keeping staff around here. It's a good thing Colleen isn't superstitious like you two, or you'd be scaring her away with all that talk of ghosts!"

Colleen was silent. She wasn't as untutored on the subject as they thought. She remembered her conversation last week with Gordon MacNabb—the story about a spirit called The Grey Lady...and the Ghruamachd. The very word had a ring of menace, and she felt a shiver go up her spine. Maybe she wasn't as superstition-free as Liz thought.

"I'm going up to check on Mr. MacNabb," she said, and signed in quickly. She hurried up the stone staircase, taking the steps two at a time. As she rounded the corner near the old man's room, she careened into a slight figure coming the other way. They fell against the wall together, each grabbing the other's arms for support.

"Oh, Simon, I'm sorry! I almost took you right out." Colleen smiled at the young man, who gulped and looked down, shuffling his feet.

"It's all right, Nurse Colleen. You can't hurt me." Simon Reid looked at her from under stubby eyelashes. "You're just about the only one here who's smaller than me. But way prettier," he added, and blushed to the roots of his light brown hair. He coughed to cover his embarrassment. "Anyway, where are you going in such a hurry?"

"I'm checking on Mr. MacNabb," she said. "Did you hear about Mrs. Buchanan?"

The boy's face darkened and he looked away and then back at Colleen, making steady eye contact for the first time. "Aye. And it shouldn't be."

"What do you mean?" she asked, frowning, but a part of her wasn't surprised to hear him say it. It was true that Mrs. Buchanan wasn't that old, by Balfinnan standards: only eighty-four. Her weight had been a problem, but there was nothing wrong with her heart. Still...

Simon's opinion mattered. He was different—in tune with the environment like no one she had ever known. When she'd asked him to keep an eye on Gordon MacNabb, he'd agreed without asking why. Almost as if he knew something about what the old man had told her.

She knew Simon thought he could see ghosts. He'd confided once that he had seen the Grey Lady not once, but several times. She hadn't believed him—or at least she hadn't believed that he'd actually seen a ghost—but it was obvious that *he* thought he had. And his sincerity was moving. For some reason she was drawn to this shy young man, and she trusted his instincts, if not his interpretation of them.

He leaned closer to her, though the hall was empty.

"I'm worried about Mr. MacNabb, too," he whispered. "He shouldn't be talking so much about the other ghost, not where anybody can hear him. It's evil, and evil doesn't like to be discovered."

"He calls it a Ghruamachd," Colleen said. "Such a weird name."

"It means 'grimness' in Gaelic," Simon said with a shudder. "But this thing is so much worse than that. I can't see it," he admitted, "and that's odd. But I feel it—its hatred." Simon cast a hopeful glance at Colleen, willing her to believe, to understand. "And that's strange, too. I've never met a ghost I could feel but not see, but maybe it doesn't want me to. Maybe it wants something here and it's mad because it can't find it. I just don't know!" He threw his hands out in frustration. Then he shoved them into the pockets of his overalls. "I'll keep a watch on Mr. MacNabb, when I can," he said, and straightened his slender body to its full height. "But you need to tell him to be quiet about the bad ghost. It's not safe."

With those words, he was gone.

Colleen knew as soon as she entered the room that

it wasn't going to be easy to keep Gordon MacNabb from talking. The old man sat straight up in his bed, arms crossed over his skinny chest, a look on his face like a winter storm waiting to wreak its vengeance.

"Weel, took ye lang enuff! Did ye hear? Noo dae ye believe me?"

"Shhh, Gordon. Yes, I heard. Mrs. Buchanan was overweight, and she didn't take care of herself. It's sad, but there's nothing more to it than that."

"Don't ye ken? Ah thooght ye had sense! She didna jist die. She was murrdured!" MacNabb was shaking like a leaf. "The Ghruamachd is killin' off awl us auld folk, an' Ah'm no gonna have mah birthday!" Tears ran down his face, tracing the deep wrinkles on his aged face. "Ah want mah birthday!"

Colleen stumbled into the kitchen an hour later, drained of energy. She had finally calmed Gordon MacNabb down enough that he'd gone off into a fitful sleep, but she didn't hold out much hope that he'd keep quiet about his Ghruamachd. She hoped Simon was wrong about the evil he'd sensed in the castle, but she didn't have much hope there, either. Something *was* wrong, and it was stupid to pretend otherwise. She wished she could just run away like the others, but she had nowhere to go and she had to stay for her residents.

Arabella Morton brought over a cup of tea. "Here, lass. Looks like you might need something a mite stronger, but this is the best I can do."

"Thanks, Mrs. Morton." Colleen took the dainty china cup and gave the cook a look of gratitude. "This is exactly what I need right now."

"Mrs. Buchanan would've been happy to see how much everybody is greetin' for her," Mrs. Morton said. "She always said people couldn't wait for her to die, but of course she didn't mean it. I have to say, I was surprised it was her. I'd have said she'd be the last to go."

Colleen sighed. "Yes, the people who complain the most seem to be the ones who have the fiercest grip on life. Well, I suppose the doctor will decide if an autopsy is needed."

Mrs. Morton looked startled. "Autopsy? I thought she had a heart attack."

"They don't know how she died," Colleen told her. "But she wasn't sick. I'm sure her family will have something to say about it."

Mrs. Morton folded her tall body into a chair across from Colleen and tucked a black strand of hair behind her ear. "I'll be honest with you, lass, this place sometimes gives me the willies. I wouldn't go up on that second floor if you paid me. There are rumors about it, especially the burned-out part."

"The ruin?" Colleen looked at her. "What really happened there, anyway?"

"Oh, it was during the Great War. The family lived there then, when Balfinnan was a hospital for wounded soldiers. A nurse killed herself up there, and a few days later a fire started and almost burned the whole place to the ground. They managed to keep the damage to just that one section, and it's been that way for almost a hundred years."

"But now Mr. Anderson's going to have it restored, right?" Colleen leaned forward. "I mean, he's hired an architect and everything."

"Well, if you ask me, that's a mistake. They should just take down the whole thing!"

Colleen was surprised by the vehemence in the cook's voice.

"But why? Wouldn't it be lovely for Mr. Anderson to have the castle back the way it was?"

Mrs. Morton shook her head, doubt written across her plain face. "I suppose you're right, lass. It's not Mr. Anderson's fault what happened way back when, now is it?"

A shadow darkened the kitchen doorway, and they looked up to see a disapproving glower on the face of the housekeeper, Mrs. Murtaugh. "You're wanted," she said to Colleen. "And I don't think it's my job to track down nurses who want to spend time gossiping when there's tragedy in the house."

"Oh, leave her alone, Morag!" Mrs. Morton shook her head at the woman. "She's having a cup of tea, for heaven's sake. Lord knows we all need one today."

"Hmmph!" was the housekeeper's response. "Well, Arabella, that's just lovely, but Mr. Anderson wants to see all the staff in his office, if Nurse Fitzgerald can bear to leave her tea. You, too." And with that, Mrs. Murtaugh turned and marched out of the room.

"She hates me," mumbled Colleen as she stood. "What did I ever do to her?"

"Probably just got up today, that's all it takes." Mrs. Morton furrowed her eyebrows in imitation of the surly housekeeper. "Ach, lass, don't worry about her!

Morag Murtaugh never met a day that she couldn't turn gloomy. It's not you—she's just passionate about this place and her job, and she thinks she's the only one that cares about Mr. Anderson. Ridiculous woman."

"Well, I'm going to continue my plan of staying out of her way. She can't hate me if she doesn't see me, right? Thanks, Mrs. Morton. The tea was lovely."

"You're welcome, lass. Anytime. Now, we'd better get on."

Graham Anderson looked up as Colleen squeezed herself into the little space and gave her a warm smile. It flowed over her like the sun coming from behind a cloud, and suddenly she felt a little taller, a little more energized, ready to take on whatever the world had to offer.

It's his gift, she thought. *No wonder Mrs. Murtaugh wants to fight his battles. I do, too.*

A little voice whispered in her head that she was very possibly going down a familiar road, but she chose to ignore it. He treated her the same way he treated every other staff member...didn't he? Except that he knew her story and had chosen to believe in her anyway. That alone was enough to put Colleen firmly in his camp.

She pulled herself back to the moment to hear Anderson say, "—and the family wants answers. They don't want an autopsy, though. I almost wish they did." He looked around the room. "Mrs. Buchanan was old, but she wasn't senile, or fragile, or near death from any known cause. There was simply no reason for her to die. And the fact that she did die in spite of all that concerns me very much. She was our resident, our family. I feel somehow as if we failed her."

Colleen felt a chill go through her at his words. *Near death from any known cause.* Contrary to public opinion, old people were not liable to pop off at any moment for no reason. They were likely to suffer from aging ailments like dementia, heart issues, joint pains, yes. But if none of those things were present, why had Mrs. Buchanan died? She caught a look from Aidan and gave him a wan smile.

"I want you all to carry on as usual," Anderson was saying, "but be extra aware. Something is going on here—something I can't explain. No, Miss Gilles, not something supernatural, and I'll ask you not to repeat nonsense like that in future." Dolly flushed and looked at the floor. "But there is something odd going on, and I swear I'll get to the bottom of it." Anderson looked around at those assembled once more. "This care facility is my dream, and I will not let anything get in the way of its success. You can be very sure of that. Now, you may go about your work. When I know what arrangements Mrs. Buchanan's family has made for her funeral, I'll let you all know, and I hope that as many of you as can will attend. Thank you. Now, Nurse Fitzgerald, Mr. Reid: can you please stay behind for a few moments?"

Several people in the room turned in surprise to see Simon wedged against the wall at the back. Anderson waited until the others were gone, and then pulled up a chair to form a tight circle of three.

"I asked you two to stay because I trust your instincts." Colleen looked up in surprise, and Anderson glanced her. "I wasn't completely truthful just now, when I told Dolly Gilles that nothing otherworldly was happening." He sighed, and his look was grave. "Simon, you may have wondered why you were hired at Balfinnan. Your family was skeptical when I asked for you—yes, I specifically asked for you to come here. They told me I was making a mistake, that you would never amount to anything."

Simon hung his head.

"But I knew your grandfather, Simon. He and my own grandfather went to school together, and they stayed in touch. He used to talk about you with pride. 'Fey,' he said. 'Simon is a seventh son, and seventh sons are special. The lad's odd, but in a good way. He sees things others don't.'" Anderson paused. "Is that true, Simon? Do you see things that others don't see?"

Simon and Colleen both stared wide-eyed at Anderson.

"There are things on this earth that can't be explained by science or logic. I don't understand them, but I'm willing to suspend disbelief because I don't know what else to do. Nurse Fitzgerald," he said, turning those intense blue eyes on her. "I have watched you with the patients, and I know that you, more than any of the others, have their confidence. I want you to listen—I know you already do that, but now I want you to be even more vigilant. In the short time you've been here, you have established trust with them. The residents know you and love you." His look was tired but amused. "Oh, yes, I also listen to those in my care. They speak very highly of you. If they're upset, or sad, or don't feel well, it's you they ask for."

Colleen was speechless. He'd talked to the residents about her? Why?

"There is something not right in my castle," Anderson lowered his voice. "Something I can't explain. People are dying. I know—" he put up a hand in a warding gesture "—elderly people die. It's the natural way of things in a care home. But that's not what's happening here. Some of these people should not have died. It wasn't their time." He looked at them, his face bleak, the blue eyes troubled. "I think that something is killing my residents."

A voice whispered in Colleen's mind. She jerked in shock, looked around the room and then at the others. Anderson seemed unaware, but Simon was staring at her, concern reflected in his eyes.

He had heard it, too, she thought—a voice with a distinctive Irish lilt.

You're in danger. Be careful.

CHAPTER 10
A FRIEND INDEED

"What's wrong? You look as dour as a Scot!"

Colleen looked up to see Aidan standing at the edge of the patio. He was smiling, but his brow was creased with concern. He turned a lawn chair to face hers, sat down, and gave her his full attention.

That was one of the things she liked best about Aidan—his ability to focus completely on his companion. His entire body stilled and it seemed as if she was the only person in the world. Quite a gift, she thought, with a surge of affection. It warmed her and eased some of the tension she'd been feeling since yesterday's eerie meeting with Anderson.

"Nothing, really." She looked up at him and decided he deserved better than that. "How long have you been here at Balfinnan, Aidan?"

"About three months, why?"

"Have you noticed anything different going on lately? Oh, never mind, you wouldn't. You're always outside." Colleen shook her head and sighed.

"You might be surprised. I am allowed inside the building now and then," he said. "As long as I take my boots off. I can be quite civilized."

"Oh, I didn't mean that! You're such an idiot." Colleen looked up to see his grin and laughed. "I just meant that you wouldn't be inside enough to pick up on any weird things that might be happening, that's all."

"Do you mean the ghosts?"

"No, not exactly, but that's part of—" *Ghosts? He knew?* "What do you mean?" Colleen kept her tone carefully level. "I only know about the Grey Lady. Are there more? Is that even allowed?" She tried to appear nonchalant and amused, but could tell by the tremor in her voice that it wasn't working. She was a terrible actress. Kate had pointed out on more than one occasion that the only person she could fool was herself.

Aidan burst out laughing. "Allowed? Ach, lass, who's going to tell a ghost that he can't haunt the place because it's already full? No, some keeps have many ghosts flitting about the place. Edinburgh Castle, for one." He eyed Colleen. "Balfinnan used to have just the one, the Grey Lady, and she's fairly recent by Scottish standards. But I've heard there're two now, so maybe the other one decided to come and keep her company. Might have something to do with the preservation," he added thoughtfully.

Colleen felt a familiar chill work its way up her spine. She heard the echo of Mrs. Morton's voice. *There are rumors about it, especially the burned-out part.*

And suddenly, with no warning, her eyes flooded and her shoulders began to shake. The worry about keeping her job, the tension with Simon and Gordon, the sudden death of Mrs. Buchanan...and the growing feelings she might be having for her boss. Yes, especially that last bit. It was all too much.

And then Aidan had his arms around her and was hugging her, giving her the gift of his empathy and his friendship. She stiffened for just a second and then let herself fold into his chest, allowing his warmth to seep into her heart.

"There's more, though, isn't there?" His voice was gentle. He released her and pushed himself back into his chair.

She couldn't tell him. He was her best friend here, and if she could tell anyone about her confusion about Graham Anderson, it would be him, but she couldn't. She just didn't know what to say. Graham had been sending her subtle messages ever since that horrible conversation about her references...or was that just wishful thinking on her part? The truth was she didn't trust herself with men anymore.

But there *were* things she could talk about with Aidan. She found herself telling him about her fears for Gordon MacNabb, and about her connection to Simon who swore he had felt an evil presence in the castle. Most of all, the suspicious deaths at Balfinnan. He listened without comment, his grey eyes never leaving her face.

"What you need," he announced when she wound down like a broken toy, "is a day away from here."

"I know," she told him. "I was supposed to go to

Edinburgh to see Kate this weekend—Kate's my best friend—and I was going with Aubrey but she doesn't feel well—she's pregnant and has morning sickness—and Finn won't let her out of his sight, and I don't want to take the train by myself—"

"I'll go with you," he interrupted.

Colleen stared at him.

"I'll go with you," he repeated. "I have a couple of days coming, and Graham won't mind. We'll take the train from Inverness to Edinburgh; it's a lovely ride, about three and a half hours, and your friend can meet us at the station or we can take a cab to her."

"Really?" Colleen felt a weight the size of a standing stone lift from her chest. "Are you serious? You'll go with me? Oh, Aidan, I love you!"

A strange look passed over his features, and then he laughed. "Whoa, lass. Don't go getting all soppy. It's just a wee rail journey!"

As Colleen skipped through the kitchen on her way back to work, an errant thought suddenly presented itself. *He called our boss Graham. How well does he know him?*

Colleen stared out the window as the train rumbled south through the Highlands. She felt her spirits growing lighter the further away she got from Balfinnan House, but at the same time something in her heart cried out at the separation. How could a place claim a hold on her so quickly, and yet frighten her to her core?

She watched sheep in the fields, placid and heedless of the train flashing past, and felt envious of their single-minded attention to the job of eating.

"There're more sheep than people in Scotland," a voice penetrated the fog in her brain.

Colleen turned to look at Aidan. He was dressed in khaki pants and a blue sweater that turned his eyes the color of the hills in shade, and an attempt had obviously been made to tame his wild dark hair. He looked even more handsome out of the work clothes he wore at Balfinnan, and the two girls eyeing him from across the aisle seemed to agree. *They probably think we're a couple*, she thought with amusement, and wondered what he'd do if she reached for his hand. Probably run for his life, she decided. Better not.

He was staring at her now, and she realized that her thoughts had wandered off again. It seemed to be happening a lot lately.

"Um—other than the airport, I haven't seen anything of Edinburgh," she said. "And I haven't seen Kate in three weeks. She's been my best friend since we were kids, and now there's Aubrey. She's here in Scotland, too. We're like The Three Musketeers."

"Kate's a detective?"

"Yes, she works for the police with her husband Jack. They just got married last year."

"And what does Aubrey do?"

"Aubrey works at Mackintosh Book Store, but she's been taking classes in writing at the College in Inverness, where her husband Finn works. He's a professor of Scottish history there."

"Oh—I know Finn. Finn Cameron, right?"

"Yes!" Aidan was full of surprises. She would have thought a gardener and a college professor ran in different circles, but Inverness was a small city and maybe they'd known each other as kids.

"Did you go to school together?"

"Sure did: Finn and I, and Graham, too. Graham was two years ahead of us, but we hung around with him in school. We used to make fun of him because he was rich but his clan didn't have a chief. Stupid stuff. He got me the job at Balfinnan, so I guess I'm forgiven."

Well, that explained the familiar use of Anderson's name.

"Aidan isn't really a Scottish name, is it?"

"Aye, it is, but my guilty secret is that I'm really Irish." He grinned at her look of disbelief. "Dinna tell anyone, lass, they'll drive me out of the Highlands!"

"And how did you end up in Scotland?"

"My mam was from Dublin. My dad went over there to work in the Jameson Whisky distillery, met Mam, and stayed. She died when I was three, and Dad brought me back and raised me right here in Inverness—his hometown. So you decide...am I Irish or Scottish?"

"Well," Colleen narrowed her eyes at him. "Does your clan have a chief?"

He roared with laughter. "Well done—and it most certainly does. And what about you? Where'd you get the red hair?"

"Oh, I'm American, born in New Jersey," she told him. "My mom was a second generation Irish-American, but my dad was born in Kilkenny. So I guess I'm more Irish than you, sir!" She punched him lightly on the arm and was rewarded with an exaggerated wince.

"Small but mighty," he muttered, then grabbed her arm and pointed out the window.

"Look, way over there just in front of the hills. That's a Scottish red deer. Not so many of those as sheep—you're lucky to see one. Isn't he beautiful?"

"Oh, he is! And what's that? The white building with the fancy letters? Is it a distillery?"

"It is indeed—the Dalwhinnie distillery. It's a very good Highland whisky. They give tours and such— have you had any whisky?"

"I have. It's the only Scottish food I like," Colleen said. "Do *not* ask me what I think of haggis!"

"Not a fan myself," he admitted. "Not all Scots live on haggis and black pudding, you know. I haven't played the bagpipes since primary school, and I only wear a kilt for special occasions. Are you disappointed?"

The banter continued as the train rolled on, and when they finally pulled into Waverly Station in Edinburgh, Colleen realized that for three and a half whole hours she hadn't thought about ghosts, or death...or Graham Anderson.

"Fitz!" a beloved voice shrilled through the throng, and Colleen was wrapped in a bear hug from her best friend Kate Bianchi. Kate MacDonald now, Colleen reminded herself. A Scot.

"Kate, this is Aidan," Colleen said. "He works with me at Balfinnan."

Kate gave Aidan a shrewd look that might have wilted a lesser man, and then put out her hand. He bypassed the hand and gave her a hug, eliciting an approving look as Kate studied him for a moment, then turned back to Colleen.

"Jack's meeting us at The World's End. It's as old as old gets and very cool. He went earlier to get a table because it's Friday night and impossible to get in after six o'clock, so let's go!"

"As old as old gets" was putting it lightly, Colleen thought, as they squeezed themselves into a corner table in what seemed near total darkness. How on earth did they see what they were serving? Or eating?

And then it didn't matter. Her eyes adjusted, she and Kate started arguing as if they'd said goodbye to each other yesterday, and in minutes the men were in a deep discussion about something called shinty, which apparently was a game where men tried to club a small ball into the opponent's net as hard as they could.

"And did you see MacRae bring his caman down on Ritchie's? Out of line, but if Middleton hadn't tackled him it would've worked. MacRae's always been a sneaky bastard."

"Aye, wish he was on our side."

Kate rolled her eyes.

"Is that the game they were playing in *Outlander*, where they tried to kill each other with hockey sticks?" Colleen asked her. Her friend nodded.

"They'll be at it for a while, and then they'll probably get into football—soccer to us—and maybe rugby. It's incomprehensible to me, but at least it means I have you to myself. Let's go outside for some air."

Out on the Royal Mile, Kate turned and faced

Colleen. So—" she pierced her friend with her gimlet detective's eye. "How's the romance going?"

Trust Kate to cut to the chase.

"I don't know what you're talking about. But Kate, so much has happened in three weeks!"

She filled her friend in on the strange happenings at Balfinnan, her growing bond with the shy young janitor, her run-ins—and mostly avoidances—with the surly housekeeper, and her new friendship with Artemis the sheep. She didn't mention Graham Anderson, but Kate's beagle nose picked up the scent immediately.

"So, don't tell me you've soured on the next Mr. Fitzgerald already! That's not like you at all, Fitz!"

Colleen hesitated, but there never had been a chance of misdirection with Kate. She sighed.

"Graham is...sort of a work in progress," she said. "I admire him so much, and I think he's fond of me, but I'm afraid. He's exactly my type, which is scary." She tightened her lips at a snort from her friend. "I'm not stupid, Kate! I know I shouldn't judge men by their looks, and I'm working on it! But Graham is different. He feels the same way about the residents as I do. He found out about my awful references and still gave me a chance to explain!" She shuddered at the memory. "And he believed me. He's been seeking me out for advice on patient care when I know he doesn't have to, and he just...looks at me in a funny way sometimes, almost as if he wants to say something and he's afraid to. Maybe he was hurt once, too. Oh, I can't explain it, but I like him, Kate, and I think I'm falling for him a little, and it scares the hell out of me!"

"Um hmm. And what about Aidan?"

Colleen looked surprised. "Oh, I love Aidan! He's become the best friend I have over here next to you and Aubrey. He's sweet, and funny, and pretty damn adorable—I can't count the times he's pulled me out of a funk and made me feel better just by talking nonsense or taking me to visit the sheep. He has this ability to just *listen*, you know? I told him all about John, and he was suitably appalled and supportive."

"He seems terrific," Kate said. Colleen nodded, her expression reflective.

"There's one thing, though. What I can't figure out is why he's wasting his time working as a gardener. He says he was friends with Finn and Graham in school, and both of them went on to university and are very academic. I mean, Aidan seems smart enough, so why work such a menial job?"

"You know what you sound like?" Kate shook her head in disgust. "A snob, that's what! Maybe he's pursuing a doctorate in herbology or something. Maybe he had the chance to go to university but he turned it down to be near his sick granny. I swear, sometimes I can't believe you! You just don't see it, do you?"

"See what? What's wrong with you?"

"What's wrong with *me*?" Kate's brown eyes grew wide. "I should leave you to your own misery, really. The problem isn't with me, it's with you! Can't you see what's right in front of you?"

Colleen gawked at her. "Aidan? He's a *friend*, Kate. A very good friend, but that's all. Graham—"

"And if you could get your head out of your ass and drag your eyes away from the sainted Mr. Anderson for two minutes, you'd see what I see. That man in there is perfect for you!"

Colleen burst out laughing. "Oh, Kate, stop it! That's ridiculous. Aidan's not my type at all. Besides, he's never even made a move in that direction, not that I'd let him. I told you, we're just friends. Now drop it, please, before one of us says something we'll regret!"

"Augghh!" Kate ran both hands through her dark curls and took a deep breath.

"Okay, Fitz. Have it your way. But don't get mad when you find out too late that I'm right, as usual."

Remember it all, every insult, every tear. Tattoo it on the inside of your mind.

Janet Fitch

SCOTLAND, 1918

race sat at the edge of the sleeping soldier's bed. His name was Alexander, and he was dying.

She couldn't remember ever having these feelings before. She had never dared stare at a man like this, but she couldn't take her eyes off him. It didn't matter anyway. He had been unconscious, burning up with fever, since he'd been brought into Balfinnan Hospital yesterday. But the fever only enhanced his looks, made him seem radiant, otherworldly. He was the most beautiful man she'd ever seen.

She looked around to make sure they were alone, and then reached out and took his dry, hot hand in her own large one. She had never touched a man like this, not with hope in her heart. There had never been an opportunity in all her twenty-two years. No man had ever asked her to walk out, none had wanted to touch her that way.

Sometimes she thought that the fates were playing a cruel joke on her to name her Grace. She was the opposite of the word—large-boned, heavyset, with a face that her stepfather had once laughingly described as a "pudding" when he thought she couldn't hear. The cruel taunt had sunk into her psyche to rest with all the other thoughtless jibes that had come her way for as long as she could remember.

But she refused to give up. There had to be more out there than her village, with its rough-mannered boys who spent their time at the pub and made rude comments to her when she passed on her way to the market. Somewhere there was a man who would treasure her, love her for herself. She just had to get out of this tiny Highland village and find him.

The war came, and the boys began to leave. They stood around in small groups pretending to be brave, but Grace could see the fear in their eyes. They were nicer to her when they were afraid, asking her to pray for them when they were gone to the killing fields of France. And she prayed, all right, but it was not the prayer that they were looking for. Many of them never came home, and most of those who did were changed, broken shells of the cocky lads who had gone off to war such a short time ago. She was glad to see their pain.

Grace's life changed with a poster at church, advertising for girls to study as nurses. Her parents, glad to be rid of a gloomy, unmarriageable daughter, were more than willing to scrape up the money to pay for training, as long as it would take her out of their way. And Grace found that here, finally, was something she could do well. She had been born a Beaton, of the hereditary medical kindred known throughout Scotland, so nursing was in her blood. Helpless patients were not so quick to dismiss her; on the contrary, they were grateful for her care. For the first time, she was the one with the power. Her oath raised her up, made her an angel of mercy. Nursing gave her a reason to go on and took some of the pain away.

The soldier stirred, but his eyes remained closed. She wanted him to look at her, to see her and know that it was she who was there for him, she who would bring him back from the brink. She continued to hold his hand, but there was no movement, no sign of awareness at all.

Grace didn't move, afraid to lose the tenuous connection. She imagined that he curled his fingers around hers, that he was holding her hand. He needed her! It was all she could do not to cry with the wonder of it. She was going to save him if it took everything she had. And he would know she was the reason he was alive. He would be so grateful, and over time that gratitude would turn to love. For her.

At last she placed his hand on the bedspread and stood to go. She had to bring his fever down, and for that she needed ice and more compresses. Humming with new purpose, Grace went down the hall to fill a basin. She hurried back to the soldier's room, afraid to leave him alone for more than a few minutes...and stopped short just outside the doorway, sloshing the water over the edge of the basin and onto the floor.

He wasn't alone. Inside the room stood a girl, staring at the soldier with shock on her lovely features. Tiny, almost elfin, she was everything Grace could never be. Lustrous red hair curled enchantingly around the edges of her nurse's cap, and the drab grey uniform was like a gown on her trim figure. As Grace watched, transfixed, as a terrible foreboding filled her mind.

Alexander Macleod stirred, and his eyes opened. Focused. Widened. Two sets of blue eyes stared at each other for an endless moment.

"It's you," he breathed.

He reached out to the girl and she took him in her arms, murmuring that she wouldn't leave this time, that she would stay with him as long as he needed her.

Grace backed away from the sheer power of the emotion before her. It was over before it had begun. It had been a dream, and she was a fool. White-hot rage rose up and threatened to choke her as she stumbled down the hall away from the room that had held such promise only moments before.

The hate swirled, grew, and became a living thing.

CHAPTER 11
OLD TOWN

olleen slept poorly that night. When she did drift off, she dreamed of tall, blond warriors stalking her around the streets of Harrington, New Jersey, pulling out claymores and fighting for her hand and then linking arms and marching off together, leaving her stranded in a street filled with blood. The images shifted, and she was sitting in the meadow behind Balfinnan watching two clans charge each other, targes up and daggers out. One clan was tall and blond, the other had untamed dark hair, and they hacked and stabbed at each other until only two were left.

"That one's perfect for you," bleated a voice at her side, and she turned to find Artemis the sheep, dressed in a tartan cloak and eating haggis from a silver plate with her curiously human fingers.

"Which one?" said her dream self, but her wooly companion only shrugged and kept eating.

You're no help, Colleen thought, but the sheep was gone and she found herself awake and staring at the ceiling.

Bleary-eyed, she stumbled into the tiny flat's kitchen on Saturday morning to find everyone else already there waiting for her.

"About time you got up, Lady Jane," said Kate, "you must have slept well." But her sharp dark eyes were mocking. Not a morning person at the best of times, Colleen glared at her and poured herself a cup of black coffee.

"Jack's taking us on a personal tour of the Old Town," Kate went on, ignoring the look. She gave her husband a fond glance as he dug into a plate of eggs and bacon and washed it down with coffee.

"Did you grow up here?" Aidan asked him.

"No, I'm from Aberdeen. But I went to university in Edinburgh, and I've been here ever since." Jack smiled. "Would you believe I've never been on a tour of the city? The only places my mates and I knew were the purveyors of fine drink." He shrugged. "I did a little research, and I think I've cobbled together a reasonable guide to the higher points of Scottish history and culture as it pertains to the Old Town."

As they walked from the car park to join the throngs of tourists flocking the medieval section of Edinburgh like birds searching for grain, Jack told them that they'd be starting at Greyfriar's Kirkyard.

"Is a kirkyard the same as a graveyard?" Colleen asked him.

"Aye, it is. I think you'll like it. Do you like dogs?"

Colleen was startled by the abrupt switch in topic.

What did dogs have to do with a graveyard? She should have had another cup of coffee.

Jack caught her look and laughed, green eyes lit with humor. "Greyfriars Kirkyard has one special grave, right near the gate, that honors a very loyal resident. He had to be buried on unconsecrated ground because he wasn't a member of the kirk...being a dog. Scottish Terriers are not religious enough, according to the church, but I'm thinking this one was probably a better person than a lot of the people buried inside. His name was Greyfriars Bobby."

Across from the entrance gate to the famous kirkyard, the statue of a small dog had been erected.

"He's a Skye Terrier," offered Aidan. "We had one when I was growing up—very loyal animals."

"And this one proves your point," Jack said. "Greyfriars Bobby belonged to an Edinburgh policeman. His owner, John Gray, died when the dog was only three years old, and for the rest of his life, Bobby sat guard on his master's grave here in the kirkyard. People fed him when they came to visit their own relatives, but he never went far from his master. He died right there when he was sixteen years old."

Colleen felt her eyes welling as she studied the statue of the little dog. Jack was right. Greyfriars Bobby put humans to shame.

"What a lovely story!" she said, her voice thick, and Jack smiled at the success of the first item on his list.

He continued the tour, leading them a short distance to a large square where tourists sat eating breakfast and enjoying the unusually balmy weather.

"This is the Grassmarket," Jack told them. "It's a lovely area, full of specialty shops and really good food, but it has more dead people than the kirkyard. Lots of haunted pubs and such."

Does everything in Scotland have to be about ghosts? Colleen shivered. Aidan turned and looked at her curiously, but she pretended she hadn't seen. She knew she'd been avoiding him all morning, sticking with Kate and hanging on Jack's every word. She wasn't sure why, but Kate's comments the night before had erected a wall between them...a wall he knew nothing about. She knew it wasn't fair, but she couldn't help it. He probably hadn't even noticed anyway, being a guy. She made an effort to smile at him, and was rewarded by a brilliant grin that did nothing at all for her tortured soul. Aidan stepped up to walk beside Jack once more, and Colleen let a space open up between them as she tuned back into Jack's spiel.

"In World War I, a German zeppelin dropped a bomb right on the Grassmarket," he was saying, "and eleven people were killed. But that's nothing to what went on during medieval times."

Kate dropped back to walk with Colleen. "Jack loves death and dismemberment," she said. "Probably his cop heritage. Never too many bodies for him!"

"I heard that!" her husband called back. "But you're right. Look at all those people just enjoying their fancy lunches. They might not be so sanguine if they knew that from 1661 to 1688 over a hundred people died on the scaffold right where they're eating, in full view of the public. It was called The Killing Time. Not our finest hour, I'll admit."

He stopped them in front of an ancient inn with a white deer on its sign.

"Looks innocent enough, right?" said Jack. "But the White Hart Inn has a dark history, going all the way back to 1516, and it's supposed to be haunted."

"Of course it is," muttered Colleen, to the delight of her tour guide.

"That one looks okay," she said, to change the subject. "Maggie Dickson's Pub. Sounds pretty innocuous, but I suppose you'll tell me she was a famous axe murderess who still haunts the place."

"Well, lass, you're brilliant, you are!" Jack grinned at her. "That pub is named after Half-Hangit Maggie, who murdered her own baby."

Colleen gasped. "Why on earth would they celebrate a child-murderer? That's taking it a bit too far, isn't it?"

Jack put up his hands in defense. "I didn't make the history, I'm just reporting it! But Maggie isn't famous because of her crime. She was hanged in the Grassmarket and her body was taken away back to her hometown to be buried. On the way, she woke up and was right as rain! Scottish law says a person can't be hanged twice for the same crime, so Maggie lived out the rest of her life free as a bird. That's why she's called Half-Hangit Maggie— they never finished the job!"

"Ugh. Are there any places in Edinburgh where a murder or execution didn't take place?" Colleen asked, hands on hips.

"Might be," Jack said with equanimity. "But they wouldn't be very interesting, now would they?"

The group left the Grassmarket and began the climb toward Edinburgh Castle, looming over them on its volcanic outcropping in the center of the city. Just outside the walls of the castle was a huge paved area that Jack told them was the esplanade.

"It's pretty new. Only built in 1753," he said. Kate looked at Colleen and both smiled at the idea that something built in 1753 was "new." It was the dawn of history for their own country. "It was built to show-case the military. If you'd been here in August, Colleen, you'd have been able to come with Kate and me to see the Royal Edinburgh Military Tattoo, which is pretty damn impressive, I'll tell you!" He looked at his wife affectionately. "Kate has a special affinity for bagpipes."

Apparently it was their private joke, and as they didn't see fit to share, Colleen didn't ask. Probably had something to do with ghosts. Sometimes she felt positively left out of the party, as the only one of her friends who hadn't seen a real ghost. And it would be just fine if she never saw one, she told herself. Just fine!

"The castle's history is mostly military," Jack said as they forced their way through hordes of tourists from every place around the globe. "But here," he stopped and pointed to a marker, "is a memorial called The Witches Wall. It pays tribute—a bit too late, mind you—to a large number of women who were burned at the stake in the sixteenth century for being accused of witchcraft."

"I'm sure they're grateful for the tribute," Colleen said, but the sarcasm was ignored by their guide.

"Mary, Queen of Scots came to the castle to give birth to her son, who was later crowned James VI of

Scotland and James I of England. Didn't do her much good in the end, though."

Kate interjected, "Mary seems to have hung out at a great many castles in Scotland. Finn took us on a tour to Eileen Donan, and he said she haunts that one, too. She seems to have died in a lot of them, because a lot of castles like to claim Mary as one of their ghosts."

"Well, Mary isn't the only ghost in Edinburgh Castle." Aidan spoke up. "I remember a school trip when I was a wee lad. A lot of former prisoners are supposed to haunt the place. There's a head-less drummer—lots of people lost their heads back then—and his drumming can be heard playing on the battlements. I think they were trying to scare us, though. Don't know how much truth there is to it."

"Oh, it's true," said Jack, "or at least the reports of drums are. They say if you do see him, it means danger is coming to the castle. So if you see a drummer who's missing his head, close your eyes!"

By the time they reached the last stop on Jack's tour, Colleen thought she would drop any minute from exhaustion. It had been a great day, but if it lasted much longer she'd be seeing headless drummers herself.

"And now," Jack intoned as he led them back down the Royal Mile, "the pièce de résistance. The crowning achievement of Jack MacDonald Tours—the Tolbooth!" He brought them to a stop in the center of the street. "The Tolbooth prison stood right here for almost 400 years, until its demise in the early nineteenth century. Public hangings, beheadings, dismemberment—it all happened here," he told them, pointing to a heart-shaped mosaic in the street. "This was the place to be if you were a political prisoner. From 1785, executions were carried out right here, and a gallows was erected so that the public could view the hangings of prominent political figures who had run afoul of the current government. There wasn't much else to do in those days, so hangings were a real treat.

"But that wasn't all the entertainment provided," he went on. "Torture was a big part of the Tolbooth. People got to enjoy the boot, which was some sort of device that crushed the foot slowly, or the pilliwinks, which is a whimsical name for thumbscrews. If you hadn't done much, you might get lucky and just wind up in the jougs."

"All right, I know I'm going to be sorry, but what are jougs?" asked Colleen.

"Thought you'd never ask. The jougs were metal collars put around a prisoner's neck, and then he was chained to wall outside for the populace to throw things at him and call him names."

"Charming."

"But those were the common criminals. They used to put the heads of important figures on spikes and leave them there for months. If you were especially famous or notorious, you got to have your head displayed on 'the prick of the highest stone', a spike on the Tolbooth's northern gable that faced the High Street. One head was there for ten years before it was taken down to make way for the next lucky tenant."

Colleen's attention was arrested by an old man

who shuffled by and stopped suddenly beside the stone mosaic. As she watched, the man spat on the heart, before moving on without a look at the gaping tourists.

"For good luck," said Jack. Colleen shook her head in bewilderment. Scots. She backed away from the heart, her stomach churning at the thought of how much spit had collected on that spot over the ages.

By the time she'd fallen into the twin bed in Kate's tiny guest room, Colleen was sure her dreams would be even worse than the night before, but this time she slept like a rock. Jack's tour, though somewhat dour and lugubrious, had been exactly what she needed. Balfinnan seemed like a dream, its ghosts a part of the distant past.

Sunday was spent shopping with Kate while the men went to a local tavern for the game. Although Kate said nothing more about Aidan or Graham, she'd planted the seed and Colleen knew it was something that would have to be resolved sooner rather than later.

Kate was wrong. She didn't want to hurt Aidan, and she shouldn't have to. Aidan was a friend. A woman could have a man as a best friend, no matter what other people thought. She wasn't going to lose him. She was going to have her cake and eat it, too.

Graham was the right man for her. She could feel it in her heart. This time she wouldn't rush it, though. She'd take her time, get to know him before committing herself—find out if he even felt the same. She knew there was something there; she'd seen how he looked at her when he thought she wasn't watching. A woman knew when a man wanted her. The feeling of anticipation curled deep inside her, warm and tingling.

The trip back was somewhat awkward. She and Aidan were alone together for the first time since they'd arrived in Edinburgh, and what with Kate's comments and her own insecurity rolling around in her head, Colleen felt tongue-tied and confused. He carried the bulk of the conversation, while she spent most of the time in her own personal Twilight Zone.

Damn Kate! Why did she have to cut right to the heart of the matter with such unerring efficiency? She always seemed to understand what Colleen was thinking...and nine times out of ten didn't agree with it. All right, Colleen could admit she was a romantic screwup, and not just in her own love life. Kate had been right about Connor, too—the big gorgeous Scot who had romanced Aubrey. Colleen had been sure he was the right choice for her friend, and in the end he'd turned out to be a criminal and had almost gotten Aubrey killed. *No wonder nobody listens to my romantic advice.*

But sooner or later her luck was bound to change. The laws of chance were on her side, and who said Kate knew everything about romance? They were best friends, but very different people. Colleen was going to have to figure it out on her own—it was her business, and she knew her friends were going to be proud of her in the end. With renewed courage, she said goodbye to Aidan and trudged up the hill to Nessie's...and the Owls. Some things just couldn't be avoided.

CHAPTER 12
TURNING POINT

Colleen and Liz Dunnet sat in the huge kitchen of Balfinnan, notebooks in hand.

"Okay," Liz mumbled, between bites of a pilfered scone. "We've got the decorations and the music. Old Harry's getting in a bagpiper who's nearly as old as Gordon, so who knows how he'll manage to play, but that's who he wanted. Mrs. Morton's got the food handled, and now all we have to do is decorate the ballroom the day of the party and we're ready."

"Dolly wanted to have a céilí, " said Colleen. "Is that like an Irish dance party?"

"C-e-i-l-i-d-h here, and yes it is." Liz snorted. "It's a mad country dance party, and just the thing for people in walkers and wheelchairs. She's completely daft, that one."

"Well, I don't know, but I think this time she's got the right idea. Maybe not a ceilidh...but dance music brings a party to any occasion, no matter how old people are. It takes them back to their youth, even if all they can do is tap their feet and sing along."

Liz sighed. "I suppose you're right. I'll look into some locals and see what I can dredge up."

"I will not have wild music in this castle!" They looked up to see Mrs. Murtaugh glowering from the doorway. "These people are sick, and I'll not have them put at risk for a few minutes of frivolous shenanigans!"

"They're not sick," Colleen protested. "At least, most of them aren't. They're just old, and tiptoeing around, reminding them of that, does more harm than good!"

Mrs. Murtaugh looked down the length of her long nose at Colleen. "Well, we'll just see what Mr. Anderson has to say about it," she warned. "And does Mrs. Morton know you've been dipping into the scones again, Nurse Dunnet?" Without waiting for an answer, she turned on her heel and marched out.

"Ugh, I loathe that hag," Liz muttered under her breath. "And I must say I'm proud of you. Never saw you stand up to her that way before. You're growing a hide, you are!"

Colleen blushed. "Well, I just figured she can't hate me any more than she already does, and it pisses me off when people act as if our residents all have one foot in the grave and shouldn't be allowed any fun, just because they're old!"

"Aye, I'm with you on that. But you'll never change Murtaugh. She was born dour, and she'll be dour till the day she shuffles off." She stood and brushed the last crumbs of scone from her uniform, and then tilted her head. "Why don't *you* go and talk to Mr. Anderson, Colleen? He seems to have a soft spot for you."

Colleen felt her cheeks reddening again. "I don't know what you mean, Liz." She busied herself clearing the papers from the table so she wouldn't have to meet her friend's eye. After a few charged seconds she said, "But maybe I will do that. If I get to him first and explain what we want, I'm sure he'll understand. He feels the same way we do."

"I'm sure he feels the same way *you* do. But I say, whatever it takes." And with those cryptic words Liz was gone.

She didn't go straight to Graham's office, though, and she refused to dwell on the reason for her procrastination. At noon, she wandered outside. The weather was Scottish, which meant it looked like rain, felt like snow, and the clouds seemed locked in an eternal battle with the sun for supremacy. Hunger clawed at her stomach, reminding her that she and Liz had been so busy with the plans for Gordon's party that she'd skipped breakfast.

She hadn't seen Aidan since their return from Edinburgh on Sunday. Three days ago, but it seemed like a lifetime. She stood on the patio and looked around expectantly, but he was nowhere in sight. Where would a gardener hang out if he wasn't having lunch with her? She cast a suspicious eye at the darkening sky and decided not to go traipsing around looking for him, not when her mind was occupied with her impending visit to Graham's office, and her memory kept replaying Kate's words from last Friday.

Kate was wrong this time. Graham was different.

He felt the same way she did about their residents, and she'd never heard anything but positive comments about him. He had resurrected his family's castle and turned it into a nursing home, determined to give people in the twilight of their lives a chance to live with dignity. He'd been nothing but professional with her, at least in front of other people. And yet somehow they knew. She wondered how many besides Liz had noticed. Had Aidan?

She stood a little longer, listening as the wind picked up, bringing with it an occasional bleat from the moor. Odd, it was lunchtime, and Aidan was almost always here this time of day. A weight settled into her heart and she clasped her arms around herself to ward off the sudden chill. There was no point being out here freezing to death...alone.

For the rest of the afternoon, she pasted a cheerful smile on her face and went about the business of caring for the needs of her residents, but a depression had settled somewhere in the vicinity of her heart and ruined a day that had started out with the fun of planning a party.

As the sun sank behind the Highland Hills, she steeled herself and turned down the corridor to Anderson's office. It was time.

"Come in." His voice rang out, strong and resonant.

Colleen hesitated, took a deep breath, and pushed open the door to stand in front of his desk, hands clasped together to control their slight tremor. "Um...sir...Mr. Anderson..."

He looked up, smiling at sight of her. Her mouth dried up, all the water going to her knees and making them shake. "Graham, please," he said. "I would've thought we'd gotten that far."

"Graham, then. I—we—Liz and I that is—wanted to talk to you about Gordon MacNabb's party."

"You want to provide wild, untamed music that is guaranteed to send him and most of my other residents to their graves—am I right?" His eyes sparkled with mirth, and Colleen relaxed.

"So she's been here."

"Aye, she has, full of dire predictions of death and destruction, legal action, and whatever else you can think of. Did you actually think I would listen to that nonsense?"

"Well, no...not really, but—"

"Colleen, don't you know me better than that by now?" His voice was gentle. There was that water in her knees, threatening to ruin her magnificent achievement of standing upright.

"Y-yes, well I think so, but you're still the boss."

Graham stood up and moved around the desk to stand in front of her. "Is that all I am to you?"

Everything stopped. Colleen stared at him, her eyes widening. What did he mean? What did he *want*? She felt like a beached fish with its gills heaving in helpless futility, wondering how she'd gotten stranded on the sand. She summoned her voice from somewhere in her frazzled mind.

"N-no. You're more than that. You're a wonderful, caring, lovely man." What the hell was coming out of her mouth? Who was saying these things? Kate was going to kill her!

And then all thoughts went out the window.

Graham reached out and pulled her into his arms, crushing her to his chest as if his life depended on it. His lips lowered to hers, and he captured her mouth with a hunger that stole her breath and left her weak. Her arms went around his neck and she answered that kiss with a passion she'd thought she'd never find again. He smelled like heather and whisky and clean Highland air, and she was lost in the sensation of kissing him.

Minutes passed—and then the spell was broken as he pushed her away.

"I'm sorry," he whispered. "I had no right to do that. I've been fighting this for so long, and I have no right—"

"You have nothing to be sorry for," she said when she could breathe again. "It isn't just you. I've been wondering about this—about us—and I wondered if you felt the same."

"Yes. No!" His voice was harsh, raspy, filled with pain. "You don't understand! I—we can't do this!"

Colleen jerked back at his tone. "What?"

"I'm sorry!" he said again, turning his back on her and walking away to look out the small office window onto the grounds of Balfinnan. "Please...you need to go now. Before I—please!"

She couldn't remember leaving, didn't know how she got out of the office, but somehow she found herself on the second floor heading for Gordon MacNabb's room. The old man was sitting in his armchair, reading, but he looked at her with sharp, beady eyes and snapped the book shut.

"Ach, lass, come 'ere." Without another thought

she dragged a desk chair across the room and sat down next to him. He took her hand in his bony fingers, and she felt the waves of his compassion pass through them and into her heart. He didn't ask what was wrong, and she didn't tell him. It didn't seem to matter. In that moment, she loved the irascible, cranky, wonderful old man more than anyone in her whole life. "It'll be aw reit, lass."

He patted her hand, and somehow, she knew it would be. Graham had kissed her. It didn't matter what had happened after that, what might happen from now on—he'd kissed her, and he'd meant it, and it might have been the best kiss she'd ever had.

And then he'd thrown her out as if he was ashamed of that kiss. It confused her and dampened the joy of that moment, making her feel desperate and needy. Because now he knew how she felt about him. Her face flamed as she remembered just how well she'd shown him *that*.

Well, the next step was up to him. She didn't know what his problem was. She wasn't going to make a fool of herself chasing after him or making moony eyes every time they met in the hall. But it was going to be hard, because she was pretty sure she was falling in love with him.

Colleen felt a thrill go through her at the acceptance of that feeling, and her spirit refused to back away from it. No matter how this ended, she'd been well and truly kissed and she was going to treasure the memory. Pulling herself together, she squeezed Gordon MacNabb's bony hand and stood up.

"Thanks, Gordon. I do love you, you know."

"Ach, lass, gie on wi' ye!" he said, but she thought his eyes seemed suddenly damp, and knew he was fighting to keep the severe look on his face. She stood in the doorway for a minute and wondered what she was going to do when this wonderful old man was gone.

She went downstairs and stood by the sign-in sheet for several minutes, for some reason unwilling to drag herself back to Nessie's and another evening of wrestling with her own thoughts—or worse, fending off the usual interrogation by the Owls.

She looked down the hallway and saw the crack of light under Graham's office door. She knew he had rooms at the back, off his office, and as far as she knew he seldom left the castle. But she didn't want to see him right now, and he certainly didn't seem to want to see her!

Still, she couldn't leave. She decided to make another round, just to make sure everyone was comfortable. Flora gave her a curious glance as she climbed the stairs, and Colleen mustered a smile as she passed. She checked each of the residents and made sure they had their evening tea, their favorite books, and their nighttime medications handy. Slowly she felt her spirits begin to rebound.

They were cathartic, her old people; they elevated her. How could she be such an emotional baby when these people had much worse problems to deal with? Their health was failing, some lived in constant pain, and many had families who never visited and seemed to have forgotten them. All they had was the staff at Balfinnan. She and Liz, Flora, Graham, Simon—even

Dolly—they were the only family some of these old dears had, and she'd be damned if she let them down.

She finished on the top floor and started down a corridor that led away from the occupied part of the castle, hoping to avoid Flora and find the old servant's staircase that Liz said offered an alternative route to the ground floor. It was supposed to come out behind the kitchen next to the side door, but she hadn't yet found the time to look for it.

The doors along this corridor were closed, and tentatively turning the knobs confirmed that most were locked. It wasn't terribly smart to explore unknown hallways at night, but she couldn't really get lost, could she? The castle wasn't *that* big. Besides, wasting time trying the doors meant she could put off the drive home to her lonely room at Nessie's a little longer.

It was dark here. Heavy draperies shut out any possible light on this end of the third floor, and the passageways for the poor souls who'd had to traipse up and down the narrow stone in years past had side turnings that meandered off into the gloom to who knew where.

The corridor ended. There was a door, but this one wasn't locked. Probably the servants' staircase, she thought in relief. She opened the door and stopped, confused.

This wasn't a stairwell; it was too big. Not heated, either—she could feel the cold damp Scottish air swirling around her ankles. She couldn't see more than five feet ahead of her, but lack of vision sharpened her remaining senses, and she detected an odd odor. The smell of burnt wood crept into her nostrils, and suddenly Colleen knew where she was. She'd found the upstairs entrance into the burned-out section of Balfinnan.

She turned to retreat, and then a sound came to her out of the darkness, freezing her to the spot. Someone was up here, *in the ruined wing*, crying.

Had one of the residents wandered away from the occupied area of the castle and become lost and frightened? But she'd just checked, and all of them were safely tucked up for the night. Still, someone was crying. Frightened—or hurt. And Colleen was a nurse.

She stood for a moment on the threshold, irresolute. The sound came again, ahead of her in the gloom. Someone was up here, and now she recognized that cry. It wasn't fear, or pain. It was heartbreak. It hadn't been so long ago that Colleen had cried with that kind of agony, the feeling that life was no longer worth living because of a loss too great to bear. And her heart melted for whoever was hiding in that room, grieving. She had to help, if she could. She took a step forward... and then another—and stopped in shock.

Out of the darkness came a young woman. She was small, about Colleen's own size, and dressed in a nurse's uniform. But not a modern uniform like those worn by the nurses at Balfinnan. This one was grey, and long—it skimmed the tops of her black buttoned boots. An apron in a lighter grey covered the dress. On the bodice was a large medical cross, like the ones Colleen had seen in textbook pictures from the early years of nursing.

The girl had pale skin and wore no lipstick. In fact,

there was no color about her at all except for the eyes: a startling blue in the perfect whiteness of her face. From beneath the old- fashioned cap, grey hair curled onto her forehead.

Grey hair? But the girl was young, not more than nineteen or twenty! Suddenly, Colleen's heart went still as the impossible stopped her where she stood.

The girl put up her hand in a warding gesture, and shook her head. Her lips didn't move, but the words formed in Colleen's mind as if they had been spoken out loud. Words spoken in a lilting Irish accent.

Go back. You are in danger here.

Colleen's mind shut down. She backed up into the dark hallway, slammed the door, and ran back the way she had come, not stopping until she reached the nursing wing and the huge main staircase that led to the ground floor, where she held onto the newel post and bent over, gasping for breath.

She was no longer left out of the party. She'd just met her first ghost.

CHAPTER 13
THAT WHICH WAITS

The dark figure glided into the great library and stood for a moment, studying the shelves. All the books and papers, journals and documents, everything collected over the centuries by previous owners of Balfinnan Castle was all here. Once the right document was found, this cursed pile of stone could be left behind forever.

The Ghruamachd liked the name it had been given. *Grimness*, in the old tongue. A fitting description, indeed. Every moment spent living this lie fed its fury. The hatred was thick enough that it should be written clearly for all to see. Blind fools! When the enemy smiled, dripped compliments, said that nothing would be possible without its help, the Ghruamachd wanted to tear off the mask and kill, watch its own hand do the deed and see the life drain from those eyes.

If only a knife could be used—in its mind, one had already been picked out from the castle's vast collection of weapons. The knife would slide between the ribs as shock transformed that hated face, just before the body slid helpless to the floor. The Ghruamachd would stand over its victim, watch the eyes widen in shock and then cloud in pain and confusion—and it would smile.

But that was impossible. It couldn't be done that way, much as the mind was soothed by that image. There were too many things that could go wrong. This form that the Ghruamachd used could not be found near the scene. The surrogate was too well known, and Balfinnan was a hive of energy, teeming with people who saw too much.

No, what had always worked would have to do. It would be poison, and the Ghruamachd must be content with hearing the news from others. The means were not really the important thing; it was the end that mattered. Maybe the surrogate could arrange to find the body, take a little time to enjoy the triumph before running out and screaming for help. It was a delicious idea—but again, impossible.

The surrogate would be a suspect if found alone with the victim. No—mustn't let rage and hatred drive away cunning. This was not a mere killing—it was an execution, and one that had to be planned carefully. The Ghruamachd could not be swayed by human emotion—could not move until the time was right.

It was annoying, though. The condemned *should* know why. If an enemy were to be executed for a crime committed by another, there should be an understanding of the justice of the act, the reason for paying the ultimate price. If the Ghruamachd was to be judge and jury, the guilty one should have to face it, admit the crime and understand the reason for the sentence.

Maybe the surrogate could leave a note—but no, then the victim would be on guard, and that just wouldn't do. It had to be done quickly, and with no warning, so as not to risk the collapse of everything that had built to this.

Time was precious. Imagination could not be allowed to distract from what needed to be done. One step at a time, and nothing more was possible until the paper was found. Maybe it was gone, destroyed so many years ago in that other cursed room, but the Ghruamachd refused to acknowledge that possibility. Finding the document was secondary to the main task, but it had become an obsession over the years.

The creature cast a glance around, glad that this form blended into the gloom so well. The library was dim and shadowed, perfect for the purpose of this visit. So far, the old man had been the only one to see the guise the surrogate took during its night wanderings, and no one listened to those old nutters.

Almost no one. That Irish nurse listened, and that creepy young janitor who sneaked around and was so adept at hiding. What was his game? No more than a lad, he was, but he seemed older than anyone in this damned castle. He'd need to be handled with care. He didn't fit into the plan, but he could be dealt with if it became necessary.

There. On the shelf was a book. It wasn't lined up straight like the others here, almost hidden between two larger volumes, and the spine was cracked from use. Many hands had held that book, that much was obvious. The Ghruamachd shrugged, hovered its hand over the book and then pulled it out. *Balfinnan House, a Forgotten Highland Jewel.*

The creature seethed in fury. Jewel? This place? Maybe a fake gemstone. Whoever wrote this drivel must have been a romantic, or didn't know what the Ghruamachd knew. The author's name was at the bottom—*Thomas Kemp.*

The Ghruamachd opened the cover and looked for the publication date. 1920. So, after the Treachery. Had Thomas Kemp been a friend or colleague of the Andersons? Something about this book had the senses tingling. Or maybe they were the surrogate's senses—it hardly knew anymore.

The dark figure skimmed its fingers over the pages until it reached the last chapter, entitled "1881-1920, the Anderson Years." Knuckles whitened and it ached to throw the book across the room, but a compulsion to read about a family's destruction had taken hold.

History—and Thomas Kemp—recorded the turn-over of the castle as a gift from Malcolm Beaton to his great friend Duncan Anderson, in gratitude for Duncan's saving his life in war. But that was a lie. The Beatons knew the truth, and had passed it down to each generation so none would forget.

The Ghruamachd knew the story by heart. Every family has a black sheep, and Malcolm Beaton was theirs. A wastrel and a gambler, the bastard had spent nearly every cent of the family's wealth by the time he met a minor lord and con man in the card game that would change everything. His adversary kept the whisky flowing and the markers piling up, and when the sun rose the next morning, the reprobate was in possession of Balfinnan and Malcolm was a broken man.

If only Thomas Kemp were still alive, so he could be found and killed for perpetuating such filth. Hatred rose up like a red mist, threatening to stop the breath in this body. With a low howl, the Ghruamachd ripped the offending pages out, crumpled them into a ball, and shoved them into a pocket. As if that would erase the past. The fury subsided, tamped down with supreme effort. This wasn't the reason for the visit.

A rustling in the corner put a stop to mental wanderings, and the dark creature's head snapped up. There was nothing there; it had probably been a rat. There were more important things to worry about than rodents. The time for vengeance was coming.

The Ghruamachd looked at the book in its hands and wondered. Something was wrong with the binding—sharp eyes caught a thread that was coming loose near the top. With rising excitement, the creature began to pick at the thread, and was rewarded when the top of the spine suddenly came away from the cover to reveal a tiny compartment.

Could it be? Would the fools have hidden it in such an obvious place? Maybe...after all, they would have no reason to think someone was searching for it after all this time. Abandoning caution in its haste, the figure worked its finger into the crevice and pulled free a small wad of vellum, folded so cleverly that it appeared to be a part of the binding itself.

Fingers shaking, the Ghruamachd spread the paper out and began to read the spidery, wavering script. The page was torn on one corner and part of a name was missing, but there was no doubt that this was the document it had sought for so many years, what it had failed to find long ago—this small piece of paper that held the truth of a family's destruction and the motive for revenge. A sense of triumph roared through its mind.

And now it was time to move forward. The figure folded the paper carefully and placed it into another pocket of the black robe. Reaching up with hands that no longer shook, it pulled a black hood over its features before hurrying from the room.

Simon Reid stood in the shadows at the edge of the library. He stared at the door through which the figure had gone, his frail body shaking as if gripped by a fever. He had not seen the thing's face, but he'd felt its fury, its hatred...and its triumph. It was the same feeling of utter evil that he had experienced in the hallway outside Mr. Burns's room the night the old man died, but this time he had glimpsed the source of that evil. He had *smelled* it. And the sensation that chilled him to his bones wasn't fear of the supernatural, because this wasn't a ghost.

The Ghruamachd *was human.*

CHAPTER 14
THE FACE OF FEAR

olleen stared at the ceiling in the big bedroom that had once been Aubrey's, then Kate's. She had called in early this morning and told Mrs. Murtaugh she was sick and wouldn't be coming in today. The housekeeper's harsh voice said that she hoped Colleen would be feeling better soon, in a tone that sounded as if she'd better. Well, the joke was on her.

She wasn't going back. Even the thought of it made her sick to her stomach. What she had seen last night was impossible, unreal...and yet she *had* seen it. And her brain refused to compute. Her mind was stuck in the off position, unwilling to accept that she had really seen a ghost, and that the ghost had talked to her.

She should have been better prepared. Aubrey had gone on and on about her curse and her ghost, and about that book in Angus's shop that talked to her and smelled bad. Colleen had listened, but not believed a word of it. Her mind simply refused to admit that such a thing could exist outside the laws of science.

She and Kate had discussed it, and they had decided it was just Aubrey's imagination working overtime to explain the weird things that went on in this crazy country. But then Kate had come to Scotland and found her own ghosts. Kate, the practical one, the cynic of their group. And Colleen had gone back to her modern country and told herself she was glad not to have been caught up in the hysteria. They'd get over it, those two. Maybe they were having her on, sharing a joke at her expense.

She'd been wrong. Horribly, horribly wrong. Because much as she tried to deny it, every time she closed her eyes she saw that beautiful white face, heard those eerie words echoing in her head.

Go back. You are in danger here.

Was she losing her mind? She hadn't been sleeping well, worry about Graham and Aidan and Gordon had her running on fumes. But that was nothing new, was it? A nurse was often overtaxed and fatigued; tragedy and loss and lack of sleep were part of the profession. Besides, deep down she knew she was perfectly sane. Which meant that, much as she wanted to disbelieve it, what she had seen last night was real.

The Grey Lady was real. Gordon MacNabb was right. And did that mean that there was a bad ghost, too, as he claimed? The Ghruamachd, or whatever he called it?

Not that it mattered, because she wasn't going back. Now she knew why Balfinnan couldn't keep staff, and she was totally on board with that. Staying in a place with real, honest to God ghosts wandering around— ghosts who pointed at you and talked in your head— that was the exact opposite of okay. Which meant that Liz, Mrs. Morton, Flora, and Dolly couldn't have seen the Grey Lady, because they were still there. Simon and Mrs. Murtaugh didn't count; Simon had always seen ghosts, so he was used to it. Mrs. Murtaugh was scarier than any ghost, and they probably knew better than to show themselves around her.

She would spend today figuring out what she was going to do next. Without Balfinnan. Without Graham. Without *nursing*. She wouldn't be there for Gordon MacNabb, or all the other residents she'd come to love. She would miss his party, the most important thing in his life.

She'd miss Aidan.

And how could she live without nursing? She'd been given a chance, offered a reprieve from a life without her calling, and she was damn good at it. She would be throwing it all away. She'd never be able to face Old Harry again, and he spent most of his time right here in the same house.

Her phone rang, and she reached for it blindly.

"Colleen?"

Damn.

"H-hello, Graham."

"How are you feeling? I was worried when Mrs. Murtaugh said you were sick."

"I'm all right. Just a little queasy this morning. Graham—I have to tell you—"

"Wait, let me say something first." His voice

sounded strained. "I'm sorry about what happened yesterday."

He's sorry. Sorry he kissed me. It was the best thing that's happened to me in the last six months, and he regrets it. Well, that's par for the course.

Her voice was dull. "That's okay. I'm sorry if I acted—"

"No!" Now he sounded breathless. "I'm not sorry about that! You don't understand—it's not you. I've wanted to kiss you for a long time. Please believe me!"

Colleen felt as if she were slogging through quicksand. "But then why—"

"I can't explain. Not yet. But I had no right to force myself on you. I have feelings for you, Colleen, I need you to know that. I can't act on those feelings, and I had no right to give you the idea that I could. But I don't want to lose you. We need you here. Think about Gordon MacNabb; what would he do if you missed his party?" A long sigh came over the line. "Someday—" He broke his sentence off and she heard the edge of his frustration. "I'm asking you to trust me, Colleen. I can't give you anything. Not now. But will you stay?"

"I—I don't know, Graham. I'll let you know by tomorrow."

"Please think about it."

She clicked her phone off and lay back on the pillow. *Think about it.* Thinking about it—all of it—was all she'd been doing since last night. Her head was spinning from the thinking.

Time passed while thoughts coalesced, dissipated, ran through her head and retreated out of her grasp. She dozed, woke up, stared at the ceiling.

At some point she looked at the old-fashioned clock Nessie kept on the nightstand. Noon! She should get up, put on some clothes, decide what to do. Start packing.

A soft knock on the door had her jerking upright in the bed.

"Colleen?"

Gladys. The last person she needed right now. She wouldn't be surprised if they were all standing on the other side of her door, waiting to pounce. The Owls knew instinctively when something was off, and none of them had ever heard the word privacy.

"Yes, Gladys?"

"There's someone here to see you. He says he'll wait."

Wait? Wait for what? Wait—he? Was it Graham?

Her voice trembled. "Tell him I'll be down in a few minutes, okay?"

And suddenly all the lethargy left her. She threw on a pair of jeans and a sweatshirt emblazoned with the faded words OF COURSE I'M AWESOME, I'M A NURSE, then grabbed a pair of socks and her sneakers, and ran into the bathroom. The image that stared back at her from the small mirror looked like someone just escaped from a lunatic asylum. Her hair stood in matted patches of red curls all over her head, her face was pale and blotchy, and the eye makeup she hadn't bothered to take off last night was smudged and ran in streaks down her face.

She groaned. The ghost she'd seen last night had been much prettier than this, and she was dead! She realized with a small shock of relief that her sense of humor had survived the experience, and mustered a weak smile for her mirror self.

"Okay, you're going back. You know you are, so just let's get on with it. Wash that face and do *something* with that hair, or whoever's downstairs will think *you're* the Grey Lady."

Twenty minutes later she walked into the sitting room, expecting to see the Owls waiting in their customary positions, primed for business. But there was only one person in the room, sitting in Old Harry's chair and reading his newspaper.

Aidan.

A mingled feeling of surprise and relief flooded her senses as she gawked at him, and then it morphed into curiosity.

"Aidan? What are you doing here?"

He folded the paper and looked at her.

"Came to get you. You look like hell, by the way. Are you really sick?"

"Yes—no. Sort of. What do you mean, you came to get me? For what?"

"Simon told me you were in trouble."

Simon! How had he known? She hadn't seen him last night during her meeting with the ghost, or afterward when she broke the all-time flight record running down Balfinnan's hallways. But then, nobody saw Simon unless he wanted them to, and she had been moving so fast she could have won an Olympic ghost-escaping race. Which was pretty much the idea at the time.

A feeling of warmth spread through her. Two of her favorite people were watching out for her. She took a deep breath and just let the words fall out of her mouth. "I saw the ghost. It was a bit of a shock."

"Aye, I thought it might be that. It was pretty shocking the first time I saw her, too," he said. "Nothing quite prepares you for that, does it?"

"*You've* seen the Grey Lady?" Colleen gaped at him. "When? Where?"

"Right after I got to the castle, and a couple of times since," he said with a shrug, as if seeing a ghost came with the job description and she should have expected it. "And where? In the burnt-out section. I spend a lot of time there, of course."

She narrowed her eyes at him. "Of course? Are there lots of flowers to be tended in order to keep the ruin looking lovely?"

Aidan gave her a puzzled look, and then his face cleared and he began to laugh.

"So *that's* why you keep asking me questions about the plants and flowers! I was flattered you thought I knew so much! I'm sorry—didn't I tell you?"

"Tell me what?"

"I'm not the gardener, lass. I'm the architect! I'm the one who's trying to reconstruct that horror to its former glory." He erupted in fresh gales of laughter at the expression on her face.

Colleen stared at him in shock. She raked her memory for the questions she'd asked him since that first day, and then a flush of shame engulfed her when she remembered her conversation with Kate. She had thought he was the gardener and automatically consigned him to a part of her mind reserved for laborers and the uneducated. Unworthy of *her*, of all people—a disgraced nurse with the worst references on record. A few weeks ago she'd been looking at a career working at Poundland!

She put her reddening face in her hands and sat down like a sack of potatoes on the couch. Kate was right—she was a snob. She'd never realized that such a seam of prejudice ran through her, never thought she cared about class. She was stunned to realize that he was most likely more educated than she was, and worse, afraid that he would guess just what she was thinking.

Peering between her fingers, she caught his amused expression. He was just Aidan—her Aidan, her friend and confidante. He was the same guy he'd been before he told her he was an architect. Not just an architect, but a *preservation* architect.

"Anyway, now you understand why I was slightly more likely than most to see the Grey Lady, aye?" Aidan was saying. "My office is out there, near the damaged part of the castle. I just help out Old Archie because the work is more than he can handle at his age, and because you learn a lot about life from old codgers like him. He's a walking history book! Also, I like sheep."

As Aidan talked, Colleen felt herself relaxing. There was no use beating herself up —all she could do was file it away as a life lesson and do better from now on. But there was no denying that his admission had changed the way she saw him. An educated man was also her type.

Now she understood his relationships with Finn and Graham. It must have been university where they'd known each other, and that was why Graham had sought him out and given him a job when he'd opened his castle up. All the pieces fit.

And Aidan had seen the ghost! Just knowing that he had shared her experience made the day brighter, her decision not to run more sensible.

"Um, Aidan? What was the ghost doing, when you saw her?"

"It's been more than once, lass. She seems to stay around the ruined section, maybe because that's where she died. And I've heard her more often than I've seen her. I work late some nights, and my desk lamp is the only light out there. Several times I've heard her crying."

"I heard that!" Colleen nodded in excitement. "Last night I was doing my rounds, and I decided like a fool to try and find the old servants staircase on that end of the castle." She told him about wandering down the dark hallway on the second floor and finding the unlocked door. "And when I opened the door it was cold, and I couldn't see anything. But I heard crying, and Aidan, it was the most heartbreaking sound I've ever heard! As if someone had lost the only thing that mattered in the world, and life wasn't worth living! Great, gulping sobs that tore a hole in the air."

"Aye, that's how it sounds," Aidan said, his voice thoughtful. "But Colleen, you said the air in the room was cold. What did you mean?"

"It was almost as if there was a door or window open to the outside," she said. "I couldn't see; it was too dark. And then I took a step forward to see if I could help whoever it was...and that's when I saw her." She shivered at the memory of that beautiful white face, that pointing hand. "She—she talked to me," she said, and watched the shock cross his features. "She said something like 'Go away. There's danger here.' She was pointing right at me, and I turned and ran. I'm lucky I didn't break my leg going down the stairs, and I decided right then and there I was never going back.

"But Aidan, I'm so grateful to you and Simon—that you came to find me and make me go back. Because I didn't want to leave, but I was just so scared. As far as I know, Americans don't deal with a lot of ghosts. It's certainly not a common occurrence in New Jersey. I *couldn't* leave my residents; I know that. I have to be there for Gordon, for his party, and for Graham—" She stopped, realizing that she was babbling, and looked up to find Aidan staring at her with a strange look on his face. "Sorry. I got carried away."

He didn't answer, and for the first time she noticed that his face was drained of color, his eyes a dark grey and his brows furrowed.

"What's wrong?"

"She talked to you," he said.

"Well, her lips didn't move, but I heard the words in my head."

"And she warned you about danger."

"Yes. Why?"

He took a deep breath and stared at her, unblinking.

"Because you've just described the room where the Grey Lady died. Where she hanged herself. If you had walked any further in, you would have fallen three floors to the ground. A great chunk of the floor is missing in that room, and the room below it."

Colleen stared at him, unable to think, to form words. Aidan took her gently by the shoulders and shook her until she focused on his face.

"I think the Grey Lady saved your life."

CHAPTER 15
THE THEORY OF RELATIVITY

olleen stared at Aidan, stunned by his rev-
elation. In her memory she could see the
clear blue eyes of the ghost, the white face
and the graceful pointing hand, the details of the
old-fashioned uniform, and the curls that somehow
she knew would once have been red, like her own.

"Gordon was right," she whispered. "She's not evil.
She's there for a reason, but it's not to hurt anyone."

"Seems so," he said. "Scottish legends are full of
the tales of spirits that stay behind to haunt the
places where they met their deaths. Most ghosts are
sad, but not malicious."

"But why is she still here? Aidan, she died a hundred years ago! If she was innocent of the crime she
was accused of, why did she hang herself in the first
place? And what is she looking for now?"

Aidan shrugged. "Who knows? Some say they stay
behind to right a wrong, or to fix something they

couldn't while they were alive. Some may stay to warn of the danger that caused their death."

Colleen realized that they were having a conversation about something she had thought impossible—the stuff of fairytales—less than a day ago, and now it felt as natural as breathing. She remembered the stories she'd only half-listened to, the tales of Aubrey's and Kate's ghosts.

"Aubrey saw a ghost once," she said, her voice sounding far away. "She said the woman had stayed behind for seven hundred years, waiting for someone to break a curse. And the someone was Aubrey. When the curse was broken the ghost went away. Finn's writing a book about it, and he said it hasn't been seen since."

"When we were in Edinburgh," Aidan said, "Jack told me a ghost led them to find Finn when he was in trouble. Just like what happened with you: a ghost saved Finn's life."

"But why is my ghost haunting Balfinnan?" Colleen missed Aidan's smile at the words "my ghost." She was too busy remembering more. "I think she's still grieving for her soldier, and that's why we both heard that crying. She's reliving the night he died, over and over. Something's keeping her from going to him. Oh, Aidan, we have to help her!"

"I like your spirit, lass!" He put both hands up in a warding gesture when Colleen's head snapped up. "No pun intended. Sorry."

She glowered at him under lowered brows, and then gave up and laughed. He was incorrigible, and exactly what she needed right now. He kept her grounded in a world gone mad.

"You're ridiculous," she said fondly, and stood up. "Anyway, we can't figure it out by sitting here, can we? And I have to get back to Balfinnan so they don't think I've quit."

"You took a sick day, right?" he asked her. "That means you have the rest of the day free, and tomorrow you can go in as usual and no one will know any different. I'll leave my car here—let's walk over to Angus's Book Shop. Didn't you say your friend Aubrey works there? And maybe I can catch Finn; he's there sometimes working on his book. After that, maybe I can show you some things in Inverness that aren't on the tours."

"Okay, I guess you're right." Colleen said. Although it felt like weeks since she'd run for her life out the front doors of Balfinnan, it had all happened last night—less than a day ago. She'd told Graham—

"Oh, I have to call Graham! I told him I'd let him know if I was staying by tomorrow, but he's probably worried."

"You talked to Graham about this?" Aidan's voice was flat and he seemed glued to the chair.

"No, not about this, but he called this morning to see how I was." She wasn't about to tell him what else Graham had wanted to talk about—it wasn't anyone's business. Besides, she wasn't sure how he'd react. She wasn't even sure how *she'd* react.

"Colleen..." His voice had gone even lower, and now there was some gravel mixed into the familiar tones. "You don't *fancy* him, do you?"

"Aidan, I think that's between him and me, don't you?" She tried to keep her voice gentle, but to her ears it sounded sharp and defensive.

His shoulders slumped. For a minute he said nothing. Then he sighed and looked up.

"You're right. I don't want to tell you what to do. But I—he—" He ran a hand through his hair. "Just be careful, aye? I don't want to see you get hurt." He forced a smile that didn't come near his eyes, and then pulled himself together and stood up. "Ready to go see some of the wonders of the Highlands?"

"Sure. Just give me a minute." She called Balfinnan and left a message for Graham that she would be in the next morning, then collected her coat and joined Aidan outside on the walkway. They walked down the path to the road, up another hill and down into the Town Centre, mingling with the tourists on the High Street. Angus's Book Shop took center stage on Church Street, which was appropriate since it was located in an ancient church.

They were in luck. Aubrey was at work, sitting behind Angus's desk.

"He won't let me work in the stacks anymore," she whispered to Colleen. "He's worse than an old mother hen. The baby's not even showing yet, and if this is what I have to deal with for the next seven months, I'm going to go insane!" But she cast an affectionate look at the bandy-legged old Scot who was stacking books in the section marked "Mystery."

"Aidan," Colleen said, "this is Aubrey—Finn's wife and one of my best friends in the world."

"Hullo," Aidan said. "Good to meet you. I was sorry to miss your wedding; I was away in Ireland visiting my mam's family, but Finn's one of my best mates from uni. Is he here?"

"No, it's Thursday. He has classes till six. But then we're going to the Waterfront; they have a great new singer there. Why don't you two come?"

Aidan looked at Colleen. "Are you up for an evening with the locals? They get in some great talent on Thursday nights."

Colleen hesitated. "Well, I'm supposed to be sick..."

"You're sick? What's wrong?" Aubrey looked alarmed.

"Long story, but no, I'm not sick. Tell you later," Colleen sighed. "You're probably the only person in the world who would believe it, especially coming from me." She turned back to Aidan. "Okay, but if anybody from Balfinnan shows up, it's on your head!"

They left Aubrey to her books and her Scottish guard dog and walked down to the river. The Ness was higher than Colleen remembered it, and running fast.

"It's tidal," Aidan explained. "And it runs fast because it has to travel a downhill path to the Beauly Firth from Loch Ness, and not much room to do it in. The whole river is only about six miles long. Has some of the best salmon fishing in the Highlands, though. You'll start to see fishermen as we get closer to the islands."

"Islands? In a river this narrow?"

"Aye, lass, and they're magical. You'll see." He refused to tell her more, and they walked in companionable silence along the walkway bordering the river. Passing the suspension bridge that she, Kate and Aubrey had bounced over on their way to the Highland Games—it seemed so long ago now—they came upon another, smaller bridge. Identical to its larger brothers that spanned the entire width of the

River Ness upstream, this one ran from the bank to a large island less than a hundred feet away in the middle of the river. They crossed, and Colleen's eyes widened in delight.

Before them stood the largest pine tree she'd ever seen. Seven feet around, its trunk stood at the edge of a path straight out of Hansel and Gretel. The path curved around other trees almost as huge, with benches that seemed to grow out of the ground. Above them, lining the path, fairy lights were just visible among the low-hanging branches of the trees.

"Oh, Aidan—it's beautiful, and you're right, this place is magical," she breathed. "I want to come back here when it's dark and see those lights lit up!"

"Well, it's only a wee distance from Nessie's, lass—you can come any time." He grinned at her reaction to the beauty of the Ness Islands. "But that's not all that you'll find here." His voice lowered. "The magic's not all beautiful. Wait till you see what they get up to at Halloween. Come on."

She eyed him warily, but he winked at her and continued on. They rounded a huge tree and Colleen jumped in fright. There, stretched out from the river almost to the path, was a huge creature with a gaping mouth, staring right at her out of beady eyes. It didn't move, and once she'd managed to shove her heart back down where it belonged, she could see why.

It was a huge tree, with a face carved out of a bulbous section of its trunk. A split formed the mouth, and some enterprising soul had painted in green nostrils and tiny white eyes.

"Very funny," Colleen said, but a moment later she

was laughing with Aidan. The Scots loved their monsters, she thought, and if they couldn't find them, they made them.

By the time they staggered up the path to Nessie's, it was late afternoon.

"I'll wait while you get ready, is that all right?" Aidan said, "and then we can drive to my house, which is just down the road. We'll come back here, leave the car and walk to the Waterfront, if it's not too much exercise for someone who's recently been ill," he added in a solicitous voice, eliciting an exaggerated glare from Colleen. "The pub's only a wee bit further down the other side of the river."

"I think I'll live," Colleen said in a dry voice. "I love walking around this city, and the company's bearable." She pushed open Nessie's front door and walked in to find the Owls all back in their customary places in the sitting room.

"Here's where I get my revenge for that Ness River monster," she murmured to Aidan. "I'm going to get my shower and get dressed for tonight, and *you*," she fixed him with an evil grin, "are going to experience the Spanish Inquisition!"

Colleen marched him into the sitting room and announced, "I'd like you to meet my friend, who will be keeping you company while I shower and change. His name—"

"Gie on in here, Aidan Shaw, ye wee scamp. Bin busy over thaur at th' castle, aye?" Old Harry put down his paper and a broad grin spread over his face. "How's yer dad?" The old man looked at Colleen. "Gie on wi' ye, lass. We'll bide wi' yer laddie."

"Hello, dear," said Gladys. "My Ronnie was just telling me the other day how much he's missed seeing you around here. Sit here right next to me. Ronnie, scoot over and make room for Aidan, would you, dear?"

Colleen rolled her eyes and stomped her way upstairs. She should have known.

Later, as they walked in the growing darkness across the Ness Bridge at the end of the High Street, she asked Aidan, "How do you know the Owls? You've never been to Nessie's before, have you?"

"Oh, aye, I used to hang out at Aunt Nessie's all the time when I was a wee lad," he said. "But I've only known Old Harry for a few years, and the others not long at all." He watched her eyes grow huge. The smirk on his handsome face was a work of art.

"*Aunt* Nessie's? Nessie is your aunt?"

"Aye, she is. Great aunt, really. My gran's sister was married to Nessie's brother."

"Nessie has a brother?" Colleen's head was spinning. She wondered if Aubrey knew that. Nessie had always seemed such a mysterious figure, like Angus. It had never occurred to Colleen that she could have *relatives*. It seemed that everyone in the Highlands was related in some way or other, though, so she shouldn't have been surprised. She felt as if a trick had been played on her. Here she'd thought Aidan was her secret, and it turned out he knew everybody she knew and was probably related to half of them! It made her feel isolated, left out of all the fun. It was stupid, she knew, but she couldn't help it.

She *was* an outsider here—the only people she'd known when she arrived last month were Aubrey,

Kate, Finn and Jack. She suddenly felt lonely in this place. She was tired of the teasing and the secrets, the camaraderie that other people had. Even Aidan, who'd been born in Ireland, was a part of this place in a way she could never be.

"What's wrong?" He had stopped under a street-light and was looking at her, his grey eyes dark with concern. "I was joking about the walking...if it's too much—"

"No, it's not that. I'm just feeling a little alien all of a sudden—like a tourist who's stayed too long and keeps trying to get off the bus." At his puzzled look, she mustered a grin. "I think too much. Let's go have fun!"

Hours later they pulled themselves up the steep path to Nessie's, laughing and gasping for breath. Aidan stopped on the patio and leaned back against the top of the wooden railing that bordered the path.

"That's some climb. Did you have fun?" he asked.

"I did. You were right. The singer was amazing. When he sang 'Flower of Scotland' at the end, I felt the hair stand up on my arms. And he did it a capella! Thanks for making me go."

"I had fun, too. I haven't taken time off the job—well, except for Edinburgh." He paused as a thought seemed to strike him. "Now that I think about it, I've taken more time off since I met you than I have in the last three months! You're bad for business, lass!"

"I'm sorry, Aidan, you won't be in trouble, will you?"

He pushed himself off the railing and stood staring at her. Something flickered in his grey eyes, and then he bent and placed his lips on hers in the lightest of kisses. Colleen was so startled that she barely registered the fact that she would have kissed him back had he not straightened and ended it so quickly.

"I'm just teasing, Colleen. I keep my own schedule, and I've given Graham more of my time than he deserves!" His tone was light, but there was an underlying edge to the words. The air went out of the evening, and a minute later he was jogging away down the path to his car with a backward wave as he disappeared around the corner.

There's definitely something going on with him. She ran a finger over her lips where he had kissed her. Where she had hoped he would continue kissing her.

Damn, it was going to be another night spent staring at the ceiling.

All the secrets of the world worth knowing are hiding in plain sight.

Robin Sloan

SCOTLAND, 1918

"I want you to take over the care of Mr. Macleod, Bridget. It means you'll be giving up your normal rounds for a while—just until he's stable. Is that all right with you?"

All right! It was wonderful, and Bridget thought Mr. Anderson knew it. In the two weeks since Alexander Macleod had been brought into Balfinnan near death from the infection in his leg, she had lived a kaleidoscope of emotions. The sheer wonder of what she felt for this total stranger, the joy and the recognition she felt when she'd looked into his eyes for the first time in two years, the agony of fearing she could lose him again after finding him. She had thought of him often as the war raged on around her—and here he was. Possibly dying. It had been beyond rough, those first days.

He shouldn't have been here in the first place. Balfinnan was not near the front, not where the most seriously injured soldiers were taken. But his life had not been in danger, not then. It was during the long trip home to his native Scotland that infection set in, *and by the time he reached Balfinnan he was burning with fever and delirious.*

He hadn't been conscious while the doctors pondered the fate of his leg, while they discussed the possibility that it should come off if he were to have a chance. He awakened for the first time to find Bridget looking into his eyes with amazement, and recognized her immediately, even in the throes of his delirium. In fact, he told her he thought she was an angel, come to take him to heaven. He had dreamed of her, not knowing who she was.

It wasn't easy, and it wasn't a sure thing. There were many nights when he begged her to let him die.

"I can't bear the pain, Bridie!" he whispered through clenched teeth on his worst days. "I don't want to live a cripple!"

"Alex, you know I can't let you leave me," she would tell him, her voice hoarse from worry and fear. "What would I do without you?" She would rock him, as she had in that hideous tent at the Somme, until he quieted and slept. And then she was free to give vent to her own fears, and to the dawning understanding that she would wish to die herself without him.

It became obvious to others at Balfinnan that Bridget was Alexander's lifeline, that she was physically and emotionally keeping him in the land of the living with all the strength and will she possessed. And slowly, against all odds, he began to heal. Although the doctors were using new techniques against infection, saving more and more lives that would have been lost just two years before, Bridget's love provided the medicine Alexander needed. His glorious blue eyes cleared, *the red flush along his incision faded to a healthy pink, and the lines of pain on his drawn face eased.*

One day he was able to sit up, and a week later he took his first baby steps, leaning on Bridget for support.

"How do you do it, Bridie?" he asked her. "Where do you get the strength? You're such a wee bitty thing, I'm afraid I'll crush you!"

"Nurses are stronger than they look, Alex. And you're not so much of a challenge, you know; all the meat's worn off your bones and you're light as a feather!" But she gazed into his eyes and knew that he would come back to her, strong and hale again, and her heart sang.

He talked to her of Skye, his island home, and told her that one day he would take her there to see the fairy pools and the mountains that reached to touch the clouds. They began to dream of a future together away from war and death and the devastation created by men.

The staff loved them, loved the joy that surrounded them whenever they were together, and began planning for a wedding. Even the other patients joined in, teasing Alexander when he limped by on Bridget's arm, telling him he shouldn't let a wee lass push him around so. Their love filled the halls of Balfinnan and echoed through the rooms where injured men recovered from the injury and illness brought by the obscenity that people were calling the Great War.

But not everyone was happy. There are those for whom the very idea of joy is an alien thing, an untouchable emotion that flees before the jealousy and anger inside. Grace haunted the corridors of Balfinnan like a ghost, avoiding the two lovers and sliding away when the rest of the staff began their insidious chatter.

Few noticed, for Grace had never made friends easily, and her presence made others uncomfortable. No one knew of the hatred that seethed in her heart for the two who had destroyed her only dream of the happiness she now knew would never be hers.

The rage swelled and grew and filled her being until she could think of nothing else. He was supposed to be hers! She was the one who was supposed to save him and earn his love. She wished he had died when he'd first come to Balfinnan, before the Irish witch had ensorcelled him. She wished he had died...

And a plan began to form in her mind.

CHAPTER 16
SIMON SAYS

olleen dragged herself into Balfinnan on Friday as if she'd chosen lead-lined boots as a fashion statement. Everything felt heavy—her head throbbed, her eyes were itchy, and her body kept telling her that it just wanted to sit down. *Karma.* You could always expect it to come calling when you played sick.

She gave herself a mental slap and continued to the sign-in desk. She wasn't sick. Not physically, at least. But as a nurse, she knew that too much mental or emotional turmoil could wreak havoc on the body, and she'd had plenty in the last two days. She'd seen a ghost and been kissed by two very different men—men who both meant a great deal to her. Her mind was in turmoil; she needed sleep. This lying awake staring at the ceiling in the darkness would have to stop or she'd be no good to her patients. Her personal life was going to have to get off this ride and let her work.

She kept her promise to herself for the rest of the day. She didn't see Graham all morning and decided to stay in the staff room with Liz for lunch to catch up on what she'd missed yesterday. At least, that was the excuse she gave herself. It certainly wasn't that she was avoiding Aidan. That would be cowardly. *But you are a coward*, the irritating voice in her head told her. It sounded smug.

The sun began to drop over the mountains as the workday finally came to a close. Colleen stumbled into the room reserved for staff and stared at herself in the mirror over the sink. Dark circles had taken up residence under her eyes, accentuating the pallor of her face. *I look like a ghost myself! I've got to pull myself together.*

As she buttoned her coat in the front hall, the door to Graham's office opened and she froze in place. Simon came out, and behind him Graham stood in the doorway, a tense look on his face. He started to close the door and then noticed Colleen standing in the foyer and became still. He took a step into the hallway and then shook his head, turned around, and went back in, closing the door softly. Colleen sighed. Whatever was bothering him, it hadn't changed. She wasn't going to let it ruin her life...but it still hurt.

Simon continued down the hallway toward her, stopping three feet away and studying her face. His eyes widened.

"You've seen something."

Colleen gaped at him. "You're positively spooky, Simon! Do you read minds, too?"

The young man blushed. "N-no," he said, so earnestly that she laughed.

"I was just kidding—sort of," she said, and then stopped and looked intently at him. "But I think I owe you an apology. You do see things, don't you? Things that aren't there—like ghosts."

His blush deepened. "Aye."

"And you know I've seen her, don't you? The Grey Lady? You told Aidan I was in trouble."

"Aye, I saw you running, and I figured you saw her. It's how most people act."

"Well thanks, Simon. You were right, I *was* in trouble, but you and Aidan helped me. I was scared, but I'm not anymore."

"Y-you're welcome, Nurse Colleen. And I'm glad."

The boy's face wore a look of gratitude. Did no one ever thank him, or praise him? Her heart went out to this shy young man. Graham was right—Simon was special. Bright and intuitive under the shy exterior, and kind.

"Simon, I need your help to understand what happened. Can you show me the room in the burnt-out section? The one on the second floor? Where the nurse died?"

"Aye." Without another word, he turned and started toward the staircase. No questions, no advice. Her heart warmed toward him even more as she followed him up the staircase.

They didn't speak as they climbed; speech would have been inappropriate for this adventure. Colleen had said she wasn't afraid, but that was a lie. She could feel her feet slowing as they neared the door at the end of the long corridor, and if Simon hadn't been right there beside her, she didn't think she could have actually gone back. As they stood in front of the door he reached out and took her hand in his. In that instant he was inscribed on her short list of most-loved people, and she was so grateful for his presence she found herself fighting back tears.

Simon reached into his overalls and brought out a torch. He unlocked the door and trained the light ahead into the room in which Colleen had stood only two nights ago, listening to the sounds of crying. Tonight the room was silent, but her hand felt clammy in Simon's and the blood rushed from her head, leaving her dizzy and swaying. *Shock*, her nurse's training told her. *Just breathe and you'll be fine.* Shock at seeing that gaping hole in the beam of the torch, inches in front of where her feet had been two nights ago. She had lifted her foot to take that next step, and then the Grey Lady had appeared.

"He was right," Colleen whispered when she could breathe again. "Aidan said she saved my life, and he was right." A rush of gratitude swept through her and for a second she wanted to see the ghost again and thank her.

Bridget. That had been her name. A real name for a real person, someone who had lived, and loved, and died before her time.

"Simon, is that why she's still here? Because she died too soon? Or maybe because her death was violent?"

Colleen heard the desperation in her voice and ignored it. This...*person*...was the reason she was standing here. They were connected now, and Colleen wanted to know everything about her: her family, her childhood, the reason she had become a nurse. Did she have sisters and brothers? Had her parents still been alive when she died? Did they have to come to Scotland to claim her body, hear the lie that she had killed her lover and live with that lie echoing in their hearts through the years?

Because it *was* a lie. Colleen knew without a doubt that the woman she had met could never have done what they said she did. There had been compassion and courage in that white face, and a will of iron.

"Why did she stay?" she asked again. "Was it because she died in sin? Is she stuck here because she committed suicide?"

Simon didn't answer. He pulled Colleen back out into the hallway and closed the door.

"It should have been locked," he said, almost to himself. "I told Mr. Anderson about what happened to you, and he was furious. He said that door has always been locked. He kept asking me if you were all right, so I told him you were fine. You are fine, aren't you, Nurse Colleen?"

"Yes, Simon, I'm fine. But you're not answering my questions. Why is the Grey Lady still here?" She turned and faced him, tension written on her face. "I need to know."

He sighed. "I don't know, not for sure. It's not like I sit down with ghosts and we have tea and talk about our lives. Ghosts don't share a lot." A hint of amusement colored his narrow face, making him look suddenly very young. "I do get feelings from them, sometimes, even when they don't say anything. Sort of a vibe, I guess you'd say." He began walking down the hallway toward the massive staircase, using his hands like a conductor to make his points. "Sometimes I think they stay behind because they never got a chance to tell a loved one goodbye. But that can't be why the Grey Lady is here. The only person she loved was already gone." He stopped on the stairs and looked at her, his face sincere. "Maybe you have the right of it, Nurse Colleen. She wasn't the only one who died a violent death. Alexander was poisoned, and no one's seen his ghost around here, or at least no one's said. And I think I would have seen him, if he was here. But Alexander was murdered, and Bridget killed herself. So maybe she wasn't allowed to follow him."

Colleen noted that at no time was the idea brought up that Bridget had been the one to murder her lover. So Simon felt it, too—the certainty that she had been innocent.

She pulled her nurse's cap off and tucked it into her coat pocket. With no awareness of her action, she ran her hands through her curls until they probably stood up around her head like a red halo. "But it just doesn't make sense. She was from Dublin, right? So, most likely she was a Catholic. She would have *known* that suicide was a sin. She would have believed that she'd be damned forever. Why would she do it, if it meant she could never be with him?"

Colleen was beginning to feel slightly sick, her natural compassion and refusal to admit defeat mixing with fatigue to create a miasma of sadness and anger in her mind. Here she was, standing on a staircase with the castle janitor, trying to make sense of something that had happened a hundred years ago!

These people were dead and gone; nothing could help them now.

But that part of her mind that ached to fix things, to make them right, wouldn't let go. The woman had saved her life! Shouldn't that be a good enough reason to allow someone into heaven? It wasn't fair! And suddenly she was sitting on the carpeted steps of Balfinnan Castle with her face in her hands, crying her heart out. For a ghost.

A soft hand patted her back, and she looked up at Simon through misty eyes. She sniffed and stood up, stumbling the rest of the way down the stairs in a daze. It was more than time to get out of here. She had her hand on the huge knob of the castle's front door when Simon's voice stopped her.

"There's something else."

The tension in his voice had her turning to focus on his face, which suddenly resembled that of a much older man. Something else? What more could there possibly be than what had already happened?

He came forward and leaned close.

"Remember last week, when Mr. Graham said that he thought something was killing his patients? When he told us to be careful and pay attention?"

She blinked at him for a second, and then it all came back. How could she have forgotten that secret little meeting Graham had called? That Irish voice in her head, warning her that she was in danger? What was wrong with her?

What's wrong? Oh, could it be that since then you got kissed and tossed out by Graham, and kissed by Aidan before he ran away? That the first parts of those occurrences were wonderful, and the second parts not so much? Could it have anything to do with the fact that you've since met a ghost with that same Irish accent, and she kept you from falling three stories to your death? Could it have anything at all to do with the fact that everybody around here is either dead or crazy, and that you're probably losing your mind, too?

Simon was waiting patiently for her. She dragged her eyes up to meet his, and said, slowly and carefully, "Yes. I remember."

"Well, I wasn't going to say anything—Mr. Anderson told me not to tell anyone, but I think you should know. There's more than the Grey Lady haunting this castle, and the other one is not like her. Not at all." He waited, as if he were parceling out bad news in little bits so as not to alarm her. Too late for that.

"You mean the Ghruamachd, don't you?" She felt a chill like cold damp fingers clutching at her spine. "Gordon MacNabb's evil ghost. You actually think it's real?"

"Oh, yes." Simon's whisper was even lower. "It's real. But it's not a real ghost."

Colleen gaped at him. "Is it or isn't it?"

"It's not a ghost at all. The Ghruamachd is a person. A living, breathing person. Or part of it is. And that's worse than any ghost. A ghost can't really hurt you. But this one can, and it's the most evil thing I've ever seen or felt. I want you to know because I think that's who Bridget was warning you about in Mr. Anderson's office."

So he *had* heard the voice, too. The chill grew and enveloped her, blotting out the foyer.

"Are you all right, Nurse Colleen?" Simon's worried voice came to her through the fog. The nausea was back with a vengeance.

"I'm fine," she lied. Blindly she patted Simon on the arm and watched him walk slowly away, concern creasing his young face. Of course he could see right through her, she thought. It was Simon, after all. She turned and stumbled out the door, heading for the car park. She'd had her fill for one day; it was time to go home to the relative normalcy of the Owls.

Hers was the only car left in the park, and suddenly the darkness seemed to pull in around her, choking her. She shook off the feeling and forced herself not to run the rest of the way to her car. Its solid metal frame steadied her, beckoning her back to the real world, to things modern and mechanical and familiar.

Nevertheless, her hands shook as she fumbled her keys out of her purse, and she dropped them twice before she got the door unlocked and threw herself into the driver's seat.

She started the car and backed out of her spot, facing the vehicle toward Inverness, Nessie, and weirdness she could handle. From now on she was leaving work with Liz, or getting someone to walk with her to her car. How many people had to tell her to be careful before she listened? It was nothing short of stupid to ignore people who had her best interests at heart. Anyway, her fears might be groundless, caused by nerves, lack of sleep, emotional stress, and...and ghosts and Ghruamachds and things that went bump in the night.

A light glinted in the rearview mirror as she reached the edge of the car park. She glanced in the mirror and recoiled. Her foot jerked off the clutch and the car stalled. The huge front door stood wide open, and lit from behind by the lights of the foyer, was a silhouette. The figure wore a long black garment, like the dress Morag Murtaugh, the housekeeper, wore. But Mrs. Murtaugh lived in a little town called Garbat, about forty-five minutes north of the castle. Colleen knew this because the woman made a huge fuss about being kept even a minute after four o'clock, blaming it on everyone except her boss.

So, what was she doing here, after seven o'clock? And if it wasn't Mrs. Murtaugh, who—or what—was standing in the huge front doorway staring at the car park?

CHAPTER 17

TIME AND TEARS

aturday dawned Scottish. Rain battered the windows in Nessie's dining room and the mountains were invisible, cloaked in a grey mist that reached down all the way to the river. Colleen sat at the huge table with her housemates, watching Old Harry dig into his full Scottish breakfast with his customary enthusiasm. She shuddered and reached for a piece of toast.

Eyes bored into her from various directions around the table, and Colleen knew without looking that the Owls were on duty. She hadn't slept well, again, and she knew she must look like something rescued from the garbage can behind the house. *Rubbish bin. Oh, who the hell cares what it's called? It's the same around the world. Not pleasant.*

"So, dear, have any plans for your day off?" Gladys's voice was a little too high-pitched, and her eyes slid to Maxine. "Are you and Aidan walking out?"

Colleen snorted. Walking out! Just what everyone needed, a lovely stroll in the driving rain. Gladys was as transparent as the window, and not the least bit penitent about it. Although she had to admit that a knock at the door, followed by one Aidan Shaw, would brighten up her day considerably.

"No, Gladys, I think I'll be spending the day in bed with a book," she said. "And I don't think I'll be seeing Aidan today."

Eyes shifted around the table again. *Do they think no one can see them?*

Gladys opened her mouth again, but was interrupted by a knock at the door. Colleen's eyes widened. Unbelievable!

"I'll get it," Nessie said, crossing from the kitchen. She disappeared into the hall, and a moment later returned with a strange look on her face. "Someone to see you, Colleen."

The table was silent. Colleen stood and retraced Nessie's steps into the front hall, fully aware that every gaze was fastened on her back.

Graham Anderson stood by the door, hat in hand, water dripping from his grey overcoat to puddle on the tile.

"Graham? Wh-what are you doing here?" Colleen reached automatically to smooth the curls that rioted on her head, and wished fervently that she'd put on some sort of makeup before slouching down to breakfast. This was the second time she'd been caught wrong-footed by a man; you'd think she'd learn.

"I came to see you." The words sent a little electric shock through her.

"Why?"

"I spoke with Simon yesterday—do you mind if I take off my coat? I'm making rather a mess here."

"Oh! Of course. Just hang it on the clothes-tree there. Nessie?" she called back over her shoulder. Can we use the library for a few minutes?" There was no way she was entertaining Graham Anderson in the sitting room, in full view of the raptor gazes of her housemates.

She led him down the hall and past the kitchen to the small room Nessie called the library. In a previous life, it had been a mudroom, and it still retained the hooks and benches that had been built into the wall for that purpose. Nessie had squeezed an old wooden desk and two small armchairs into the remaining space, and a tiny bookshelf took up the last inches of room along one wall, crammed with books on Scottish history, cookbooks, and old news magazines.

She pointed to one of the chairs and sat down in the other one. She focused on her guest and realized with a jolt that she wasn't the only one who looked a little the worse for wear. Graham's hair was combed neatly back from his forehead as usual, but he had a new growth of stubble that indicated he'd run out without shaving this morning. The circles under his blue eyes could give hers some serious competition, and he had missed a button on his shirt. He looked adorable.

She jerked herself out of her thoughts to find him staring at her.

"So," she said carefully, "you talked to Simon? About me?"

"Yes, and he told me you had a nasty shock in the

burned-out room on the second floor. That door's supposed to be locked, but why on earth did you go in there? It's under construction, or soon will be, and it's dangerous!" He sounded angry...or frightened? It didn't matter, she was getting a little annoyed with his tone. No way was he making this her fault.

"I was lost," she managed. "And to be honest, if a room is that dangerous and supposed to be locked, maybe it should have been!"

Graham sighed and put up a hand. "I'm sorry, I'm not saying you did something wrong. I was just worried. When I think what could have happened—" He broke off with a shudder.

"Why did you come, Graham?" Colleen's voice sounded thick in her ears. Was he going to explain himself at last? Did she even want to know?

"I care about you, Colleen." His voice was so low she had to strain to catch the words. She felt her blood pressure rising, her Irish temper sawing away at frayed nerves.

"I'm sorry...did you just say you care about me?" She pinned him with a hot glare. "You have a funny way of showing it, to be honest." She sat back and crossed her arms.

"I know I've been a bit of an arse. There are things I have to do before—" Again, he cut himself off. Could the man not finish a sentence? He stood up suddenly. "It was a mistake to come here. I'll go."

She jumped up and barred his way, or at least she tried to. The height difference between them was ridiculous, but she had righteous indignation on her side, and he backed up a step.

"No you won't. Not until you tell me what your problem is!"

He stared at her. The side of his mouth quivered, and he pressed his lips together tightly. Colleen backed up and glared at him, hands fisted on her hips. Was he *laughing* at her? And suddenly she saw the scene as if from a distance—a tiny woman facing down a much larger opponent, armed only with red hair and a quick temper. And as quickly as it had come, the rage drained out of her and she felt mirth welling up from deep in her body.

His eyes cleared and he exhaled, and then they were both laughing—weak chuckles born of relief that grew and expanded and filled the tiny room.

Graham bent over and grabbed the edge of the desk for support. "Your face!" he said, when he could catch a breath.

"What's wrong with my face?" she demanded, trying to recapture her annoyance between giggles.

"Nothing. Nothing at all. It's lovely. Look—the rain's stopped. Let's get out of here."

And it had stopped. Weak sunlight filtered into the tiny room, catching the raindrops on the window and turning them into jewels. Without a word, Colleen led Graham out of the library and through the front hall. She retrieved their coats in the hallway and pushed him out the door, refusing to look into the sitting room as they passed. The room was ominously silent, but she knew the Owls were there. She'd deal with them later.

It wasn't until Graham helped her into the passenger seat of his silver Porsche that Colleen realized she hadn't gotten an answer to her question. She looked over at him, opened her mouth and closed it again. His knuckles on the wheel were white and his face was set, his brows furrowed. She knew she was being a coward again, but she couldn't force the words out.

Was he regretting this already? Colleen's chest tightened and she looked down at herself. She hoped he wasn't planning to take her anywhere fancy, because the jeans and sweatshirt she'd thrown on this morning were anything but. No makeup, and her hair was a wild thing because of the rain. This was probably another colossal mistake, and completely typical.

Neither said anything until they left Inverness and were traveling along a narrow one track road through thick pine forests carpeted with ferns and bracken. Glacial rock jutted from the roadside, The steep sides of the roadway were covered by the orange husks of dead ferns and by heather, the blossoms browning now that autumn had taken a firm hold on the land.

"Where are we going?" Colleen broke the silence, her voice sounding loud to her own ears.

He seemed to come out of a distant place in his thoughts. "I don't know. I really didn't have a plan. Would you like to just drive for a while? I can show you some interesting things, if you like. And then we'll go for coffee, aye?"

Colleen didn't answer. On her right, the trees had thinned to reveal a field dotted with perfect cylindrical bales of hay. Beyond the field were rolling mounds of grass dotted with sheep, spreading down to the shoreline of a huge body of water framed by distant hills. She gasped in delight.

"That's Loch Ness," Graham told her. "Twenty-one miles long. Largest loch in Scotland, and the second deepest. Which is why Nessie loves it." His eyes crinkled and his hands relaxed a little on the wheel.

"Another magical creature, like your unicorn." She attempted a teasing voice. "What kind of country has a mythical creature as its national animal, anyway?" Her laugh died in her throat. *The kind comfortable with ghosts, that's what kind.*

"Aye, I suppose we can seem a little silly." He shrugged. "But I'm taking you to where the magic began, in a time even before the Picts."

The forest gave way to more farm fields on both sides, the bales of hay lending the scene a bucolic normalcy that belied his words. Then he pulled over, just far enough off the road for cars, if there had been any, to get by. They were alone out here, though, just two humans and the ubiquitous sheep. The silence was complete, as if this scene existed in a bubble that would burst if disturbed by a single sound.

Colleen let out a gasp of delight. There, in the middle of a field, was a standing stone. Not like the fake ones in her favorite television series, *Outlander*—this was a real standing stone. Alone in the landscape, it reared out of the ground to a height of ten feet or more, almost as wide at the bottom and tapering unevenly to a jagged point at the top.

Graham helped Colleen out of the car and together they stood at the wire fence, staring at this remnant of a civilization as old as time itself.

"We can't see them from here," he said, "but there are two more stones beyond this one that were once part of a circle called the Gask ring." He watched Colleen's face, his own reflecting the pleasure he saw there, the joy every native takes in the gift of his culture.

"Are those messages on the stone?" Colleen's voice was a whisper of awe.

"Iron Age people left no record of their language," he said. "They carved symbols that are repeated over and over on stones left all over the north of Scotland—wolves and birds and such." He watched her rapt face. "Later the Picts came and carved stones with hunting scenes and spirals, and after they became Christian they carved crosses with embellished Celtic patterns."

Colleen was silent, trying to take in the vast gulf of years between the time of these people and the present. They had loved and lost, hated and fought, just like the people of her own time. Had they recorded their deepest thoughts on materials that had not survived like the stones? Mourned each other during times of war and hunger? She felt small and inconsequential in the vastness of time, and yet the connection to these strange early people gave her strength and an odd comfort.

They returned to the car. Graham didn't speak as he drove down the narrow road, and for that she was grateful. She needed time to take this in, and it was a lovely gift.

He pulled into a car park and turned the engine off.

"Ready to do a wee bit of hiking? We're going to see the Falls of Foyers."

They crossed the road and began a long descent over steps built of wood and forest material constructed so that they fit into the landscape as if they'd always been there. The steep stairway path curved back and forth in a zigzag pattern, seeming never to end, and all the time the roar of falling water could be heard in the distance, growing ever nearer.

Finally they reached a lookout. From somewhere beneath the earth came a rush of water so intense that it seemed as if God himself had turned on a giant tap and left it for his people to enjoy. Water cascaded down the cliff for almost 200 feet before ending in the vast waters of Loch Ness. Graham told her that the falls had been a tourist destination since the early 1700s.

"Imagine how amazing the falls must have been to people traveling the loch by paddle steamer, seeing the spray rising through the trees and hearing the thunder of the water."

He turned to her, and his eyes were the same blue of the sky and as clear as the waters of the loch. She wanted him to kiss her, knew that if he did she'd be lost. A part of her welcomed the possibility, but she hung back, waiting...for what?

The moment passed. He turned and led her back up the stairs, to the car park and the waiting Porsche.

"I promised you coffee, and coffee you shall have, madam," he said, keeping his voice light. "The place we're going is just down in the glen, and it's one of my favorites."

They wound around and down the road, and suddenly the trees opened up to a valley with a long, low wooden building surrounded by fields. On the car park side of the building were the words "The

Camerons Tea Room and Farm Shop" in huge, bold letters. Smoke drifted from the chimney, rocking chairs lined the porch, and...

"Oh, my God!" Colleen pointed at the field. "Are those Highland cows?"

Graham laughed. "Aye, they are. Would you like to meet them?"

But she was already gone, running across the grass to the fence, where the most adorable animal she'd ever seen stood patiently as if he'd been waiting for her all his life. By the time Graham joined her, she and the cow were immersed in a one-sided conversation, which ran along the lines of, "Oh, you are such a handsome boy! Oh yes you are. Do you know how cute you are, with all that hair in your face? I know someone else with hair like yours. Do you go to the same barber?"

"Um...Colleen? We can come back, the cow will still be here," Graham said. He grinned at her. "About that coffee?"

Reluctantly Colleen bid her new love goodbye and turned to follow Graham around the corner and into the tea room. They spent a delightful half-hour over coffee and some of the best pastries she'd ever had. Conversation flowed naturally, and she felt the tension that had gripped her since the almost-kiss at the falls ease up.

She didn't mention the unanswered question, fearful of disturbing this tenuous harmony between them. This was enough for now, she told herself. She'd had a wonderful day, but the new Colleen was going to take it one step at a time. No more jumping in headfirst without checking first for rocks under the surface. He liked her, she liked him, and for now that was enough.

Graham went to the counter to pay their bill.

"I'll meet you at the car," Colleen told him. "I have to say goodbye to Hamish."

"Hamish?" His eyebrows went up and he shook his head, smiling. "You've named the cow?"

"Oh, no, he told me that was his name."

Colleen and Hamish said their goodbyes, and a few minutes later she turned to walk back to the car park. She rounded the corner and came up short.

Graham stood next to his car talking to a woman with long blond hair, and by the looks of it, the conversation wasn't going well. As Colleen watched, the woman reached for Graham's hand and he pulled it away. Even at this distance it was obvious that they were far from strangers. There was a history here.

Colleen stayed where she was, in the shadow of the tea room. The tension was back, and suddenly she wished she'd stayed talking to Hamish a little while longer. As she watched, the woman's shoulders drooped and she turned away, walking quickly to a small blue car across the lot. Graham stood staring after her, his back rigid. But Colleen wasn't watching him. Her eyes were on the dejected figure of the stranger, and she was sure of one thing—the woman was crying.

CHAPTER 18
BELLADONNA

Dolly Gilles pulled her coat tighter around herself and pushed her way through the forest, feeling her heart lighten with each step. Every moment away from the castle was a tiny sliver of joy, an escape from the intolerable.

She loved the woods always, but especially in October. The colors were like those paintings she'd seen on a trip to Edinburgh when she was a child, the sound of her feet swishing through the damp leaves reminded her of the firth during a storm. And the smells! She turned her face up and breathed in the fragrance of fall in the Highlands. Damp moss, rain, flowers, and needle-covered paths guided her farther away from Balfinnan House.

God, she hated Balfinnan, with its musty hallways, dark, gloomy rooms—and old people. The castle was ancient, with those repressive smells that old buildings have, but the elderly people who hung out there, just waiting to die, were the worst. They forgot how to go to the toilets, whined constantly about their pain...and they smelled. Dolly's gran had smelled like them—a combination of boiled cabbage and old urine—but she was only one person, and family. There were fifteen feeble old fogies at Balfinnan, each with his or her own particular old-person problem. Being around them was depressing, which was why Dolly took as much opportunity as she could to forage for herbs in the forest and fields around the castle.

I don't want to get old and decrepit like that. I don't know how the nurses do it—act as if they like those old trouts and buffers.

Dolly had never wanted to be a nurse. She knew she had gotten the aide job because of her ability with natural remedies—thank Mum for that—but she didn't want it. She didn't want to work at all, to be honest; she wanted to marry a rich man and never have to work again a day in her life. A *very* rich man—like that nice Mr. Anderson. He'd be a catch for sure, but who was she fooling? He'd never look at her like he looked at that pretty American nurse, with her flawless complexion and gorgeous red curls. Dolly bet that one didn't even have to use makeup. Some people just had it naturally, and the rest bought mascara and rouge.

She ploughed on, her delight in the forest fading as her spirits plummeted. She'd never gone this far before—the woods were unfamiliar here, and darker. She wasn't even sure she was still on Balfinnan land, but it was still Scotland, and still the forest. At least she might find some good mushrooms, and fennel was easy to find this time of year. If she was lucky, she might even come across some late borage, that all-round cure for aches and pains.

She giggled. Mum said borage was good for a hangover, or even as an aphrodisiac. Maybe if she gave some to Mr. Anderson in his tea...

Summer was best for healing herbs, of course. Garlic grew wild from April to June. Corn mint, mostly found from April to September, could still be tracked down by the savvy forager later in the year. Ground elder, that wild cousin to spinach, was available all summer, and dandelion grew year-round and was useful in savory stews and replenishing broth. Maybe she could find some for Mrs. Morton; the cook loved the herbs Dolly brought back. At least somebody appreciated her talents.

A twig snapped somewhere in the forest. Dolly stopped and looked around, but saw nothing. Nothing familiar at all, in fact. She wasn't worried about getting lost; the forest was in her blood and would never let her down, but she really needed to get going if she were going to have something to show for her time away from the castle. Otherwise she'd get another lecture from Liz Dunnet, the old hag, and she was tired of making excuses for her absences. You could only be sick so often. She wished she could just run up and down the halls shouting, "I hate this place!" at the top of her voice, but then she'd be out of a job and Mum would give her a skelping she'd never forget.

The trees opened suddenly to a clearing, with several waist-high berry bushes in the very center of a grassy circle. Curious, Dolly moved closer and then stopped, puzzled.

These bushes weren't growing willy nilly, as forest shrubs normally did. There was a clear order to their arrangement—circles within circles, three rows deep. They looked as if they'd been planted here, on purpose, but who would do that?

She reached out and broke off a branch, holding it to her nose. The berries looked like tiny black cherries and smelled like summer tomatoes before they were ripe. She sniffed at the leaves and wrinkled her nose. Bitter and nasty. She knew that smell.

Into her memory came her mother's voice. "Witches used it in the old days to make an ointment to help them fly. The devil's cherry, some call it, but most know it as deadly nightshade. Stay away from it, Dolly—the berries taste sweet but eating just five or six will kill you. Learn its look, so you'll know its secret."

Deadly nightshade: the other name for belladonna, one of the most poisonous plants on earth. What in the world was it doing out here, planted on purpose and carefully tended? Someone should be told about this—warned about the danger. What if a child wandered into the woods and sampled some of the lovely berries?

A smile worked its way onto Dolly's face. She would be the one to tell; she'd be the hero, the brave one, the one who made the difference. For once in her life, she would matter. And the one she wanted to matter to was Mr. Anderson. He would notice her then, wouldn't he? He'd forget about the beautiful American nurse when he realized that she, little Dolly Gilles, had saved his castle and his patients from ruin. Liz would shut up when Mr. Anderson told the staff what an amazing person she was.

Another twig cracked somewhere, closer this time, and Dolly felt a chill run up her back. She looked around again, and still she saw nothing in the trees behind her. But suddenly, the forest didn't seem so much like a friend. This was a feeling she'd never had before, this apprehension in a place that she called her own, and it unsettled and frightened her. She began to walk back the way she had come, a hurry in her steps as she reached the darkest part of the woods where the trees crowded out the hazy light. In her hand she clutched the sprig of belladonna as if it were a talisman.

Without warning a figure appeared in the gloom ahead of her on the path, barring her way. Dolly squeaked in fright and then relaxed, her heart receding to its proper place in her heaving chest.

"Oh, thank God it's you. You nearly scared the bejesus out of me!" she said, voice quivering in relief.

"What are you doing way out here, lass?" The voice was calm, reassuring.

Dolly looked suprised for a moment at the question. For a second she had forgotten why she was in such a hurry. She looked at the sprig she carried. "Oh—look what I found back there, in a clearing!" She offered the small branch up for inspection. "You don't know what this is, do you? Someone planted this out here on purpose. The gardener needs to dig it all up, right away." She straightened her spine, feeling her new importance. "This stuff is dangerous—it can kill you!"

"Oh, dear. Better show me where it is, then."

Dolly nodded happily and turned to lead the way back to the clearing.

Her head exploded in pain, a red haze of agony eclipsing the world and driving her to her knees. She braced herself on all fours and tried to get up, but her limbs didn't seem to be working. Another pain exploded in her skull, and she collapsed and rolled slowly onto her back. Her body convulsed, out of her control, and then the pain drifted away as the darkness of her beloved forest claimed her. The convulsions subsided into twitches, and a moment later Dolly lay still on the leaf-covered forest floor.

The Ghruamachd studied the blood that spattered the end of the branch it held, and a grim smile crossed its face. It shifted its gaze from the branch to the body on the ground. Dolly Gilles stared back, eyes fixed and vacant—an empty shell in which a young girl with hopes and dreams had once resided.

"Well, I'm sorry that was necessary, but some people just don't have any luck." The Ghruamachd sighed, bent down to grasp Dolly by one arm, and began to drag her through the forest.

"Let's just get you settled, shall we?"

CHAPTER 19
BROKEN BRANCH

ell, it's almost here! Are you excited for your part—?"

Colleen stopped in the door-way to Gordon's room, surprised. The old man sat in his usual chair, dressed for the day. He wore tartan trousers, a pristine white button down shirt, and a bow tie. It was Sunday, but that had no bearing on his attire. No matter what was going on around him, Gordon always presented himself as a gentleman, his pride in his heritage radiating from his wrinkled face, and eyes shining with humor and love of life. And today he was simply buzzing because he had company.

It shouldn't have been surprising that he had a guest; Old Harry came at least once a week to "have a blether" with his old friend. But this was someone she hadn't seen before.

Gordon's visitor was another old man, dressed in brown overalls. A faded yellow scarf was tied around his scrawny neck, and the cuffs of his blue shirt were frayed and dirty. He was tall and gangly, looking for all the world like an aged Ichabod Crane. He had large feet encased in brown work boots, and grey hair straggled out from under a floppy canvas hat.

His chair was pulled up close to Gordon's so that their bony knees were almost touching, and they were whispering and cackling like hens when Colleen came in. They both stopped and stared at her like guilty school children, but Gordon recovered first.

"Miss Colleen! come reit haur an' meet mah fren' Archie. Archie, thes is th' sweetest nurse th' guid Lord ever pit oan th' earth! I've tauld ye about 'er." He sat back, grinning from ear to ear as if he was presenting one treasure to another.

Archie. So this was Archibald Ferguson, the real gardener. Aidan had told her he never came into Balfinnan if he could help it, but she guessed the lure of one Gordon MacNabb was worth the torture. They obviously knew each other well. She gave the old man her best smile and extended her hand. Archie looked at it as if it might bite him, and she withdrew the hand quickly and stuffed it into her uniform pocket. Well, so much for that.

Gordon laughed. "Archie's a wee bit shy, lass, don't ye be worrit about heem. He'll like ye if Ah dae."

"I'm glad to meet you, Archie," she said carefully, still smiling but keeping her hand in her pocket. "Aidan's told me about you. He says you were a wanderer."

The transformation was instant and remarkable. The stiffness went out of the old man's body and something that might pass for a smile in a wax museum found its way onto his face. Colleen suspected it was an unfamiliar sensation.

"Ah, Aidan. Guid lad." He sat back and studied her with a critical eye. "He said ye're all right."

Despite the fact that the praise was as lukewarm as day old tea, Colleen felt a warmth go through her. Aidan had talked about her to this old man! Why did that make her feel so good?

She hadn't seen Aidan since Thursday. She felt a sudden yearning to see his face, watch his clear grey eyes crinkle when he smiled at her.

She was going to have lunch outside today, she decided, even though the weather had turned cold and windy. She missed Aidan, and deep down she knew it was her own fault. After the unsettling end to her adventure with Graham yesterday, she needed to see her friend.

Her friend who had kissed her, and then run away from her.

Colleen had never considered herself a rare beauty. She knew she was attractive to men—and she knew why. Most of them looked at her chest first, before dragging their eyes up to her face. *And knowing that hasn't stopped me from falling for the wrong ones, has it?*

John had talked about her physical attributes often. Maybe a little too often, she realized now. With time and distance, she was able to see that he was no different from all the other disasters in her love life. Smoother, definitely. But what good was that with no staying power? His betrayal still hurt, but the pain when she thought of him was not nearly as sharp as it had been. She had Graham to thank for that...and Aidan.

Those two were different—from the others and from each other. Graham had said he was drawn to her empathy and compassion, and she believed him. He'd never said a word about her looks, had he? But the physical attraction was definitely there on both sides. Just because he was her idea of the perfect male specimen didn't mean that he had to be a loser, did it? If you kept digging, you sometimes found gold.

But the memory of that woman she'd seen talking—arguing—with him in the car park bothered her. She hadn't asked him about her, and he hadn't offered any information. She told herself it was none of her business, but she knew that fear had a great deal to do with it. It didn't matter, she told herself. Everyone had a past, and it didn't need to mean anything here and now. Still, it had hung around, like a dark cloud over their afternoon. Both of them had been quiet on the way home to Nessie's. He'd given her that gorgeous smile and held on to her hand a little longer than necessary, but he hadn't tried to kiss her and he'd seemed preoccupied as he drove away.

And Aidan? She had thought Aidan was an open book, and she loved that about him. Always there with a ready smile, a comforting word—the perfect friend. And then he'd gone and kissed her. To be honest, it had barely been a kiss, just a peck on the lips really. So why had it thrown her like that?

Because I liked it. Because I wanted more. It scared me, and I think it scared him, too.

Colleen realized that Gordon and Archie were both staring at her, and forced a smile onto her face.

"Sorry, just woolgathering. I'm going to lunch now, maybe I'll see you outside, Archie."

He nodded without speaking, and she pressed Gordon's hand and left them to their visit.

Liz met her in the front hallway as she put her coat on, a harried look on her face.

"Have you seen Dolly today, Colleen? She forgot to sign out yesterday, which is nothing unusual because she skips out early most days anyway. But she was scheduled in today, and she never showed. She always calls with an excuse, at least."

"Maybe her mother *is* really sick this time," Colleen offered.

Liz shrugged. "Humph. I think I'll call her and give her what-for. I wish Mr. Anderson would just cut his losses and sack her; we need someone reliable here." She went off, mumbling under her breath, and Colleen continued on through the kitchen and out to the patio.

Aidan wasn't in sight, so she walked along the pathway that led to the moor. Maybe Artemis would give her some company while she ate her sandwich. Artemis wouldn't kiss a person and then run away, would she?

A happy bleat told her she was right. The sheep trotted up and butted her hand as if she'd been waiting for her, and soon Colleen was surrounded by wooly bodies. She suspected that they loved her sandwich as much as they did her, and parceled it out until it was gone.

"Artemis, you and your friends are just what I need right now," she told the sheep. "You don't want anything from me except my lunch, and you don't judge. You are a sloppy kisser, though." She looked at the sheep and noticed that the area around her nose was stained red. "Where have you been, Artemis? Did you get into the garden shed? Find some paint lying around?"

She looked closer and her heart skipped a beat. This wasn't paint. She was a nurse, and she knew blood when she saw it. Was there an animal injured somewhere on the castle property? She'd better find someone, now.

As if in answer to a prayer, Aidan appeared on the path.

"Well, I was beginning to wonder if you'd quit, or didn't eat anymore." His voice sounded relieved and strained at the same time. "I heard the sheep bleating, and I figured I might find you—wait, what's the matter, Colleen?"

"I think Artemis has gotten into something, Aidan. Look!" She pointed to the sheep's wooly face. "It seems like too much blood to be a small animal. Could it be one of the other sheep?"

"Hope not," he said. "I'll go hunt up Archie and we'll take a look around. The sheep don't go far, so whatever it is should be on the castle grounds somewhere." He paused. "Artemis is a wanderer, though; she likes to go into the forest sometimes. Whatever it is, Archie'll want to clean her up. Walk back with me?"

"Of course. I looked for you when I came out, but I didn't see you anywhere."

"Oh, aye. I was taking a working lunch in my office. When I heard the sheep..."

His voice trailed off. An uncustomary shyness seemed to have overtaken him.

"Aidan—"

"I'm sorry about the other day, Colleen. I had no right to—to overstep at Nessie's. Don't know what came over me. Are you angry?"

"Oh no, Aidan! I don't know if I *could* be angry with you. I was just surprised, that's all."

Aidan's face cleared and he gave her a weak smile. "Well, then, that's all right." He took out his cell phone and took a picture of the blood on Artemis's face, and then the two walked back to the castle.

It wasn't the same, though. Something had come between them, charging the air with tension. Colleen struggled for something to say, but the easy camaraderie that had been between them was gone. She couldn't help thinking it was somehow her fault, but she didn't know how to fix it. Finally, as they reached the patio, she turned to face him.

"Aidan, what's wrong?"

"Nothing. Why?" But his eyes slid away from hers. "I think I should get this picture to Graham; I'll talk to you later."

And he was gone, moving quickly away and into the kitchen, leaving her staring after him with a lump in her throat and tears in her eyes. She felt broken, as if something precious had been lost.

Liz met her in the hallway. Her normally cheerful face was pinched and her brows furrowed. "Colleen, I called Dolly's house. She's not there, hasn't been home since she left for work yesterday morning. Her mother thought she was visiting a friend—apparently she does that sometimes—but she called everyone she knows about and she's not with any of them." Liz's face was tight with worry. "I called Flora—she's on nights but I thought maybe she'd talked to Dolly before she left this morning. She hasn't seen her since yesterday. So I walked down to the car park... and her car's there. She never left Balfinnan!"

The vision of a splash of blood on Artemis's white wooly face rose up in Colleen's mind, and she felt sick. She told Liz what she and Aidan had seen and watched her friend's face blanch.

"We'd better tell Mr. Anderson," Liz said, and the two of them hurried down the hallway toward the office.

"Mr. Anderson is busy," came an officious voice, and the black bulk of Morag Murtaugh appeared out of the gloom. She stood in front of the office door like a guard dog, scowling at them.

"He'll want to see us," Liz said shortly, and pushed past her to knock. When there was no answer, she opened the door, to a shocked gasp of outrage from the housekeeper. Colleen slid in behind Liz before Mrs. Murtaugh could stop her.

Graham and Aidan were bent over the photo on Aidan's phone. They looked up as the two women barged in, closely followed by Mrs. Murtaugh.

"I told them—" the housekeeper huffed.

"We think something's happened to Dolly," Liz cut in. "She didn't sign out yesterday, she's not here today, and her car's still in the car park."

The two men exchanged a look.

"Mrs. Murtaugh, see if you can find Archie and

Simon, and tell them to come here," Graham said quietly.

"Archie's up with Gordon MacNabb," Colleen offered. "At least he was half an hour ago."

Mrs. Murtaugh disappeared up the stairs without another word.

Mrs. Morton stuck her head into the office. "What's wrong?" she asked, her eyes darting from person to person as they huddled in the tiny space.

"Dolly's missing," said Liz. "Have you seen her?"

The cook creased her brow in thought. "She came through the kitchen yesterday afternoon. Said she was going foraging. She didn't come back in that way, but she often goes straight home to organize her finds. Maybe that's what she did."

"Her car's still here," Colleen told her.

Mrs. Morton's face paled. "I'm going to make tea," she announced, and disappeared back the way she had come.

Simon materialized from somewhere, and moments later Mrs. Murtaugh came back with Archie in tow. The men collected their coats and disappeared out the front door in the direction of the forest, leaving Colleen and Liz alone in a gloomy hallway that was suddenly too silent.

For the rest of the afternoon, Colleen tried to keep busy with the mundane tasks of geriatric care, but her mind kept straying to Artemis and the splotch of blood on her muzzle, and her inattention did not go unnoticed.

"What's wrong with you, lass?" grumbled Mrs. MacLennan. "You know I like two pillows behind my back!"

"Sorry," Colleen said, and hurried to remedy her mistake.

"Nurse? Nurse!" The plaintive voice came from room five. Mrs. Draich refused to call any of the nurses by name, as if not knowing them was proof she wasn't really in a care facility, and therefore not really too old to live at home anymore. Colleen sighed and turned into the room, for once grateful for the woman's incessant demands.

The day shift ended. Flora Kemp came in early, and still the men hadn't returned. Liz and Colleen hung around the sign-in desk with Flora, unwilling to go home. Mrs. Murtaugh joined them and for once had nothing to say about their loitering after hours. She showed no signs of leaving herself, and the sick feeling in Colleen's stomach intensified.

The front door opened. Graham walked in, his tread heavy, with Aidan right behind him.

"We found her," Graham said, his voice low and gravelly. "There was an accident. It looks as if a branch fell from a tree and hit her—" he stopped, cleared his throat, and forced the next words out. "I'm afraid she's dead." He placed his hand over his mouth as if to push the words back where they had come from, and then let his arm drop to his side.

Gasps sounded through the hallway and Liz began to cry. Graham patted her shoulder distractedly and moved like an old man toward his office.

"He's blaming himself," Aidan said, as he came up to Colleen. "Are you all right?" he asked quietly, his eyes dark in the subdued lighting of the castle's hall.

"No," she said, her voice bleak. "What happened?"

"There's an old dead tree on the edge of the forest, near the moor," he said. "A lot of branches have fallen over the years, and there was one beside her—beside Dolly—that was bloody on one end. Archie thinks it must have broken off high up and come down and hit her. He and Simon are there now, waiting for the ambulance and the police." He sighed. "Graham thinks he should have had that tree cut down, but of course that's ridiculous. There are hundreds of dead trees on Balfinnan land, and the chances of someone walking under one at just the moment—" He broke off, shaking his head.

"Oh god, that's awful," Colleen said, her voice catching as she imagined a young girl lying all alone in the woods, maybe still alive and in terrible pain, for who knew how long?

"I don't think she suffered," Aidan said quickly, studying her face. "It—it was bad, Colleen. She probably died quickly. And we think Artemis came along and tried to wake her up, and that's how she got the blood on her face."

"Has anyone called Dolly's mother?" Liz had come up behind them. Her voice shook. "I should do it. I know her." She burst into tears again. "I was so mean to Dolly! Why couldn't I have been nicer? She didn't mean any harm."

"Come with me, lass. We'll go to her house and tell her mother together."

Colleen hardly recognized the soft voice of the housekeeper. Mrs. Murtaugh put her arm around Liz's shaking body and walked her down the hall and out the front door.

She sounds as if she really cares, Colleen thought as she and Aidan stood staring after them. *Why do we wait until it's too late to be nice—to tell people how we feel about them?*

CHAPTER 20
PAST SINS

In an odd way, Dolly's funeral seemed to rejuvenate the residents, as if life was more precious no matter their aches and pains. Most of them had barely known the young nurse's aide. Dolly had made little attempt to hide her distaste during the time she spent tending to their needs, and they knew it. They'd experienced it before, some from their own families. They hadn't liked her, but they mourned her. And none of the residents wanted to miss a trip outside, no matter the reason.

They were used to funerals, these old people; death was always on the horizon. Everyone wanted to go, to pay respect to one whose time on earth had been cut so short when they had been allowed to live on. And so here they were, clustered together in the small kirk that served the community around Balfinnan, hearing the words of the ancient rite that had been spoken through the centuries for those who had passed on.

The service was long. Colleen barely heard the words delivered by a vicar who looked as old as the Balfinnan residents and who kept referring to the deceased as Polly. Apparently Dolly hadn't been a staunch churchgoer, and her mother was in too much of a daze to notice the mistake. She was a Scot, and life had been hard for her family for as long as she could remember, but the idea of burying her child was one she couldn't comprehend. She would be selling her small house and moving in with her sister in Aberdeen, but she'd wanted Dolly buried here, in the place she'd been born and spent the whole of her short life.

Graham had hired vans to carry the residents the short distance to the church. As the bagpiper led the group to the kirkyard, Colleen watched the procession of wheelchairs and walkers with concern. It was raining and the air was cold. A biting wind came off the Beuly Firth and swirled around the gravesite. It mocked the mourners and drove rain into their faces to mix with the tears, as if to warn them that their time on earth was pitiful and short, but the wind and the land and the sea would go on and never think of them again.

Colleen huddled against the raw wind with Liz and Flora, wondering if this sad affair would go on forever. She looked across the circle of mourners at Graham and Aidan, dressed in the kilts of their clans, and remembered Aidan's words from the trip to Edinburgh. *I only wear a kilt for special occasions.* Her eyes filled with tears at the thought that Dolly's special occasion had come down to this—a last goodbye in a cold, wet churchyard.

But finally it was over. She walked to where Gordon MacNabb sat resplendent in his kilt and ancient tweed jacket, holding court in his wheelchair and accompanied by Old Harry and Archie. Colleen hadn't wanted him to come, citing the weather and the rough ride in a van, but he had been adamant and now she saw that she had been wrong. To her old man, death was just more proof that he was still alive, still challenging the forces of nature. His wrinkled visage was solemn, but his eyes sparkled and his posture was straight. Colleen saw the same glint in other residents' eyes, and thought she understood. Their wrinkled faces were fixed in solemn respect, but their thoughts were elsewhere. They were thinking about Gordon's birthday party.

For Gordon, she thought, as for Mrs. MacLennan and Mrs. McNally and Mr. Montgomery, a funeral was usually as close as they were likely to get to a party. But these people knew something that the cold Scottish wind did not. Dolly's death was sad, of course, but in just a week, one of their own was going to beat the odds. Gordon's birthday party would be a triumph against time and the elements for all of them. He was their hero, and in the midst of grief and sadness there was a joy that nothing in this gloomy place could hold at bay.

Colleen shook her head in wonder at their ill-concealed enthusiasm. They were a testament to the indomitable will of men to live, to make the world notice their presence. In that moment, in a windswept kirkyard with freezing rain drizzling down the back of her collar, she knew there was nowhere in the world she would rather be than here with her people.

She closed her eyes and offered up a prayer for Dolly Gilles, and for the forlorn black-clad figure of the mother who would never hear the bagpipes play at her only daughter's wedding, never hold a grandchild or celebrate another family milestone. Life was so uncertain; maybe her old residents had the right of it to find joy in simply being alive in the moment.

Everyone gathered in the old ballroom at Ballfinnan after the service. Arabella Morton had stayed behind to get ready for the wake, and her efforts were apparent by the smells that assailed frozen nostrils as the mourners straggled through the front door and into the great room.

The tables were covered with food that ignored the dietary rules in place for most of the residents. Meat pies, sausages, fish and chips, and haggis stood in proud display on tables that had been moved from the library to stand in the center of the huge space. Whiskey from every distillery imaginable stood on a large table against one wall, with large pots of tea and dainty china cups nestled up against the whisky tumblers and gin glasses.

Chairs had been grouped around the tables in the center, and in one of them sat Dolly's mother, eyes glazed and hands clasped tightly in her lap. Graham sat next to her, and on her other side, glowering out at everyone present, was Morag Murtaugh. The housekeeper caught Colleen's eye and glared at her out of narrowed slits.

The real Murtaugh was back. Colleen wondered if she had imagined the other one, fantasized the soft voice and the kind hand on Liz's back. She sighed.

The housekeeper's momentary sympathy had been just that—a fleeting lapse in the woman's true nature.

Graham stayed for only a few moments. He stood, said something to Dolly's mother, and left the ballroom, headed for his office.

Aidan worked his way over to Gordon MacNabb, where he sat with Colleen and Old Harry.

"Are you ready, Gordon?" Aidan asked him, somehow knowing exactly what the old man had on his mind. "It's only a week away now."

"Ach, laddie, it's only anither birthday. Dinnae ken whit everyone's goin' oan abit."

Colleen choked. "Why, you old faker!" she said. "It's not just another birthday! It's all you've talked about since I got to Balfinnan!" She fixed him with her best nurse's no-nonsense face. "But if it's just another birthday, then maybe we should reconsider having a party. I mean, it's a lot of work for Mrs. Morton, after all the food for the wake." She winked at Aidan. "What do you think, Aidan? Don't you think we could all go without another big feast so soon?"

He rubbed his chin with one hand. "You might be right, Colleen. I mean, there's always next year, aye?"

Gordon's face had drained of color. He gripped the bars of his wheelchair as if he wanted to leap out of it and hurl himself at his tormentors. Then he heard a soft snicker from Old Harry, and relaxed back into the chair. He narrowed his eyes at Aidan and Colleen.

"So, yoo're havin' me oan. Ye ken Ah willnae likely be here next year. That's jist pure mean, an' Ah thooght ye two waur mah friends!" He shook his head in despair.

Colleen laughed. "I'm sorry, Gordon, I just couldn't help it. And it's your own fault for pretending this birthday isn't special, you know."

"It's special to me," Aidan added. "It's not often I get to kilt up twice in one week. Or eat this much, either!"

"Humph!" was Gordon's reply.

"And anyway, what makes you think you won't be here next year?" Colleen asked him, and then she stopped, reminded of the not too distant time that her old man wouldn't be here. He focused on her face, all amusement gone.

"Ah dinna think th' Ghruamachd will lit me." His voice quavered.

Aidan pulled up a chair. He took one of Gordon MacNabb's wispy hands in his own.

"Why do you think that?" His voice was soft and he went still, prepared to give the old man his complete attention.

Without hesitation, Gordon told him about the Ghruamachd, and about his fear that the evil ghost who haunted the castle knew that he suspected it and wouldn't let him live. Colleen had heard it all before, and she wasn't listening to Gordon MacNabb.

Her attention was on Aidan. He was giving the old man the gift of his empathy, as he had so often done for her, and suddenly she was buffeted by a surge of something more than simple affection for this man who made her life here at Balfinnan so much more than bearable.

She saw the substance, the core, of a man who gave everything to those he considered friends, and remembered the feeling that had coursed through her when Aidan touched his lips to hers at Nessie's. Felt again the feeling of utter joy that had gripped her heart for those few precious seconds...before he ran away and took it with him down the path.

She wanted to grab his hand and pull him away and out of the great hall, to paste her lips on his and see if it would happen again. To see what was real. Her mind began rewinding the events of the past weeks, moving back and forth between the two men who had become so central to her heart.

Graham. She had been so certain that she was falling in love with him, but now the feeling danced just outside her senses as if it was teasing her. What *was* it about Graham that had made her feel that way? He was mercurial in his attention to her—one minute acting as if she was the only person in the room, the next closing down and shutting her out. Was that it? The mystery in his changing moods? Was that what kept her hopeful that someday there would be more?

Aidan was never moody. He was honest and forthright and funny. He understood her fears and insecurities, and he never wavered. The perfect friend.

Can't you see? That man in there is perfect for you! Kate's frustrated voice rang in her memory, reminding her what a fool she was about love. She was twenty-six years old, and still judging men by their superficial qualities like a lovesick teenager. Like she had done with Aubrey, deciding that Connor MacConnach was the perfect man for her friend because he looked like Jamie Fraser on *Outlander*! Like she had done with John, buying into his world of romance and physical attraction, following him like a lamb to slaughter, seeing him through rose— or blond—colored glasses. Mistaking a tall, muscular body for sincerity.

Her mind slid sideways again. How did Graham really feel? Were his moods caused by ambivalence toward her, or was there something else? What had that passionate kiss in his office meant? She knew what it had meant to *her*, but maybe it was a momentary lapse and he'd immediately returned to his senses. He'd certainly seemed to regret it, but then he'd made the effort to spend more time with her, taken her out and showed her his Scotland. They'd had fun, dammit! His eyes when he looked at her seemed to be sending a message that she understood all too well. Surely it wasn't just physical with him.

No. There was something there with Graham. He had feelings for her, that much was certain. That kiss hadn't been merely friendship. She thought she knew at least that much about men. So what was his problem—why wouldn't he let her in? *There are things I have to do before...* Was there something in his past?

Her thoughts shifted again as she looked at Aidan, immersed in Gordon's tale. Was there anything there, on his side? He'd kissed her, too—a very different kind of kiss. Not much more than a peck, really, and then he'd seemed ashamed of it afterward. He seemed eager to prove that they were friends—best friends, she thought bitterly—and nothing more.

A sick feeling crawled through her. They *were* friends, nothing more. She had made sure of that, never giving him—*them*— a chance to be anything else because he wasn't her *type*. A feeling of self-disgust swept through her, leaving her weak. What the hell was wrong with her?

Maybe if she talked to him...she knew if she asked Aidan how he felt he'd be honest with her. That was another thing she admired about him: his honesty. He'd tell her the truth, even if it hurt.

She couldn't ask him yet, though. Not until she understood herself where her heart lay. It wouldn't be fair to him. She had to figure this out on her own, study her feelings for both men.

Besides, it wasn't just her own heart involved here. This wasn't like a pet store, where she could make a choice of puppies and just take the lucky one home with her. In real life, the puppies had to decide what they wanted, too. *It's not all about you, Colleen Fitzgerald!*

Suddenly she couldn't take it anymore. She stood and patted Gordon on the shoulder, waved to Archie. Old Harry's eyes followed her as she made her way across the ballroom and out the door. She needed air. She had some thinking to do. She needed to examine herself and figure out just who this sad specimen of woman was when it came to affairs of the heart.

The great knocker at the front of the castle resounded through the hall, breaking up the thoughts swirling through Colleen's brain. She started for the massive door, wondering who would be calling on a day like this. Everyone who'd been at the funeral was already here.

She was shouldered aside by a large figure. Mrs. Murtaugh stomped to the door, flung it open, and froze in place. A young woman stood on the doorstep, her hand raised to sound the knocker again. Young, beautiful, her long blond hair fell in loose curls to her shoulders. Large doe eyes in a flawless face took in the formidable figure of the housekeeper, and then moved beyond her to Colleen and to the people who had begun to filter into the hall at the clangor of the knocker.

Colleen felt a storm cloud gathering behind her eyes as she stared at the visitor. Not someone she knew, but not a stranger, either. The last time she'd seen the woman, those eyes had been streaming with tears as she stumbled away from Graham Anderson in the carpark of the Cameron Tea Room.

"Come in, Mrs. Anderson. I'll take you back to your husband's office." Mrs. Murtaugh's voice penetrated the fog. Colleen saw the housekeeper's baleful eyes fasten on her as they passed. Eyes that gleamed with triumph and malevolence.

Mrs. Anderson. Your husband. As if in a dream, Colleen turned to face the others who stood in the hall. Her eyes went to Aidan—to his pale face and furrowed brow—and his expression told her everything. He'd known. Her *best friend*, who never lied to her, who'd known how she felt about Graham, had known about this. And he'd said nothing.

Of all the words of mice and men, the saddest are, "It might have been."

Kurt Vonnegut

SCOTLAND, 1918

Alexander and Bridget walked along the pathway in the gardens of Balfinnan. Their heads were close together, their voices soft. Occasionally, a bubble of laughter would rise into the spring air, only to be lost in the fine misty rain. Neither noticed the flowers, or the weather. Nor did they notice the figure that followed them at a distance, cloaked all in black and hooded against the drizzle.

Grace had followed them many times, staying just out of sight and straining to hear their voices. She wanted to know what lovers said to each other, needed to watch how they touched. It intensified her pain to see and hear their happiness, but she couldn't help herself. Her hatred had grown and eaten away at her until it was a living thing, badgering her and giving no rest.

Once she had wanted him, had thought he was different. When he was weak and helpless he would have turned to her, offered her gratitude which might—no, would!—turn to love with time. Even after that one came, there had been a chance. If only Grace had been *the one to nurse him, she would have done anything—given anything.*

She had gone to the head of the castle, Duncan Anderson. He'd been so nice when he offered her the job, told her that her exams had been stellar and he was fortunate to have her. "You're a natural nurse," he'd told her. "Not so surprising, you being a Beaton. I'm proud to have someone from the medical kindred on my staff."

But when she'd asked to be assigned to the soldier whose life was in danger from the infection in his leg, he'd refused. Looked at her coldly and said he had already assigned someone else to take care of him. He was a liar as well as a cheat.

Men were all liars, and Alexander MacLeod was the worst. He'd made her feel, made her think he was different, that there could be something between them—and then he'd chosen the other one. Grace had held his hand when he was unconscious, but now that hand was wrapped around the arm of the Irish nurse, and those brilliant blue eyes saw no one but her.

Grace wished she'd never come here. When this was over, she would leave, find work elsewhere, far away from this cursed castle with its false hope and constant reminders of her failure. She knew now that her fantasy of finding love was as fleeting as the Highland mist. Her hatred surged, dark wings beating against the inside of her chest.

A lilting laugh came back to taunt her. They were laughing at her! How could that be, when they didn't know she was here? But they were laughing, mocking her pain. It was more than she could bear.

She forced herself to turn around, to stumble back to the castle and up to the room she shared with three other nurses. They were there, squawking like rooks in the trees, ignoring her as always. She'd never bothered making friends with them, and after a while they shrugged and turned away. Now their disinterest suited her purpose.

With her eyes trained on the chattering group across the room, Grace reached under her mattress and retrieved a small bottle of pills that had once sat on the shelf of the pharmacy. She sat for a minute studying the label, and then tucked it out of sight in the pocket of her uniform. It was time to give back.

"Tell me again about Skye, Alex."

Bridget pulled up a chair next to Alexander's bed and watched while he took his medicine. She sat on the edge of the bed and took his hand, feeling his pulse strong and sure under her fingers. It had been such a near thing. She would never stop thanking God for bringing him to her, not once but twice. She hadn't understood the gift the first time, in that terrible tent on the Somme, but now that he was healing she never wanted to let him out of her sight.

"Skye is the most beautiful island in the world, Bridie. I can't wait to show it to you. On a clear day the mountains reach up to touch the sky, and their feet reach to the sea." He coughed and cleared his throat. "When it's raining, the clouds come down and fold the tops of the mountains into a grey cloak. And every-where—every—" He coughed again.

241

Bridget leaned forward. "Are you all right, love?"

There was something wrong with his eyes. They were dilated, but the room was bright. His hand began to tremble in hers, and his breath rasped in his throat.

"What's wrong?" Bridget took his pulse again. It was racing, and now he was shaking uncontrollably.

"I—can't—" He tried to swallow and his eyes grew large with terror as his throat closed.

"Alex!"

The hallways of Balfinnan Castle were quiet in the late evening, heavy with the calm that accompanies sunset and the onset of darkness.

And then a scream split the air and reverberated down the corridors and out into the night. It went on and on, a keening borne of excruciating grief and suffering. Footsteps sounded on the stone floor as others raced to find out what kind of pain could cause such a sound, drawn by the sheer agony in that scream. Among them was one who knew what they would find, one whose face wore a small smile, though it was quickly suppressed.

It was just beginning.

CHAPTER 21
BETTER THAN ME

"Are you even listenin' to me?" The petulant voice sliced through Colleen's fog, and she jumped.

"Of course, Mrs. MacRae," she said, pitching her voice low and trying to regain the soothing tone that used to come so easily. Mrs. MacRae, a tiny, spidery woman with advanced arthritis and bad knees that confined her to a wheelchair, glared at her in disgust.

"I dinna understand where your mind is these days!" she said, shaking her head. "Ye used t' be the one knew just what I needed when the pain got real bad, but these days yer just not...there."

Guilt filled Colleen's tired brain. Mrs. MacRae was right. Her mind hadn't been on the job lately, but she thought she'd been covering pretty well. Trust her residents to cut through the bullshit.

"Yer upset about that woman says she's Mr. Anderson's wife, aren't ye?" Mrs. MacRae was ruthless. If you wanted honesty, or even if you didn't, you could count on finding it in Balfinnan House.

"Not upset, really," Colleen hedged. "Just...surprised." A snort told her how well that one had gone over. "I'll get you an icepack for your knees, Mrs. MacRae," she said, and patted the old woman's arm.

She hurried out of the room and leaned against the wall in the hallway. Did they all know? Was everyone laughing at her? No, the residents would never laugh. They'd have her back and fight for her happiness like ancient warriors—accent on the ancient. But there was nothing they could do about this.

She'd done it again—fallen for a married man. Was there something in her DNA that put out a neon sign saying, "Sucker here, please take full advantage?"

Colleen wandered down the first floor hallway. She needed to be alone for a few minutes, and the best place for that was the great library; nobody ever seemed to be there. She entered the cavernous room and threw herself into a high back leather chair, closing her eyes. Maybe the books that filled the floor-to-ceiling shelves would send some wisdom her way. God knew she could use it.

"Oh, hello." A soft voice came from the chair across from her. Colleen jerked and found herself staring into the huge brown eyes of the woman who had come to the castle's door a week ago. Graham Anderson's wife. She struggled to her feet, prepared to go. "No, please don't leave on my account." The woman put out a hand, and something in the other woman's face stopped Colleen where she stood.

"I—I was just—I have to—"

"Please. I need someone to talk to. I don't know what to do." There was desperation in her voice. "You're a nurse here, aren't you?"

"Yes." Colleen sighed and sank back into her chair. This was the last person in the world—besides maybe Graham or Aidan—that she wanted to talk to, but it was against her nature to be unkind, and it was obvious that the woman was in distress.

"I'm Olivia. Olivia Anderson." The woman twisted a ring on her finger. "Although I don't think it'll be Anderson much longer." Her voice had thickened, and was that a tear making its way down her face? Oh, shit, it was. Colleen's nurturing instinct kicked into place.

"Why? I mean—what's wrong?" she asked.

"He doesn't want me," she said. "It's been too long. We have nothing in common." The woman sat up straight and looked at Colleen with those magnificent eyes. "I was a fool to come here, to give it one more try. It's been too many years." The woman looked away and laughed, a dry sound in the huge space that turned her voice bitter. "But what about love? Shouldn't that count for something?"

Colleen sighed. "Tell me about it." She sat up straight and prepared to give Graham Anderson's wife her full attention.

"We met in university," Olivia said, her voice thin and distant, like the past she was remembering. "It was love at first sight." She looked up. "Can you understand that? Not just for me—he loved me, too! I know he did!"

"What happened?" Colleen's voice was soft. It was the voice she used with her residents when they were frightened about the future or in pain. And this woman was definitely in pain.

"We got married three weeks after we met, and lived in a tiny flat in town near the university. It was perfect. Everything I'd ever dreamed about." Olivia looked at Colleen, anguish written across her lovely features. "Have you ever felt like that? Like nothing could ever go wrong if you were together?"

"Um—ahh—yes. I have."

"But it did go wrong." Olivia's voice had sunk to a low murmur, laced with sadness. "After a while, he started to get restless." She sighed. "I don't know how well you know him, but Graham is driven."

"Driven?"

"Yes. He's always been obsessed with his dream for this castle. At first he told me everything. His father had died two years before, and Graham inherited Balfinnan." Olivia's voice tightened. "I tried to understand—I tried so hard! He talked about how his great-grandfather and his grandfather had frittered all the family money away and had to close Balfinnan down. The castle was close to being sold for taxes, but Graham's father turned it all around, made money in real estate and the stock market and saved the place. But he never opened it back up."

"Graham said his family was greedy. All they lived for was money—making it, spending it. All except for his great-great grandfather, who had opened his home to the wounded in the first World War. Graham idolized him, wanted to be just like him." Olivia looked down at her hands. She seemed to have forgotten Colleen was even there. "He took business courses in university, spent all his time studying. His friends tried, but nothing distracted him from his goal.

"Until he met me. He said I saved him from being a bore." A small smile played around her mouth, but was quickly gone. "For a while it was enough. I was enough. But then the obsession began to take him over again, and he began staying at the library every night. He hardly ever came home. He forgot how to have fun. He forgot me."

Olivia's voice caught on a sob. Colleen reached a hand out and put it on the other woman's arm, but she didn't seem to notice. "So I left. He didn't come after me. I don't think he even realized I was gone for awhile, and then one day he called and asked me why." Her eyes flashed with a sudden anger. "He asked me why, but he didn't ask me to come back. It was over for him—but not for me. We never divorced. It's been ten years, and we're still married—for what that's worth." Olivia looked at Colleen, her eyes bleak. "I never stopped loving him. Do you think that's pathetic?"

"N-no, of course not." There was something about this woman that reached into the innermost recesses of Colleen's romantic psyche and squeezed her heart. "Olivia—" She stopped, cleared her throat, and began again. "Why are you here now?"

Brown eyes fastened on Colleen's face. The woman cleared her throat.

"I saw him two weeks ago at a tea shop we used to go to, way out in the country, and it all came back as if it were yesterday. I knew I was still in love with him, and I wanted to give us one more chance." She took a deep breath and looked down at her feet. When she raised her head, Colleen could see the tears pooled in those lovely eyes. "But he wasn't happy to see me. We argued, and he told me to move on and find somebody else. 'You're better than me,' he said. So I ran away before I could break down in front of him. I knew it was no use." She sighed, a long, shuddering breath that rocked her slim frame. "I came to Balfinnan to tell him I would give him a divorce. He's been gentle with me. He wanted me to stay for a while so that we could work things out in a civil manner. Graham is always civil." The bitter edge was back, and Olivia stood suddenly. "Thank you for listening. You've been very kind."

She pressed Colleen's hand and turned to leave the library. At the doorway, she turned and looked back.

"You know what I think?" she said, almost to herself. "I think he's found somebody else."

"No." Colleen's gaze focused on the other woman, and she took a long breath. "I think he still loves you. Go to him—give him another chance."

Aidan glared at the blueprints on his desk. He'd been at it for over an hour now, and had absolutely nothing to show for his time. He rolled up the offending documents and shoved them onto the shelf. The definition of insanity, someone had said, was doing the same thing over and over and expecting a different result.

Well, he *was* insane. A fool. He'd gone completely radge, and had no one to blame but himself. Why had he let Colleen go on mooning after fecking Graham Anderson, when all the time he'd known the man wasn't available? Graham was an emotional cripple; his only true love was Balfinnan. He could have told her that. Wasn't that what friends did for each other? All that time he'd spent with her, talking and laughing, and he'd said nothing.

No, protested a voice in his head. *You did try to tell her. You warned her not to get involved with him.* Aidan squelched the voice for the liar it was. He hadn't tried—not really. He'd stammered something weak and tepid and she'd snapped his head off. So, like the coward he was, he had mumbled something about not wanting her to get hurt and dropped the subject. And sure enough, she'd gotten hurt.

There had been plenty of opportunities. Their friendship wasn't all fun and games; they had serious talks, too. She'd told him about her lover in New Jersey— her *married* lover—and never once had he opened his damn mouth and said, "Oh, by the way—did you know Graham's married?" It would've hurt her, and maybe she'd have been mad at him for being the bringer of bad news, but she'd have got over it. Not like now.

Even now, a week later, he saw her face every time he closed his eyes, drained of color as she stared at him in Balfinnan's hall and read the truth in his eyes. She'd known right away that Olivia wasn't a surprise to him, and her look of betrayal was seared into his memory. She was lost to him in that moment, as a friend...and as anything else. And he'd never realized how much that would hurt. It was like a vise on his heart, squeezing him dry.

She hadn't spoken to him—hell, she'd been avoiding him like the plague since the day of Dolly's funeral. She took her lunch inside, and stuck to Liz like a burr when she wasn't working. He'd responded by trying to drown himself in work, but most days were like today; the plans blurred and his brain was soggy mush when he tried to think. If he kept this up, Graham would fire him—*the bastard*—and maybe that would be for the best.

He could leave this cursed castle with its sadness and death and broken friendships and pick up the pieces elsewhere. He was good at his job. He'd had several offers before Graham had come looking for him, some of them certainly more prestigious than this one. But Balfinnan had called to him, with its history, its ghosts, and the challenge inherent in resurrecting that ruined piece of the past. It hadn't only been his friendship with Graham and the chance to live and work so close to his hometown that had solidified his decision to come here. Balfinnan had gotten to him on a level he'd never felt before. And then of course there was Colleen. *Had* been Colleen.

He didn't want to leave. He wanted to finish this job, see the restoration of the once noble castle take shape under his hands. He wanted to share it with Colleen, watch the wonder on her face. See her lovely face warm with pride.

He sat very still, eyes closed, and pictured her face. Her blue eyes that danced with mirth when she talked, the single dimple on the side of her mouth that deepened when she laughed. A warm glow spread through him at the memory of her voice, teasing him and responding to his jokes. He thought of the trust she had placed in him when she'd been confronted by the Grey Lady. Her kindness toward Simon, when so many others ignored the lad altogether. Her love for the residents.

He couldn't lose her. Aidan sat up straight, his eyes widening. He realized that he had just entered dangerous territory. It had snuck up on him when he was at his weakest, when he was powerless to deny his feelings. Well now, when it was too late, he was facing those feelings. Unless he was very much mistaken, he was in love with Colleen Fitzgerald.

And wasn't that just wonderful? That he hadn't realized how he felt until he'd lost her. She hadn't spoken to him in a week, and had he gone to find her? Made her listen to him, hear him say he was sorry? No, he'd just frozen there in the hall, pinned by her eyes, and then slunk away in disgrace. Eejit!

Aidan ran his mind over the problem like one runs a tongue ulcer against a tooth just to feel the pain. He forced himself to see the scene that day in the hall through her eyes, and it made him sick.

He didn't think she was really in love with Graham. He would have known if she was, wouldn't he? But she'd cared something for him. She had feelings for him, and she'd been made to look a fool by that odious Mrs. Murtaugh, with her smug smile and hateful smirk as she'd paraded Graham's wife past her in triumph. Colleen had looked to her best friend for support, and had seen the truth on his face. It was a betrayal of the trust they had shared—almost as if he had lied to her.

If she wouldn't talk to him he couldn't apologize, or beg her forgiveness. But he had to try, and tonight was the perfect time. It was Gordon's birthday party and everybody would be there. He frowned. Colleen would never miss this party, and somehow he'd get her aside, even if he had to threaten to make a scene. Simon would back him up, and so would Gordon. She'd have to listen to him if he mustered his troops.

He realized he felt better than he had in days. He had a plan, at least. He turned off the desk light and stood to go. If he hurried, he could get home to his flat in Inverness to shower and change. Normally he wouldn't have cared, but tonight he wanted to look good for this party.

A stirring of air moved the papers on the desk, and Aidan turned, curious. There was nothing there, no reason for wind with the door and windows closed. As he stared toward the corner in the darkness, he felt the hairs on the back of his neck come to attention, the familiar shivering start at the base of his spine. *She* was here.

He stood very still as the slight breeze solidified—if one could call it that—into the form of a woman. A tiny woman, with white skin and piercing blue eyes. Dressed in a nurse's uniform from a time long past.

The Grey Lady stood staring at him for a long moment. He could feel the weight of her pain like a damp blanket in his mind, pinning him down. He'd felt just that same pressure each of the two times he'd seen her before. Not frightening, just impossibly depressing. It made him feel helpless, as if there was something she wanted him to do that he couldn't.

But tonight there was something else. A sense of urgency that passed from the figure as she locked eyes with him. Fear—it was naked fear. And that made no sense. What did a ghost have to be afraid of? She was dead, her need to fear anything long behind her. So if she wasn't afraid for herself, then *who*?

The Grey Lady opened her mouth, and Aidan's jaw fell open in a macabre imitation. She'd never done that before, either. Colleen had sworn that the ghost had spoken to her, but it had never happened to him.

Words appeared in his mind as he read her lips.

He needs you. Help him.

"W-who?"

But the ghost was gone.

CHAPTER 22
CO-LÀ-BREITH MATH

airy lights twinkled from the branches of potted trees placed throughout the ballroom at Balfinnan House. A huge table groaned under trays of food. In the center of the table, a four-tiered cake sat, resplendent in blue and white icing, and atop the tower flew a miniature saltire, its white cross against the blue field proclaiming that this party was being held for a Scotsman. A tiny cake sat to the side, also decorated in blue and white and labeled in icing, "100." It was Gordon's own cake, proclaiming a man's achievement in a land that honored time and tenacity above all else.

Colleen had dressed carefully for the occasion, in a form-fitting moss green dress that brought out the streaks of gold in the red curls that fell to her shoulders and caught the lights in the ballroom. She knew she looked good. Gordon deserved her best, she assured herself, while a little voice repeated *liar*, like a broken record in her head.

She told the voice to shut up and forced her attention back to the room. All the residents were present, dressed in their idea of party attire. More tartan than she had ever seen in her life was draped, cinched and folded around skinny limbs and rotund figures, making her favorite people look like an aged reenactment of *Braveheart*.

Mrs. MacLennan was wrapped in an arasaid that was two sizes bigger than needed and held together with a huge clan brooch emblazoned with a coat of arms bearing the head of a stag between two crowns. Her eyes danced with the pleasure of so much company.

Mrs. MacNally had waddled over to the food table and was eyeing the spread with predatory eyes. Gordon's small cake had a smear on its side, and was that a bit of icing on the collar of the woman's lace blouse? Colleen gave the old lady a stern look. Mrs. MacNally rewarded her with wide eyes and an innocent smile as she sidled away from the table.

Colleen sighed and continued her observation of the residents. Damn it—there was Miss Curry, who was ninety if she was a day, wearing something diaphanous that she undoubtedly thought was sexy. The gown exposed much more wrinkled cleavage than needed to be seen by anyone as she leaned over and whispered into Mr. Montgomery's ear.

The poor man was leaning as far over the other side of his wheelchair as he could manage, risking a fall onto the floor. Miss Curry's spidery hand kept fondling the folds of his kilt, and it was obvious the octogenarian had had all he could handle. He looked terrified. Flora swooped in and wheeled his chair away, earning a grateful smile from the erstwhile romantic victim. From across the room, Colleen saluted Flora, and was rewarded by rolling eyes and a wry grin from the other nurse.

Most of the staff was already here. Simon was barely visible where he stood in the shadows by the doorway to the hall. Mrs. Morton raced in and out, adding still more delicacies to the buffet table. Liz bustled around the room, checking to make sure all their plans had been carried out properly and clucking when something seemed out of place. Flora deposited Mr. Montgomery safely among a group of male peers and then moved among the residents taking pulses and giving out medications.

Colleen smiled, a feeling of affection for her colleagues sweeping through her. It was a party, but this was also a care facility. Together, Liz and Flora were seeing to both of those functions. It was time she joined them and did her part. She moved into the room, but stopped short.

Graham had entered and was making his way toward the guest of honor. He looked wonderful. His Anderson kilt, with its sky blues and forest greens, brought out the color of his eyes and contrasted with his burnished blond hair. His eyes met Colleen's and his brows furrowed before he looked away.

Gordon MacNabb, oblivious to the undercurrents swirling around the room, sat grinning like a small boy at all this work that had been undertaken just for him. He said something that made Graham throw back his head and laugh.

Colleen waited until Graham had finished his brief conversation and moved away before she joined Gordon and pressed a kiss to his ancient forehead. The old man flushed a deep red.

"Ach, lass, yer makin' mah heart race. Ur ye tryin' tae kill me afore Ah hae mah cake?"

"No, you old rascal, I would never do that. And, since you mention it, try to remember that the little cake is for you, not the big one. Can you do that?"

He tried to look offended, but the grin gave him away. This was a man who'd been born two years after the ending of the first World War. A man who'd spent a century on this earth, making his own mark on history. He deserved his cake.

Colleen looked around the room and noted that not only Old Harry, but all the Owls were here, sitting at a circular table at the side of the room. Gladys was carrying the conversation as usual, and Maxine's foot tapped to the beat of the Celtic music coming from the band in one corner. Ronald looked bored without his television, and Old Harry sat as still as a statue, watching his old friend and mentor with a proud smile on his face.

The Owls may have been facing each other at a round table, but Colleen had no doubts that they were tuned into everything in the noisy ballroom. This evening would give Gladys fodder for a week. On the upside, maybe it would take her mind off Colleen's love life, which seemed to be the usual topic of conversation in Nessie's sitting room.

What love life? the small voice in her head butted in, and Colleen tried to shake off the sense of depression the words brought. This was Gordon's night, and there were worse things than a fractured romance or two. She looked around again at the gaggle of ancient residents and resolved to try to be more like them. They'd loved and lost, probably lots of times, and here they were, lined up and ready to party on.

A prickling began at the nape of her neck, and she turned to see that Aidan had entered the ballroom. His kilt, with its symphony of rich reds and dark greens, set off the dark sheen of his flyaway hair and coordinated with the short black jacket, kilt hose and vest. Colleen forgot her anger and just stood staring at him. He looked like a model for an upscale kilt shop.

He turned as if he'd felt her gaze, and stared back at her as if uncertain of his next move. That look was what did it.

Grow up, Fitzgerald! The voice in her head wasn't bothering to stay small. *You're an adult, for goodness sake. You know you're going to forgive him, so stop your pity party and get on with it!*

Something about the look on her face must have reassured him, because Aidan held up a hand and beckoned her. Without a second thought, she went. When she reached the doorway, he grabbed her hand and pulled her out into the hall.

Now he'll apologize, and I'll make him squirm, but then I'll forgive him—because I'm an adult.

Then she realized that they weren't alone in the hall. Simon had moved up close and stood waiting. Something was going on here—something that had nothing to do with apologies or misunderstandings or forgiveness. She looked more closely at Aidan, and saw that his grey eyes were dark with concern. He raked a hand through his dark curls and held her with his steady gaze.

"I saw her, Colleen. She talked to me."

"Who? Oh—Olivia? It's all right, I talked to her, too. She's actually very sweet."

"Olivia?" Aidan looked startled. "What are you talking about?"

"Well then who? Am I supposed to guess?"

"The Grey Lady."

Colleen stared at him, and then swung to face Simon. He was watching her intently. His calm demeanor settled her nerves and dampened her frustration. She turned back to Aidan, trying to copy Simon's posture.

"Okay. What did she say?"

"She told me to help him."

"Who?" This was becoming more like *Alice in Wonderland* by the moment! Were they having her on? No, Aidan's sincerity couldn't be more evident.

"I don't know." He held her gaze. "She said, '*He needs you. Help him.*' Her lips were moving, and I heard the words in my head, just like you said. And she sounded frightened. I think she wants me to help someone right now, which means someone at the party. Don't ask me how I know, I just do!"

"Well, practically everyone at Balfinnan is at the party." Colleen closed her eyes and scanned her memories of the ballroom and its inhabitants. "Mrs. Morton, you, Simon, Liz, and Flora—" Her head snapped up. She looked up and down the hallway and whispered, "Mrs. Murtaugh isn't there."

"Well, the Grey Lady said to help *him*. And even though Mrs. Murtaugh is as big as a man, I don't think she is one."

"Don't make fun of me," Colleen snapped. "I'm just trying to think."

"What if it's one of the residents?" Simon spoke for the first time. "It's the residents who've been dying, isn't it? They're the helpless ones."

What makes you think you won't be here next year?
Ah dinna think th' Ghruamachd will lit me.

"I think it's Gordon," Colleen said. She stared at the men before her, waiting for them to laugh at her fantasy. But the laugh didn't come.

"He always talks about the Ghruamachd; he thinks it's trying to kill him. I know he's old, but—" Then she remembered something. "Simon, you saw the Ghruamachd! You said it wasn't a ghost; it's a real person, right?"

Simon was nodding his head. "I've been watching for it, but I think it knows I'm there. I haven't seen it since that one time. I did tell Mr. Anderson, but he just said to keep watching."

Aidan was staring at them. "And neither of you saw fit to tell me about this? Gordon told me about the Ghruamachd at Dolly's funeral, but you didn't think I could help if I knew it was real, and not a ghost?" He looked hurt.

"I'm sorry, Aidan, I wasn't sure how much of it I believed myself. But now that we know it's real, we have to figure out what it wants. If Gordon's right, why?"

"Why?" Aidan gave her a puzzled look.

"Why would anyone want to kill him? He's a hundred years old, for God's sake! What kind of threat can he possibly be to anyone?"

"He talks, Nurse Colleen." Simon's eyes, almost green tonight in the light of the hall, were earnest. "He talks a lot, about things he sees...and about the past. What if he knows something that could hurt the Ghruamachd, something from a long time ago? What if it thinks he's a danger?"

Colleen tried to recall the stories Gordon MacNabb had told her. So much of it was garbled Scots that was barely comprehensible, but most of it had to do with the story of the Grey Lady.

"His mother worked here during World War I," she said in a low voice. "She was here when the Grey Lady—her name was Bridget—supposedly killed her lover and hanged herself in that burned-out room. But Gordon's mother didn't think Bridget was guilty, and—" She stopped, afraid to go on.

Aidan's voice was gentle. "And?" he encouraged.

Colleen took a deep breath. "And after I met her, I agree with him. I don't think she could ever have killed her lover. I think she's crying for him, still."

"I think you're right," Aidan said, in a low voice.

"What?"

"I heard her too, remember?" The look he gave her was steady.

Colleen felt a warmth spread through her, beginning in her head and sifting downward until her heart felt as light as the mist that rose from the loch on a rainy day. He believed her! It was the most ridiculous story she'd ever heard, and he believed her.

"Now that we've gotten that settled," Aidan said. "What do we do next? If we think Gordon is in danger, how can we help him? I think he's as safe as he can be right now, surrounded by all these people, but we have to watch him closely."

He raked fingers through his hair in frustration. "We don't even know for sure it's him, and if it is we don't know what he's in danger from! I wish ghosts would give a little more information."

"I'll keep an eye on him," Simon volunteered. "You two have to be more careful than me. Nobody notices me, even when I'm right there." His voice held no bitterness, just the knowledge that to most people he was invisible. Colleen's heart went out to him. It was their loss. There was so much more to Simon than they could ever imagine.

They returned to the party and split up to monitor the room as best they could. Colleen stood against the wall so that she could see the entire room, and Simon and Aidan took positions just behind Gordon MacNabb's chair.

"Co-là-breith math," yelled Old Harry, lifting his whisky glass. "Happy birthday!"

Gordon was at the center of a bevy of well-wishers, receiving gifts and handing out pithy sayings like a Highland Yoda. The female residents had done their best, knitting mufflers and mittens with arthritic hands. Mrs. MacLennan had painted a portrait of Gordon in the gardens of Balfinnan, smoking a pipe. It looked suspiciously like a skinny garden gnome, but Gordon beamed from ear to ear and Mrs. MacLennan blushed like a girl.

Old Harry marched over with the gifts from the Owls. His own gift was an odd fishing lure that, judging from Gordon's grin, must have held a secret meaning between the two. Gladys had contributed a jar of homemade marmalade in a knitted cozy. Maxine gave him a book of quotations about nature, and Ronald had donated a CD collection of British comedies. Most of the gifts were utterly useless for a housebound centenarian, but Gordon examined each with care, his eyes gleaming.

Liz came over to where Colleen stood. "He's enjoying himself, isn't he?" she said, her voice fond. "I don't know if I want to live to be a hundred, but if I do I want to be just like him."

"He's amazing," Colleen said, her voice cracking. "I hope he lives another hundred years."

The cake was cut and distributed. Flora brought Gordon's special cake over to him and then joined Liz and Colleen to watch the residents dig in.

"Just look at them," she said. "I don't care what anybody says, this is the best nursing job there is. You can learn so much from them, can't you?"

"Yes, you can—" Liz stopped. "What's wrong with Mrs. MacNally?"

They turned and looked at the old woman, sitting next to Mr. Montgomery. Her face was flushed and she was shaking, tremors wracking her plump body. Liz knelt beside her chair.

"Mrs. MacNally! Can you hear me?"

The old woman turned slowly toward her.

"Mama?" she said. "How nice of you to—to—" Slowly she toppled from the chair into Liz's arms, still shaking.

"Call an ambulance!" Liz yelled. "She's having a seizure!"

Time seemed to slow down for Colleen. She looked at Mrs. MacNally, at the icing on her collar, and then at Gordon MacNabb, his fork frozen halfway to his mouth, and something clicked.

"Aidan! It's the cake!"

Aidan reacted instantly, knocking the cake out of the old man's hand. Simon scooped it up before it could hit the floor and disappeared in the direction of the hall.

Liz looked up at them in relief. "Her color is better. She'll need to go to Raighmore to be checked out, but I think the worst has passed."

Mrs. MacNally was loaded into the ambulance and taken off, and slowly the noise in the ballroom returned as the shock wore off. It was obvious the party was over. The staff assisted the residents to their rooms, the Owls took their leave, and Mrs. Morton began, with shaking hands, to clear up the remains of the food. Colleen rolled Gordon MacNabb's chair toward the ancient lift, her own hands shaking on the handles. As they reached the hallway, Gordon's voice rang out in aggrieved rage.

"Ach! Whaur's mah cake? Ah niver got mah cake!"

CHAPTER 23

THE ICING ON THE CAKE

The staff was once again gathered in Graham Anderson's tiny office, but this time he was not the one seated behind the desk. Constable Sam Brodie, out of Inverness, looked at the pale faces of those crowded into the small space and cleared his throat.

"First of all, I want to tell you that Mrs. MacNally will be fine. She's resting comfortably at Raighmore Hospital, and will be back when she is released by the doctors there." His eyes narrowed. "I understand from Mr. Anderson here that this is not the first accident that has happened at this facility recently." The silence in the room grew and expanded as he looked from face to face, watching for a reaction.

No one moved. No one shuffled, or sneezed, or looked away from his direct gaze. Every eye in the room was focused on him and him alone, as if they were caught in a still life painting. He needed to shake them up.

"Mrs. MacNally's collapse last night was not due to her age or her health." He paused for a long moment, letting the tension build. "She was poisoned."

Gasps filtered through the room, and people began to look at each other. Some in fear, most in confusion. Three in recognition. A dark-haired man dressed in jeans and a green jumper locked eyes with a pretty young red-haired nurse, and then both looked at a much younger man almost hidden in the shadows. Interesting. Constable Brodie filed that away for future reference.

"What do you mean, she was poisoned?" A harsh voice demanded. "That is impossible!"

"And you are?" Brodie asked politely.

"I am Morag Murtaugh," she said, her voice dripping ice. "I'm the housekeeper here, and this is not the kind of facility where people get poisoned!"

"I see," said the policeman, looking over his glasses at her. "Thank you for your information."

Mrs. Murtaugh gasped and narrowed her eyes to slits, but Brodie turned his attention away from her. There was a snicker somewhere in the crowd, quickly suppressed. The constable continued as if he hadn't heard it.

"The poison used was a common one. Atropa belladonna, or atropine, known to many by its more fanciful name, deadly nightshade. But there is nothing fanciful about its effects." Brodie looked around at the wide-eyed group in front of him. "Atropine is used in medicine to save lives. It can be employed to treat Parkinson's disease, and as a painkiller. It's the drug of choice for something called bradycardia, where a patient's heart rate slows to a dangerous level. But when given too much—and too much is a very small amount—the patient becomes a victim. The nervous system is blocked and functions like heart rate and breathing are compromised. The symptoms include dry mouth, enlarged pupils, and hallucinations. If untreated, the victim can lapse into a coma and suffocate. Mrs. MacNally was suffering from mild symptoms of atropine poisoning." Constable Brodie paused. "You have atropine in your hospital pharmacy here at Balfinnan. Or, I should say, you *had* it here. All supplies of the drug have been confiscated, and tests are being run. Tests, for instance, like fingerprinting."

There was a rumbling in the group.

"You think one of our medical staff poisoned Mrs. MacNally?" a black-haired middle-aged woman wearing an apron choked out as she fisted her hands. "I know these people! No one here would do that!"

"And you are?"

"Arabella Morton. I'm the cook here." She sat up straight, her expression belligerent.

"The police don't think anything, Mrs. Morton. We don't make assumptions like that. What we do is investigate. We ask questions, do tests, run theories. Contrary to what you see on television, the police are not in the business of accusing people of crimes without proof."

Mrs Morton was radiating indignation. "But—"

Constable Brodie interrupted her. "I also did not mean to imply that hospital supplies are the only possible source of this poison." His voice was silk. "Belladonna is a plant. It has sweet berries that, when collected and juiced, can become a very effective poison. Only a few drops can be fatal. It could be added to a drink, or food—cake icing, for instance."

Mrs. Morton's eyes widened. Her mouth opened, but no sound came out. She sank back into her chair, shoulders slumped, and made a great study of her hands.

Constable Brodie sighed and rubbed his temples with his fingers. After a moment he looked up at his audience again.

"Now, you may all go back to work. I'll be talking to each of you, to see if there is anything you can add to this investigation. May I ask—" He spoke briefly to Graham and consulted his list again. "Nurse Fitzgerald, Mr. Shaw, and Mr. Reid to stay back for a minute, please? You stay as well, sir," he added to Graham.

The others in the room looked relieved. They moved toward the door, trying not to hurry, and squeezed out into the hall.

"Close the door, please, Mr. Reid." The young man did as asked and joined the other two in front of the desk.

Constable Brodie studied them for a few minutes. They betrayed the nervousness one might have expected in this situation, but that was all. He sensed no guilt, which struck the policeman as interesting after the silent communication he had witnessed earlier. There was something, he was sure of it, but he was damned if he could put his finger on it.

Graham drew up another chair next to the young

woman. She stiffened but didn't look at him, her clear blue eyes focused on the constable.

Well, might as well just lay it out.

"I couldn't help but notice that you three didn't seem surprised to hear that Mrs. MacNally was poisoned," Brodie began. No one said anything for a minute. Then the man in the green jumper spoke.

"We weren't—not exactly. We didn't know it would be poison, and we didn't think it would be Mrs. MacNally, but we thought something might happen at the party." His grey eyes were steady.

"Indeed," said Brodie. "Would you care to explain that, please?"

"We believed that Mr. MacNabb might be in danger from...someone."

"Really? And why was that?"

"It's hard to explain. We had no proof, but Mr. MacNabb thought so, and we believed him."

Graham spoke up. "Mr. MacNabb is one of our residents. He can be quite imaginative. Still, it was his party, and it was his cake that seems to have been poisoned." He paused. "Mrs. MacNally is—well—a bit eager when it comes to sweets, and apparently she couldn't resist tasting the icing."

"I see." Brodie was silent for a moment. He turned his attention back to the man with curly dark hair and calm grey eyes, who sat patiently across from him. "So you thought Mr. MacNabb was in danger, and Mrs. MacNally, in effect, saved him." He went on, his voice reflective. "She had just a small taste of the icing, and you saw how it affected her. If Mr. MacNabb had eaten his cake, I have no doubt I would be investigating a murder today."

The red-haired nurse's blue eyes filled with tears, and she swiped them away with an impatient gesture.

"But," continued the constable, "you still haven't explained why you thought Mr. MacNabb was in danger. In danger from whom, did you think?" He snapped his head around to look the nurse straight in the eye. "Can you add anything, Nurse Fitzgerald?" The words came out with whiplash-inducing force. The nurse jerked and a flush rose in her pale face.

"N-no, it's just like Aidan—Mr. Shaw—said. We thought—"

"I told Nurse Fitzgerald that Mr. MacNabb said someone was going to hurt him," the man in the green jumper interjected smoothly. "She's a very caring nurse, and I'm afraid I upset her with my theory. She agreed to keep watch with me, and it's a good thing she did. She saw that Mrs. MacNally had icing on her clothing, and she made the connection to Mr. MacNabb's cake. She saved his life." The man sat back with his arms crossed over his chest.

Constable Brodie studied him for a moment, and then his gaze moved back to the nurse. She was staring at the young man, too, and her face bore a faint look of surprise.

He sighed and sat back in the desk chair. "Well, that's all for the moment. Thank you for staying. I may have further questions, but you may go now."

He watched them leave the room. There was more to this than they were telling; he could feel it. Constable Brodie was a shrewd judge of character, and he thought that Nurse Fitzgerald and Mr. Shaw had been telling the truth. They just weren't telling all of it.

"You were right, sir," he said to Anderson, who was staring at the doorway. "There's something odd going on here."

Then his eyes snapped up to the door that had now closed behind the three. Three? His brow furrowed. There had been a third person in the group. A much younger man, a mere lad. He'd been so still and quiet that Brodie had forgotten he was there, even though he'd been sitting right in front of him.

Curious. Quite a talent, that.

CHAPTER 24
THE COST OF REGRET

"So, we're ready to begin construction, then?" Graham asked his architect. The two men were bent over the blueprints in Aidan's office.

"Destruction, more like. We want to remove the affected beams first, without endangering those not weakened by the fire."

Aidan pointed to a corner of the drawing. "The damage is not the same throughout. See, this room on the third floor is where the fire started; the devastation was greatest there. The beams will have to be removed and braced before reconstruction can be started."

Graham nodded. "I've always wondered about the fire. Was it an accident? There are no accounts anywhere in the records from that time, which is odd."

Aidan studied the blueprints again. "It's one of the smallest rooms. You can see it was accessed from the end of the second floor hallway, and there's a doorway on the right wall that leads to another corridor and from there to the back of the building, where the family stayed during the war years."

"Can we see that room?"

"Sure, as long as we're careful. It's shored up from below now. The window glass is missing, and there's that large hole right in the center that hasn't been covered yet. We'll have to walk around. Take a jacket and a couple of torches. It's dark in there, even in the daytime, and it'd be easy to fall."

Aidan closed his eyes, remembering Colleen's frightened face when she looked at the room in daylight and realized how close she had come to plunging through that hole. The night he'd come close to losing her. He swallowed.

Things had been better between them the last few days. She'd forgiven him, but he wasn't sure he was ready to forgive himself. Gordon's party and its aftermath had intervened, and they hadn't had an opportunity to discuss the elephant in the room.

He opened his eyes again to find Graham watching him.

"What's going on with Olivia?" That wasn't what he had meant to say, but now that the words were out, he was glad.

Graham looked startled, and then annoyed. "I don't see how that's any of your business."

"It shouldn't be, but I find that it is." Aidan's voice was crisp. "Are you finally getting that divorce?"

Graham bristled and then deflated, letting out a long sigh of frustration. "She's offered to give me a divorce, and until recently I thought that's what I wanted. But something's holding me back. I'm no good at this stuff, Aidan! I don't want to hurt her." He looked up, his eyes bleak. "I thought I'd moved on, but in these last few days, seeing her again every day, I—"

"You're a good man, Graham." Aidan patted his friend on the shoulder.

"Thanks, but you're wrong. What kind of man marries a woman and just lets her walk away six months later? What kind of man knows he has nothing to offer, and still goes after someone else?"

Aidan's heart lurched. He was afraid to ask the next question, but he found he had no choice. His mouth went on without him. "You're talking about Colleen, aren't you?"

The words dropped into the room like a rock, taking his heart down with them.

Graham raised his head. When he answered his voice shook. "She's lovely, isn't she? Beautiful, but it's more than that. She cares about people. These residents—my residents—think she walks on water. She has so much to give, and she wears her heart on her sleeve, you know? I took advantage of that."

Aidan said nothing, just regarded him with his clear grey gaze.

"I think I was falling in love with her." Graham's voice was low. "No, I know I was. But what the hell do I know about love? I thought I was in love before, and look what happened!" He sat down on the only chair in the room and put his head in his hands. When he looked up, there were tears in his eyes. "Sometimes I think the only thing I really love is this castle. How pathetic is that?"

Pretty pathetic, Aidan thought, but held his tongue. Regardless of his failings, Graham was his friend, and it was the truth that he was a good man. There was simply something in his makeup that had caused this man to be so driven, to love a place more than people.

"So what are you going to do?" he asked, trying to keep the tension out of his voice.

Graham lowered his eyes again and studied his shoes. "Well, I have to talk to Colleen, of course. She hasn't even looked at me since the night Olivia showed up, and I can't blame her for that. But I've been a coward. I've mucked it all up, and I have to own it. And then I have to decide what to do about Olivia." The silence grew between them, and then Graham looked up. "I still care about her, Aidan. I thought I'd put my marriage behind me, but there has to be some reason I never pursued a divorce." He stood up. "Enough about me and my mess. Let's go look at this burned-out room, shall we? And thanks for listening and not telling me what an arse I am. I know you're thinking it."

Damn right, mate, Aidan thought, but suddenly he was more cheerful than he'd been in days.

The two men made their way up to the second floor, listening to the sounds of a working care facility. Carts rolled across stone floors, and the murmur of voices rose above the clang of bedpans and the incessant ringing of residents' call bells. Liz Dunnet came out of a closet at the end of the hall and waved to them before disappearing into another room. Colleen was nowhere in sight, and Aidan was grateful. He didn't want to see her anywhere near Graham.

Stupid. As if keeping them apart would solve everything. Colleen and Graham would have to sort themselves out, and he would just have to live with it.

At the end of the hallway, Graham unlocked the door. They stood for a moment on the threshold, studying the space in front of them. Even in the daylight, the room was cloaked in gloom. The lingering charcoal scent of the long-ago fire was overlaid by something else—a musty odor that evoked damp, rotting fabric or long-dead vegetation. Dust tickled Aidan's nostrils and he clamped down on the urge to sneeze. He reached into his pocket for a torch and made the room visible.

In front of them was the gaping hole, an obscene gash in the floor where the fire had burned hottest. It held no mystery for Aidan any more—he'd studied the ruined space before him when he first arrived at Balfinnan—but still it raised the hair on the back of his neck and called to something primitive in his soul. It smelled of death and sadness, and of time lost.

On the wall across from them the shelves flanked a fireplace, its grey stone blackened with soot. The shelves here were empty and relatively undamaged except for smoke residue, but the outside wall and window told another story.

The glass was long gone from the blackened frame, allowing the damp Scottish air to pour in unchecked. Shelves next to the window were charred and blackened stumps of wood that sagged and leaned away from the wall. Books and documents had spilled out and turned to dried lumps from the water that had been thrown against them in an effort to quench the fire.

"I don't think anyone except you has been in this room since it happened," Graham said from behind him. "They removed the books on the other three walls, but on this one there was nothing to be saved, so they just locked the door and left it the way it was."

Aidan stepped carefully around the hole in the floor and made his way to the ruined bookshelves.

"What was kept in here?" he asked.

"I think this room was originally a bedroom," Graham said, "but the family kept the most important books and documents here during the war. The rest of the books were removed to the great library on the first floor after the fire, but those on these shelves were destroyed, as you can see. Are you sure it can be renovated?"

"Yes, the walls are mostly intact, and the support beams are still in place. The shelves will have to be removed and the floor replaced, of course. It's really not as bad as it looks, but we should cover the hole with plywood until we're ready for that step."

Graham nodded. "I don't know why that wasn't done a long time ago. My mind has really been on other things, I guess, and the door has always been kept locked."

"Except when Colleen opened it." Aidan's tone was terse.

Graham sighed. "Except then. And I don't understand how it could have been unlocked that time. You and I are the only ones with keys to that wing."

"You and I...and Simon, of course...and Mrs. Murtaugh. She has keys to every lock in the castle, doesn't she?" Aidan shrugged.

"Mmm, I hadn't thought of that. Ask her if she was careless, why don't you?" He rolled his eyes and Aidan laughed at the image of Murtaugh's face if someone were so foolish as to make such a suggestion.

Aidan went back to his study of the damaged bookshelves. On the surface, it didn't seem as if the books or papers had anything of interest left to give. Most of the pages were glued together in an unrecognizable mess, and papers clung to the floor and shelves like blobs of paper mâché. He'd have Simon come up and get rid of everything before they started the work on this room.

"Well, I'm going down to my office," Graham said. "That constable is coming at noon, and I have to placate him as best I can. I'm afraid if he doesn't get anywhere in his investigation, he's going to close us down." His face was drawn. "And then where will my people go?" He skirted the hole and turned at the door. "I want to tell you again how much I appreciate your friendship, Aidan. You know I never had a lot of close friends, even at university. You and Finn, and maybe Charlie, and that was about it. I guess Olivia was right when she told me I was too obsessed to have fun."

As he went out the door, Aidan heard him mutter, "She was right about a lot of things."

Despite his annoyance with the man, Aidan felt a surge of sympathy. He thought about what Graham had just said. *You and Finn, and maybe Charlie.* The sad thing was that he and Finn had never felt particularly close to Graham, and Charlie Magruder had barely put up with him. Graham Anderson had never been a social animal, always stuck in the library with his business books, fixated on his castle.

Aidan sighed, remembering. Reopening Balfinnan had been Graham's main topic of conversation in school, to the point where most of the other students turned away from him. His mother died when he was a baby, and his father had been too intent on turning the family's finances around to pay much attention to him, so much of his childhood was spent with his maternal grandmother.

It had been his Gran, Graham said, who inspired his quest to open Balfinnan as a care facility. He had watched the once spry woman become frail and forgetful, until his father packed her off to a nursing home without a second thought. Her grandson was her only visitor. He watched Gran weaken and fade in the sterile environment of the home, and when she died he vowed to make his castle into a place of dignity for those nearing the end of their lives.

He had done that. Aidan looked out the window at the back garden of Balfinnan House. Here in the middle of November, everything looked dead, but in the spring that garden would be filled with flowers and the residents would be out enjoying the beauty of the Highlands. These people had made this country what it was, and now they were enjoying the best it had to offer in their twilight years—thanks to Graham Anderson.

"Hats off to you, Graham," Aidan said out loud to the silent room. "You may be an arse who's after my girl, but you're all right. And I'm the arse if I don't fight for her, so fair warning there."

He walked back around to the doorway and studied the room as a whole. Three wooden beams ran across the entire space beneath the peaked ceiling, but something was out of place. The central beam was the only one that showed major fire damage, and it seemed to have been confined near the ruined section of shelves and the window. Odd, that.

He'd assumed that the fire had started in the center of the room because of the hole in the floor, but that made no sense. If it had started there, wouldn't it have burned across the whole beam, and from there to the other three walls?

Then he saw something that made a chill run up his spine. Burned into the wooden beam was a braided pattern that looked familiar. It ran across the wood from the wall to the center, and stopped there.

A rope.

The fire hadn't started in the center of the room. It had started—or perhaps had been started—at the bookshelves, and then run up the wall and across the beam. The chill was growing stronger. What he was looking at was important, but he couldn't quite wrap his mind around it. His brain was giving him the answer, but he was avoiding the obvious conclusion.

Why had the fire run across the beam and stopped in the center? And what was the rope for? Gordon's words floated into his mind. *She knows Ah ken...didna kill 'er loover...hangit hersel. Hangit hersel.*

Of course. Bridget had met her end in this room.

Had someone started the fire to cover up the

hanging? But no—that still didn't make sense. The fire had happened days later. Bridget's body had been taken down long before then. Everyone knew the story of the nurse who killed her lover and then herself. And anyway, the fire had started in the *bookshelves*, not where the nurse had stood in her final moments, accepting that life was no longer worth living.

The solution came to him in a rush, the way the solution to a difficult math problem suddenly appeared fully solved in his head after eluding him for hours.

Aidan realized he was shaking. He had a piece of the mystery in his hands, but it was too bizarre to accept with his eyes alone. He needed corroboration from someone he could trust.

CHAPTER 25
TWISTED VENGEANCE

"Colleen, may I talk to you?"

Colleen stared at her boss. She hadn't spoken to Graham in two weeks, not since the night of Gordon's party. The night his *wife* showed up and her world spiraled out of control.

But he was her boss, and she didn't want to leave Balfinnan. She'd known this moment was coming, but there was no way to prepare for it. She followed him into his office without a word, and sat in the chair in front of his desk, just as she had months ago. She waited.

Graham stared over her head for a minute, and then brought his gaze back to her. "Colleen, first I want to apologize, for—for not telling you about Olivia."

"Why should you tell me about Olivia?" She wanted to sound arch, sophisticated, as if it didn't matter, but it wasn't working so she shut up and simply stared at him. To his credit, he flushed a deep red.

"I was going to tell you that Olivia and I have been separated for almost ten years...that there's nothing between us anymore and we will be divorcing."

"But?" There *was* a but there, she could hear it in his voice, and Colleen was a veteran of this sort of battlefield.

We're not together. She won't give me a divorce. She says she needs me. Were the words ever any different? But there was a difference this time. This time she was stronger. She hadn't let him so far into her heart that there was no turning back.

"But I can't tell you that." Graham looked at her, pain in his blue eyes. "I thought it was true—that it was over between us, but I don't know. I just don't know!"

"Olivia deserves better."

"What?"

"I met her. She told me about university, about how you two were barely old enough to know, but it was love at first sight. She told me she'd always loved you. She still does." Colleen didn't know whether her words were consolation or torture for him, and she didn't much care. Graham just stared at her. "I don't know whether she'll take you back, but I would hazard a guess that she will...if you play your cards right."

"B-but—"

"Graham, you don't have to worry about me. I'm not in love with you. I thought I might be for a while, but I'm not." His blue eyes were round with...what? Surprise? Relief? "You're a lovely man, and I like you very much...but I don't love you. It was touch and go there for a while, but—no."

Colleen stood, walked around the desk, and gave Graham a kiss on his cheek. Then, without looking back, she left the office.

She leaned against the wall in the hall for a few minutes. *Did I just do that? Basically tell Graham Anderson to go pound sand?* She began to giggle, thinking of the look on his face. The giggle turned into a chuckle which evolved into a laugh that welled up from somewhere just south of her heart. Tears pooled and then ran down her cheeks, and she bent over to stem the hysterical tide.

"Colleen? Are you all right?" A hand cupped her face and a pair of worried grey eyes swam into focus. Aidan.

"I'm f-fine. I just told Graham I'm not in love with him." And then she was off again, laughing and crying and hiccupping.

"Oh. That's good then." His smile was brilliant as he took her arm and led her away from the office. "Do you think you can pull yourself together enough to help me solve a mystery?"

She nodded, her eyes still watering, and he led her up to the third floor and unlocked the door to the devastated room. At Colleen's raised eyebrow, he shrugged.

"I'm the architect, remember? Graham gave me a key a long time ago."

He led her into the room she remembered, but now it looked very different. The hole in the floor had been covered by a thick panel of plywood. In the corner stood a generator connected to a space heater and an electrical outlet strip, into which a floor lamp had been plugged. Light flooded the room, throwing the charred beam and damaged shelves into sharp relief. Shadows lurked in the corners the lamp's light couldn't reach, reminding Colleen that here was where she had met a ghost. She wondered what the Grey Lady thought about this invasion of her privacy.

Simon Reid was perched on a stool next to the shelves, carefully sifting through dried papers and charred books. He looked up when he saw her and grinned, that shy smile that transformed his elfin face into something beautiful.

"Hi, Nurse Colleen."

"Hi, Simon. What're you doing?"

"Trying to see if anything legible survived the fire," he told her. "So far nothing much, but there's lots to go through yet."

Aidan pulled her over to a chair that had been placed directly underneath the beam, centered on the piece of plywood.

"Stand on the chair. Don't worry—it's safe. There's a support underneath." He looked at her, eyes dark and unreadable, and placed an arm around her waist to anchor her on the chair. "I wouldn't let anything happen to you, Colleen." His voice was soft, but she felt the tension in his arm.

"I know."

"Now, look closely at that beam and tell me what you see."

"Um, burned wood, a lot of soot, some kind of gouges here in the center. What's that from?"

"Look harder."

"I don't see anything—wait—there's a kind of

pattern on this one side, and here in the center it goes right around the beam. Like a braid or something."

"Or?" He waited, holding her steady. She ran a finger over the pattern, and her eyes widened.

"A rope?" She stared down at him. "Was this where Bridget hanged herself? So it's real!"

"Oh, it's real. But now look at where the rope went around the beam and then along here." He pointed along the beam and Colleen's eyes traced it to the wall next to the bookshelf. "It's dug deep into the wood all along the beam, but especially in the center, where the noose would have been." Aidan's voice was soft.

Colleen blinked at him. He helped her off the chair and faced her with steady eyes. There was something she wasn't getting here. She waited.

"Bridget was small, right? She didn't weigh much at all." Now Aidan's voice held an edge of excitement.

"R-right."

"It puts a great deal more pressure on a beam if you're hoisting a dead weight from the floor, than if a small body falls a few feet. It's physics."

He stood back and watched her mind make its own connections.

"Aidan—are you thinking that maybe someone *pulled* her up? That she was already dead before she was hanged?" Her eyes were round. She put her face in her hands, and when she looked up her expression was set. "If that's true, then Bridget didn't hang herself. She had help." Colleen's voice was soft, and she was filled with sadness at the terror this young woman must have faced in her last moments, coupled with an odd sense of hope that this was the way it had happened. Horrible as it was, this conclusion validated everything she had come to know about the Grey Lady. "It all comes together when you look at it that way. People didn't think she killed her lover. An Irish Catholic *wouldn't* be likely to commit suicide." She stared at Aidan, eyes wide. "She was murdered."

He nodded. "I think so." He turned back to the bookshelf and studied the destruction. "Colleen," he said, raising his eyes to the rope pattern charred into the wood. "The fire burned only the half of the beam from the noose to the bookshelf, right?"

"Yes, it appears so."

"I was assuming that someone started the fire in the center of the room, because of the burned-out section of the floor." He stepped back and narrowed his eyes at the beam and its charred rope pattern. "But what if the fire burned *from* the bookshelf to the center of the beam, following the rope? It would travel along to the noose, and down the rope. If there was a carpet on the floor, the rope would fall right in the center and burn through to the wood, and then down to the floor below. It makes so much more sense that way!" He added, "And Simon and I have been wondering if maybe the fire had nothing to do with Bridget at all! What if the murderer started it to hide something in this bookshelf?"

Colleen stared at the shelves of burned papers. Simon caught her eye and gave a tiny nod.

She turned back to Aidan. "Something here was important enough that someone wanted to destroy it. Maybe something that would point to the killer.

And oh, Aidan!" Her blue eyes were huge and round. "If someone killed Bridget, then that same person probably killed Alexander! In fact, maybe his death was the murderer's real goal. Then Bridget was killed to make it look like she was guilty!"

"We'll probably never know for sure," Aidan said. "But it fits with everything we know about Bridget, doesn't it?"

"It does. Can you imagine what that poor girl went through? What a horrible, vicious, evil thing to do!" Colleen found herself choking up as tears welled in her eyes. "That's why she cries, Aidan! I wish there was something we could do to help her—tell her family the truth, at least—even if it was so long ago. They deserve to know their ancestor wasn't a murderess."

"Shhh!" Simon's sudden hiss traveled across the space. "She's coming!" He doused the lamp and pulled the plug on the generator, but not before a frigid cold settled on the room. The shadows in the corner began to take form, revolving and sending dust motes swirling out into the center of the room. Before their eyes a figure appeared, clothed in a nurse's uniform from the past. The Grey Lady had come to call.

"Come in."

Was his voice steady enough? His heart certainly wasn't. In fact, Graham was pretty sure his heart had vacated his body.

The door opened slowly, and Olivia stood on the threshold. God, she was beautiful. Had she changed at all in ten years? Every time he saw her he was reminded of the first time, at that university party they'd made him go to. *Get out and do something, Graham! You're rotting away in this library—the books'll still be there, lad!* So he'd gone, just to shut them up.

He'd been sitting on the couch nursing an ale, wondering how soon he could leave. The door opened for the hundredth time—and there she was. Slim, blond, with huge brown eyes that darted around the room. She looked like a nervous fawn poised to run, and suddenly he was beside her, taking her hand and leading her back to the couch. Just like that—and three weeks later he was a married man.

For a while it had been perfect. His shocked friends had left them alone, and that suited both of them just fine. They spent hours walking around the campus, talking. Nights wrapped in each other's arms. Olivia was a listener, so Graham told her about his vision for his family's castle. He told her about his great-great-grandfather, Duncan, and Duncan's friend, Malcolm Beaton. How Duncan saved his friend's life in the first Boer War, and Malcolm offered him Balfinnan as a gift. How, years later, Duncan offered up his castle as a hospital for wounded Scottish soldiers.

Graham had taken Olivia to see Balfinnan, and that was the beginning of the end. She found the castle cold and forbidding, and told him she'd never want to live in such a huge, frightening place. The arguments were mild at first, but after awhile they became their only conversation. Graham escaped, as always, back to the library and his vision for Balfinnan. He rarely came home. And one day, while he was buried in his books, she left.

And now here she was, and what he'd thought dead and gone was here with her. This was supposed to be their final meeting. She was going to agree to a divorce, after all these years, and he would be a free man. But free to do what? He'd never found another woman in all those years who could come near to Olivia—until Colleen. And now she was gone, too. He'd messed that chance up just like he'd ruined his marriage. Running away. What the hell was wrong with him?

"Graham?" Olivia's voice, tentative and unsure, reached through his fog. He looked up to see her still standing in the doorway, and suddenly he was out of his seat and around the desk.

"Come in, sit down." He led her to a chair in front of the desk, but instead of returning to his own leather chair he pulled up another and sat beside her. She looked surprised, but pleased. They sat for a moment in silence.

"Are we ready to do this?" she asked, her voice trembling just a little.

"I don't know." He hadn't meant to say that. The correct answer was yes, but not the true one. He reached out and took her hand, and the old electricity ran through his body. What was happening?

"I'm sorry, Livvy." The old nickname rolled off his tongue. "I'm so sorry for everything. It was all my fault, what happened. I was an arse."

Her hand was on his lips. "Shhh, of course it wasn't your fault. We were barely more than bairns, playing at being adults! I could have said something, tried to explain. I could have been more reasonable about this place."

"Well, I guess that much is true," Graham said, and his mouth quivered. "You only saw the castle once, and you didn't give it a chance. I couldn't believe you were so set against it."

"I guess I just never understood how much it meant to you," she said. "Although I probably should have—you never shut up about it. 'Balfinnan this,' and 'when I open up Balfinnan that.'" She stopped, but her smile was gentle. "We were too young to compromise, Graham. We let one roadblock sabotage our marriage. Which is why kids shouldn't get married. We're proof."

"We're not kids now."

She stared at him. "What?"

"We're adults, Olivia. Maybe we're grown up enough to change things." Graham had stopped smiling and was staring at her, his blue eyes intense.

"Change things?"

"There has to be a reason we never got divorced. Maybe fate knew something we didn't."

Her laugh was shaky. "Do you mean—"

The words burst out with sudden certainty. "I don't want a divorce, Livvy. I want to wait, see how this works out. What do we have to lose?"

He sat still, afraid to move. A long moment passed.

"Do I have to live here?"

Graham stared at her, and then realized she was smiling again. Her hand in his was damp, but she was smiling.

Olivia shrugged. "This place doesn't seem so bad

now." She jumped up and walked to the sideboard. "Can we make a toast to something? Like how insane this is?" She picked up the decanter that sat on a silver tray. "Is this the same wine? Your favorite French stuff that I can't pronounce?"

Graham laughed. "Chateau Lafite Rothschild, and yes, it is."

"Snob." Her voice was light, buoyant. Happy. Olivia poured the wine into two glasses and took a sip of hers. Her eyes widened. "Ahh, yes, Chateau Lafite... whatever. Rich, full-bodied, with a robust fruity something—"

"Shut up, and you're supposed to wait for the toast. Don't you know anything about wine?"

Olivia gave a shaky laugh and took a gulp of the wine. She cocked her head. "Nope. You know I never did. Wine is a mystery to me. But I guess I'll have to learn." She coughed, and the glass wobbled. She drank again, and giggled.

"You're a lightweight," he said, and got up to take the glass from her. Olivia staggered and coughed again. Reaching out to steady her, Graham saw that her eyes seemed unusually wide. No, it was her pupils—they were dilated, and—

"Graham?" she choked. A look of stark panic came over her face, and she clutched at her throat. "I— can't br—" Her body began to convulse as she fell forward into his arms, taking them both to the floor.

I vow you the first cut of my meat,
the first sip of my wine,
from this day it shall be only your name
I cry out in the night
and into your eyes that I smile each morning;
I shall be a shield for your back
as you are for mine,
nor shall a grievous word be spoken about us,
for our marriage is sacred between us
and no stranger shall hear my grievance.
Above and beyond this, I will cherish and honor
you through this life
and into the next.

Celtic Wedding Vow

SCOTLAND, 1918

Something was wrong. She'd gotten what she wanted, so why didn't she feel better?

It was almost too easy. Once the soldier was gone, that Irish nurse was like a walking corpse, going about the castle in a daze. Grace probably could have pushed her down the stairs any number of times and she wouldn't have noticed. But that wasn't the plan.

It had grated on her to watch the rest of the staff try to comfort the girl, but Grace knew what was coming so she put on a brave face and went along with the others. Wouldn't do to stand out.

After a few days she began to drop a comment here, a mild observation there—never to the same person, and never anything too negative. "How could it have happened? Bridget was the only one who gave him his medicine, wasn't she?" "She was awfully clingy. Maybe he was getting tired of her."

It didn't take much. Balfinnan was out in the country, away from society. The only fun around here was gossip. And when the whispers had reached enough ears, Grace made her move. A few pills like those she'd placed in his room just happened to be found in Bridget's nightstand, hidden away in a small pouch and ready for the head nurse to find when a new rumor reared its ugly head.

She could just sit back and wait then. Those who had grieved with Bridget now turned against her. They went to Anderson with the proof, and he was forced to lock the girl up in his private library, waiting for the police to come and interview her. But Grace had gotten there first.

She stood on the threshold of that room now. Holding a candlestick high, she surveyed the space. The body had been removed and claimed by the girl's wailing parents. To the authorities, the case was closed, wrapped up neatly by the killer herself. The shock of the murder and suicide was already fading as the days went on.

It was the family's private area, after all, so no one else had been present when Duncan Anderson discovered his darling little nurse hanging from the beam in his library. And of course, Grace hadn't needed to be present, although she'd have loved to see the horror on his face.

She looked at the beam where she had wound the rope and tied it to a hook on the window frame. The other end was still dangling there in the center where they'd cut the girl down. The family had moved back down to the first floor—no one came to this section of the castle anymore. Something about people hanging themselves in your library must be off-putting.

It hadn't been as easy as she'd thought it would be, getting her up there. Dead bodies don't cooperate much. But Grace was a strong woman, and sheer fury had sustained her efforts.

So why wasn't she content? The soldier who had refused her love was gone; the tart who had stolen him was gone. Was it because the girl hadn't put up a fight? Hadn't even seemed to notice or care when the rope went around her neck? Maybe—that had been annoying. But Grace didn't think it wasn't that.

No. The reason she was still here, the reason for her unease, was Duncan Anderson. Her mission was incomplete. Before the soldier, before the Irish whore, there had been a plan. Somewhere in this damned castle was the paper that would prove what Anderson had done to her family. He had robbed her father and stolen her inheritance. This castle should have been hers, as the only daughter of Malcolm Beaton, but that fool had gambled it away and now she was supposed to feel lucky to be a drudge in her family home.

Duncan Anderson's lie had shaped her existence. His fantasy had Malcolm Beaton in a starring role as the friend whose life Duncan had saved in the Boer War. The friend who was so grateful he'd gifted a castle in return. Her hands clenched and her teeth ached from her grinding them together. The whole idea was ludicrous. Who would do that? But the world loved a hero, and Anderson fit the image to perfection.

Grace had never known her father; she was two years old when he died. But she hated him almost as much as she hated the cheat who had robbed him. How could he have been so stupid as to allow their future to be dealt away in a card game? Her mother had told her he'd signed a document giving Balfinnan to Anderson in 1881, and then slunk away to live in poverty until the night he shot himself like the coward he'd always been.

Why couldn't he have managed that feat before his wife gave birth to his only child—an ugly, mean-tempered bairn that they'd tortured with the name Grace? She wouldn't be standing here now, searching for the document that could prove the truth behind the lie. She would never have met Alexander MacLeod.

She shook herself and returned to her search. Hours later, when her candle neared the end of its life, Grace had to admit the truth. The document was not here. They must have moved it to the great library, and that would take a lifetime to search. Time she didn't have: the war was ending, and the hospital would close.

A snarl twisted her plain features and she held the wick to the nearest stack of documents, watching as flames grew and began to eat away at the paper. She lit several places on the shelves and stood back, watching the fire gain momentum. When it had burned almost to the nub, she pulled the candle stub out of the holder and threw it into the blaze.

At the doorway, Grace turned to look once more. The fire was beginning to climb the rope she had tied off next to the window. With luck, the whole place would burn to ashes and take Duncan Anderson with it. His stolen castle would be consumed from the inside, just as she had been.

Surely then she would find peace.

CHAPTER 26

THE CENTRE CANNOT HOLD

Colleen waited in the hallway outside Graham Anderson's office for her turn with the police. It was chilly, but she barely noticed. The cold inside her had grown and swelled until it filled her entire body, and she didn't think she'd ever be warm again. She closed her eyes and leaned her head against the wall, remembering the horror of the last few hours.

The Grey Lady swam into her mind, standing as she had in the ruined library room on the third floor, reaching out to them with fear and sadness etched on her beautiful pale face, trying to tell them something.

Help him! she had cried, screaming into Colleen's head. Aidan's hand had crept into hers, and she knew he was hearing it, too. *Help him!*

And then she had dissipated, gone back into the shadows as if she'd never been.

Why couldn't ghosts be more specific? They'd assumed she meant Gordon MacNabb again, had wasted precious time tracking him down and reassuring themselves that he was all right. So they'd gone to talk to Graham, and walked into hell.

Graham was sitting on the floor of his office, rocking the body of his wife. Horrible, grating noises came from his mouth—the same sounds one might expect from a wounded animal caught in a trap. He had looked up at them, his blue eyes streaming, with no sign of recognition.

Colleen had tried to go to Olivia, but Graham pushed her away.

"Sh-she'll be okay," he told her, raw pain giving the lie to the words. "She'll be okay." His head bobbed up and down and his eyes begged them to believe.

Colleen turned to Simon and mouthed, "Get help," and he disappeared down the hall without a word. Aidan came up and squatted in front of Graham, but he might as well have been invisible for all the attention he was given.

"Let me help her, Graham." Colleen used the soft, soothing tone she used with fearful patients. "I'm a nurse. You have to let me help her."

But there was no helping Olivia. Her brown eyes stared sightlessly at the ceiling, and her face had already taken on the pallor of death. Colleen found her wrist. Still warm, but there was no pulse. She gave Aidan a tiny shake of her head, and he closed his eyes with a grimace and rocked back on his heels.

"We're not getting a divorce," Graham told them. "We're going to try again. Isn't that wonderful?" His voice was a monotone, as if he were a robot devoid of emotion. Shock and grief had robbed him of human-ity and turned him into an empty shell.

The ambulance came, and then the police, and suddenly the small room was filled with officials going about their grim business. Olivia was taken from Graham's arms and loaded onto a trolley, her body transferred to the waiting ambulance and whisked away to Raighmore Hospital. They had moved Graham to his rooms behind the office, where he sat staring at the wall, guarded by a constable.

"Nurse Fitzgerald? We're ready for you now." A constable beckoned to Colleen from the doorway. She moved to join him, but he shook his head and pointed across the hall to the tiny coat room behind the sign-in desk. As she entered, she saw that the space had been reconfigured for interviews. Two metal folding chairs had been placed on either side of a small table, and in one of them sat another police-man. Not Constable Brodie: this was someone new. The door closed, leaving them alone in the tiny room. The policeman stood and pointed to the other chair.

"Please take a seat, Nurse Fitzgerald." His voice was even. "I am Detective Inspector Douglas. I'll be investigating the death of Mrs. Anderson." He con-sulted the papers in front of him. "You're a nurse here at Balfinnan?"

Colleen nodded.

"I understood you were the first to arrive, and verified her death."

"Yes, sir. Mr. Shaw and I—and Mr. Reid—came in to see Mr. Anderson and found him holding her."

"Did Mr. Anderson say anything to you when you arrived?"

"He seemed to be in shock. He was telling us she'd be all right, but I could see that she wasn't." Colleen's eyes filled and she swiped a hand across her face.

"I'd like to know a wee bit more about you, Nurse Fitzgerald. American, aren't you?"

"Yes."

"And what brought you to Scotland?"

Silence fell in the room. *What do I tell him? He's going to find out about Nesbitt! He's going to think I'm a criminal!*

Douglas let the silence stretch out, his face impassive.

"M—my best friend lives here. She's a detective in Edinburgh." There. That sounded good. Detectives didn't hang around with criminal types, did they?

"And who is Mr. Shaw?"

"He's the architect Mr. Anderson hired to renovate the part of the castle that burned years ago."

"And Mr. Reid?"

"He's the janitor and night watchman." So far, so good. As long as she kept herself from babbling, she'd be all right. Just the facts, like they said on TV.

"How well did you know Mrs. Anderson?"

"I'd just met her a few days ago. She's only been here about two weeks."

"And what was your impression of the deceased?"

"We had a conversation once in the library. She seemed very sweet."

"And of Mr. Anderson?"

Watch out, girl. Say nothing. "He's my boss."

"I know that, Nurse Fitzgerald. I was asking for your impression of him."

Colleen looked at DI Douglas, feeling the tight-rope swaying under her feet. She opened her mouth, but nothing came out.

"Nurse Fitzgerald?"

"Um...he's a very good employer. Balfinnan is his life's work." She scanned her memory for innocuous information about Graham. "He told me he'd always wanted to open his castle as a care facility. He's very kind."

"Do you know Mr. Anderson well?"

Was that a loaded question, or was guilt reading more into the inspector's question than was there? Colleen felt out of her depth, and could sense panic building. She forced the bile back down and faced the implacable hazel eyes across the table.

If I don't tell him, Mrs. Murtaugh sure as hell will.

"Mr. Anderson and I are good friends. We share the same views about elderly residents. I admire him."

"Hmm." The inspector stared at her. She felt like a rabbit in a trap, frozen with fear and unable to move away from that gaze. "Thank you, Nurse Fitzgerald. You live in Inverness, correct? Don't plan any trips away for the foreseeable future, aye? We'll be speaking again."

He stood and indicated the door. Colleen forced her feet to move. She had reached the door when the inspector's voice brought her back around to face him.

"Please don't discuss anything with others here. We're looking at a suspicious death, and it's important not to spread gossip. I'm sure you understand."

She nodded automatically and fumbled for the doorknob.

Do they tell everyone not to leave town? Why does it feel as if he thinks I did something wrong?

"It's all falling apart."

Colleen looked around the sitting room at the familiar, beloved faces of the Owls. Their eyes mirrored the misery in hers, and everyone except Gladys seemed at a loss for words.

"Surely it's not that bad, dear," she said. "Old Harry says they'll get to the bottom of that poor young woman's death soon, and then everything will be fine." She gestured to the armchair in the corner, where Old Harry sat peering over his newspaper. He grunted, that odd guttural snort somewhere between a cough and a croak, and retreated behind the paper again.

"Gladys, they think Olivia was murdered. They've closed Balfinnan down and moved all the residents to other care facilities. Who knows when they'll come back, or how many will even want to?" She thought of Gordon MacNabb, who had fought being removed from his home with everything in his frail body. He'd be back, if grief didn't carry him away before the police solved the mystery. But the others?

Mrs. MacNally had never come back. Miss Curry and Mrs. MacLennan had protested the move, but who knew if, once they were settled somewhere else, they'd be willing to return. Or, if there was even a place to come back to. There were no longer any names on the waiting list.

"The police want all the staff to stay on. They said it's so we can be handy to answer questions, but I get the feeling we're all under some sort of house arrest. I'm here to pack a bag since I'll be staying at Balfinnan for a while." She shook her head. "Maybe if I'm lucky they'll let me room with Mrs. Murtaugh." A shudder went through her at the thought. "We can have slumber parties and talk about how awful the Irish are."

Despite herself, she giggled at the thought of Mrs. Murtaugh, resplendent in a black mobcap and frilled nightgown, sitting up in bed sharing girl talk about all the things and people she hated.

"You must keep your faith," said Maxine. "You are such a wonderful girl, the police will see that you have nothing to do with this terrible happening. And you will be safe, because you will have our Aidan there to protect you." Her eyes glinted and a smile quirked the edge of her mouth.

"And how is Aidan?" Gladys took back the reins of conversation. "He is staying there, too?"

"Yes, he'll be there." A feeling of relief went through Colleen at the thought of having Aidan nearby. "But this isn't a house party, Gladys. We'll just be doing paperwork. I won't be *nursing*, not until the place opens up again. And no one knows when that will happen."

Or if. In the two days since hell had opened up and swallowed Balfinnan House, she hadn't seen Graham Anderson once. Mrs. Morton took him his meals and carried back an untouched tray, and Mrs. Murtaugh stood guard like Cerberus at the gates. He hadn't come out of his private rooms, not even to check on the welfare of his staff.

She tried to squelch it, but a flash of irritation passed through her. He had a business—employees and clients. People who depended on him. Where was the driven man who had worked against all odds to reopen his family's castle to the elderly? Why hadn't he at least come out to say goodbye to Gordon and the other residents he'd said meant so much to him?

Colleen shook her head, disgusted with herself. He'd lost his wife! Who was she to judge people on how they reacted to a life-changing tragedy? She was an expert on grieving, both personally and professionally, and she should know better. It was different for everyone. Still...

Aidan wouldn't be like that. Somewhere in the deepest recesses of her heart she knew it. He was always there for the people he cared about, thinking of their needs and worries first. She remembered how he had held her when she was so frightened of the Grey Lady, how he'd comforted her when they'd found Dolly's body. He'd taken time off to escort her to Edinburgh, even though he had no reason to go. And somehow, no matter what kind of chaos was raining down all around them, he managed to make her laugh.

It was Aidan she looked for every day when she arrived at Balfinnan. He brightened her day and eased her mind. The sight of him made the sun come out even on the gloomiest Scottish day. And he was the one she turned to when trouble reared its head. Not Graham. It had never been Graham.

The thing that had been curled up around her soul stirred and blinked, sending a warm sensation through her frozen body. She sat up straight and looked at the faces of the Owls, who stared back at her with their uncanny, omniscient eyes.

"I love him." The words settled into her mind and filtered like confetti down to her heart. "I love Aidan."

"Well, of course you do, dear." Gladys's voice was tinged with humor. "It was a lot of work, but such things are meant to be."

Maxine's beautiful face split into a grin, and Ronald nodded like a mandarin. A grunt of amusement came from the corner. Living with the Owls had given Colleen the ability to screen out their intrusive babble when it became overwhelming, and she had always thought their Jedi mind tricks were mostly in her imagination, but this was too much!

"What do you mean, 'it was a lot of work?'"

Gladys clucked. "Never mind, dear. It's just that you were your own worst enemy, and you had to work hard to discover what was right for you."

Colleen narrowed her eyes. That wasn't what Gladys had meant at all, but she knew she wasn't going to get anything out of the old dear unless she wanted to spill it.

Maxine sat up straight and crossed one graceful leg over the other.

"Is it not obvious, cherie? That young man...he is just your type."

Colleen opened her mouth, and shut it again. She would never figure these people out—not even if she lived to be as old as Gordon. But just knowing that they understood what was happening to her heart was enough to make her love every one of them even more.

I love Aidan. I'm in love with Aidan Shaw. She ran the words through her mind again, picturing his calm grey eyes. They were windows to his soul, those eyes. Cloudy like the sky before a rain when he was worried or upset. Clear like the waters of the Ness when he was amused or about to say something humorous. Dark and sometimes unreadable when he studied her.

How did Aidan feel about her? When he was with her, he gave her his undivided attention, made her feel as if she were the only one in the world. But that was his gift. Didn't he treat Gordon the same way? And Simon?

Simon would climb the highest mountain in Scotland if Aidan asked him to. And Gordon had shared his deepest fears with only one other person besides Colleen. So how could she tell if he felt something more for her? He'd kissed her, but it certainly hadn't been a declaration of passion. And then he'd run away.

Colleen squared her shoulders and stood up. Well, she'd just have to find out, and she couldn't do that in Nessie's sitting room. She summoned a weak smile for her housemates.

"I'm off to pack, and then to Balfinnan. Wish me luck."

"We're wi' ye lass. Gie on wi' ye noo." Old Harry was beaming at her.

A knock sounded from the front door. Nessie bustled out of the kitchen and opened it. She exchanged a few words with the visitor and came into the sitting room, her face tight. "It's someone from th' police," she said, her voice flat. "He wants t' speak t' Colleen."

Colleen found herself shaking. Why would they come all the way here? They'd told everyone to pack for a few days and return to Balfinnan. She went to the door.

"Come in, officer. How can I help you?"

"I'd like you to come with me, Nurse Fitzgerald."

"To Balfinnan?" Her mouth was dry.

"No. To the station here in Inverness. We believe you may be able to help us with our inquiries."

CHAPTER 27

OUT OF TIME

"I found something."

Simon had come into Aidan's office with that unsettling silence that in anyone else would seem like stealth. In his hand he held out a small scrap of paper.

Aidan took the scrap and studied it. It seemed to be the corner of a larger document. The edges of the triangular piece of paper were charred and blackened. On the right side were the words "I, Malc," but the rest had been torn away and lost.

"It was pressed inside one of the books, nearly pasted to the pages," Simon offered. "I don't know why, but something stopped me when I saw it, and I got a feeling." The young janitor shrugged.

Aidan patted his shoulder. Only a fool would overlook one of Simon's feelings.

"The paper seems to be vellum of some sort. Maybe part of a will?" He looked at the words again. "It begins like a testament. Could this person—Malcolm, maybe— have owned the castle at one time?"

Simon shrugged. "That's what I thought. Balfinnan's been here since the thirteenth century, and Malcolm is a common name. So there's a good chance someone with that name might have lived here. Shouldn't be hard to find out."

Aidan looked at the tiny corner of paper, and suddenly felt overwhelmed with the futility of it all. "It's just a scrap of paper. Nothing to say as to who this person was—if he lived here or was a visitor. Maybe this was from a history book, and not about Balfinnan at all! And what are we even looking for? How will this help us prove Colleen innocent?" He ran his hands through his unruly black curls. "We're just chasing shadows!"

Simon eyed him with sympathy. "How's Nurse Colleen?" he asked, his voice soft.

Aidan looked up, his eyes bleary from lack of sleep. "I don't know. There's a constable at the door of the library. That feckin' job's-worth won't let me see her. 'Nurse Fitzgerald is helping us with our inquiries,' is all he'll say. What she must be going through!"

"I saw her two days ago," said Simon. "They don't seem to notice me much, so I slipped in and talked to her for a few minutes. She's afraid, but I told her you were worried about her and she seemed to like that."

"Thanks, Simon. I wish I had your invisibility cloak sometimes. What can they be thinking, keeping her under watch like that? If they only knew her like—"

Like I do. Aidan pictured Colleen's lovely face in his mind, the crystal blue eyes in a face like fine porcelain, the red curls that rivaled his for unruliness, the wide smile. But it wasn't her looks he was thinking of now. It was her heart—the size of Loch Ness, and open to anyone who needed help. She was a born nurse, a true healer who ensnared the souls of her patients and forced them to believe they mattered.

Like Gordon. That old man would never have made his hundredth birthday without Colleen pushing and pulling him to believe in the possibility. If Gordon knew what was happening here now—Aidan shuddered to think what would happen. Thank God he was safely—if miserably—ensconced in another care center.

And Simon. He looked at the eager face of the janitor. That young man thought Colleen was the second coming, and Aidan understood why. It was her kindness, her absolute faith that everyone was important and interesting. She had captured Simon with the simple act of caring—of listening to him.

She captured me, too. Aidan sat back and thought about that. It was true. From the moment he'd seen her wandering in the gardens of Balfinnan House back in September, searching for a way in, she'd held his heart in her hand. He just hadn't realized it at the time. She'd looked on him as a friend, and he'd been content with that much. Being friends with Colleen was the next best thing to heaven in his life, and for awhile it had been enough.

Watching her fall for Graham Anderson had been painful. Standing by while she mooned over a man who wasn't emotionally or legally available was the hardest thing he'd ever done, but he'd been afraid to lose her friendship, so he'd kept silent. And he'd almost lost her anyway, by being a coward.

When he'd kissed her outside Nessie's, he was sure there had been a reaction. What if he'd had the courage to deepen that kiss, to let her know how he felt? What if? Would Graham have even been in the picture? Because that was what the police were going on, he was sure. They'd heard about Colleen's feelings for Graham, and they were following the trail like a pack of damn bloodhounds.

He knew how they'd heard about it. There had been whispers going around almost from the first day. Once he had overheard the new nurse's aide talking to Flora Kemp. "They say she was pure raging when his wife came back. Pitched a flap right here in the nurse's station!"

To her credit, Flora had skelped the youngster a new arse and sent her fleeing down the hall, but gossip has a way of seeping into the consciousness of people eager for something new, and he knew it wasn't the last time he'd hear such nonsense. As if Colleen would throw a fit over anyone! She'd be mortified if she knew people were talking about her love life. He needed to reassure her, in case she'd heard the whispers. He had to get in to see her, the sooner the better. And the way to make that happen was right in front of him.

"Simon?"

"Aye, sir?"

"Can you get me in to see Colleen?"

Simon straightened to his full height of five feet eight inches. "Of course I can!"

Aidan looked at the scrap of paper he held in his hand. "And stay nearby. I'm with you about this paper. Call it hope or whatever you want, but we're going to find out who this Malcolm lad was, and what connection he had to Balfinnan. I just have a hunch it's important somehow."

They left the office in the waning light of another dreich day, and made their way through the kitchen and up the main staircase to the second floor. The only person in the hall was a lone constable who was seated at the door of the library, reading a newspaper.

Simon waved Aidan into the shadows and approached the man. It wasn't until he was standing right in front of him blocking the light in the hallway, that the man looked up, startled.

"Whoa, lad, I didn't see you there. What's your business up here?" The man's voice was the truculent tone of one caught slacking off.

"Sorry, sir, I just came up to relieve you. I thought you might want to take a wee break. Mrs. Morton's made scones and tea for everyone down in the kitchen."

"Can't you see I'm busy here, lad?" The constable puffed himself up. "Go on and leave me to my misery."

"That's all right then. It's just that everyone's in the kitchen, and Mrs. Morton's scones are the best around—I was sent up to watch the door for you, if you wanted a break."

The constable stretched. Boredom and scones warred with duty. Simon waited.

"Keep an eye out here then, will ye, lad?" the man said. "The door's locked and I've got the key, so it shouldn't be too much of a job for ye. And thanks."

The guard ambled down the hall and out of sight.

Simon grinned as he fished his huge key ring out of his pocket. "The door's locked, and I've got the key," he mimicked. "Did I forget to mention that I'm the janitor?"

The door opened without sound. Aidan slipped in and Simon locked the door behind him.

For a moment, Aidan couldn't find Colleen in the huge room, and then he saw her sitting in a leather armchair, reading a book as if she'd just wandered in on a break. His heart skipped a beat. She was so brave.

"Colleen?" He kept his voice low. She looked up, and tears filled her eyes.

"Aidan! How did you get in here? They won't let anyone in. Liz tried, but they told her I was—"

"I know," he said, feeling his teeth grinding. "You're helping them with their inquiries."

"Oh, Aidan, I knew you'd come!" She blinked back tears.

In three steps he crossed the room and pulled her out of the chair and into his arms. He could feel her small body trembling in his embrace, and his soul ached for her. He pulled back and looked into her wide blue eyes.

"It'll be all right, Colleen. Simon and I are working to find out who might really want to hurt Olivia, and you'll be out of here in no time. Believe me?" He took her hand in his, and his thumb caressed her palm.

"I trust you, Aidan. I always have." She looked up at him, swiped a hand across her eyes, and gave him a long look. "There's something I've been wanting to tell you, but it never seems to be a good time." Her laugh caught in a choking sob.

"Aye?"

"I don't think we can be friends anymore."

Aidan's heart stood still. Panic raced through his body like an electrical charge, and he found himself frozen in place, the anxiety threatening to strangle him. Then he looked into her eyes again, and the fear drained out of him as if it had never been. He waited.

"The problem is, I love you. I'm *in* love with you." She took a deep breath. "I've loved you for a long time, but I was too stupid to reali—"

In the next second Colleen was crushed against his chest as his arms tightened around her.

"Are you trying to kill me, lass?" he whispered into her hair. "I've loved you since the first moment I saw you wandering around outside Balfinnan, afraid to use the door knocker! You were so wee, trailing after Mrs. Murtaugh when I knew you wanted to run for the hills." He held her away from him and his eyes crinkled at the corners. "And then when Artemis liked you, well, I knew I was right."

"You formed your opinion based on a *sheep*? Maybe I'd better rethink this."

Aidan lowered his lips to hers, felt the electricity go through his body again as pure sensation overtook him. Kissing Colleen was everything he'd dreamed it would be: passionate and sweet and complete. This time he put it all into that kiss—the yearning, the dreaming, the hope he'd cherished for months. And when he finally ran out of breath he stood with his hands tangled in her hair, soaking in the love from those brilliant blue eyes until he thought he'd drown for wanting her.

His cellphone buzzed in his pocket. Simon. The text read, *Hurry!* Aidan sprinted to the door, turning at the last second.

"Have to go—but I'll be back. I love you!"

"Where are we going?" Simon held onto the door handle as Aidan's small Fiat powered through the streets of Inverness. "Are you *speeding*?" His voice swelled with admiration.

"To Angus's Book Shop, and no, I'm not speeding. Not exactly." Aidan pulled the car up in front of the ancient church that had become the home of the shop, leapt out, and raced inside with Simon right behind him.

"Whoa, laddie! slaw yerself doon!" came an irrascible voice from behind a pile of books on the desk. "Och, it's Aidan. What's got ye in sich a blether, lad?"

Aidan braced his hands on the counter. "It's Colleen, Angus. They've got her locked up at Balfinnan, while they run around like fools trying to prove she killed Olivia Anderson."

"Eejits! What's th' matter wi' th' polis! Cannae they see 'at sweet lassie wooldnae hurt a midgie?" The old man shook his head in disgust.

"Well, they seem to think she's their best suspect right now," Aidan said, his brow furrowed. "So, our job is to find them a better one. And for that we need you."

Angus puffed himself up. "Ay coorse ye do. Sae whit do we do first?"

Aidan spared a smile at Angus's inclusion of himself in the investigative team. He looked with affection at the old man who had made Aubrey and her friends part of his family, and for a moment, gratitude threatened to take him down.

"Well, the police seem to think that Colleen was jealous because she was—" He paused and then ground out the rest. "Interested in Graham, and so she poisoned Olivia's wine. But that's ridiculous."

Angus snorted in disgust. "Weel ay coorse it is. Everbody knows 'at lass is yers!"

Aidan stared at him. *Everybody knows? Had everybody known how he felt except him?* He pulled himself together and focused. There'd be time for that later.

"So, the first thing we have to figure out is, who at Balfinnan *did* want Olivia dead?"

Angus crossed his spindly arms and pursed his lips. "Probly wasnae 'er."

"What?"

The old man gave a Gallic shrug. "Whit Ah said. Probly wasnae Anderson they waur efter."

Why hadn't he thought of that? Why hadn't the police? Or had they? Graham always kept a carafe of his favorite wine on the sideboard in his office. The murderer could have poisoned the wine at any time, trusting that sooner or later he'd drink it. And that indicated a great deal of patience. Which suggested revenge, not jealousy. He took a long breath.

"I think you're right, Angus. Nobody really knew Olivia. The target had to be Graham. But who would hate him enough to kill him?"

"Ah hae a wee book er two 'at might help." Angus

went behind the counter to his inner sanctum, and came back a few minutes with two books: one a small worn volume, the other massive and new. He placed both on the table and pointed to the small book.

"At 'un is a history ay Balfinnan, published in 1920 by Thomas Kemp. But th' authur was a mate ay th' Andersons, sae it might be all pish."

"I know that book!" Simon's voice vibrated with excitement. "There's a copy in the library at Balfinnan. The Ghruamachd took a paper out of it, and was absolutely raging." He shuddered at the memory.

They bent over the small book. The last chapter was called "1881-1920, the Anderson Years," and together they read the story of the friendship between Duncan Anderson and Malcolm Beaton that resulted in Anderson's ownership of the castle.

"Malcolm!" said Aidan, stabbing the name in the book. "He has to be the one on your paper scrap, Simon. Says here he gave the castle to Duncan Anderson as a gift for saving his life." He looked up. "Duncan is Graham's hero. He used to go on and on about how his great-great-great grandfather opened Balfinnan as a hospital in World War I. Pretty damn generous, if you ask me. Who gives away his home as a gift? Did he have extra castles in his back pocket?"

Angus interrupted, tapping the larger book. "Thes 'un micht help," he said. "It jist come oot fife years ago, an' it has aw th' family trees o' th' clans in this part ay th' Highlands, reit up t' noo."

Aidan looked at Simon. "Let's start with our very generous Malcolm Beaton," he said. "Kemp's Anderson chapter begins in 1881, and that's way before World

War I. I don't think that's the war he means. We need to go back further, I think," Aidan said, turning the pages. "Weren't the Boer Wars in the late nineteenth century?" He shook his head. "Where's Finn when you need him? He'd know all this stuff."

Angus snorted. "Th' first Boer War was fooght frae 1880 tae 1881, an' th' second frae 1899 tae 1902." He wagged a finger. "A lot o' Highlanders gave ther lives in 'at war. Whit did ye learn 'at university, laddie?"

But Aidan wasn't listening. He had turned a page, and there it was. Malcolm Beaton—born 1855, died 1903. "His name seems to have died with him—all his descendants are women, which is—"

Shock ratcheted through him and the color drained from his face. It couldn't be a coincidence. The name at the bottom of the page, the last living descendent of Malcolm Beaton, was one he knew. A person who was right now at Balfinnan House, where someone had tried to murder Graham Anderson. Where Colleen was trapped in the library. His chest tightened and spots appeared before his eyes.

He'd been right. It was all about revenge.

CHAPTER 28
WORM IN THE WOODWORK

Graham Anderson's blue eyes flashed sparks as he faced Detective Inspector Douglas. The inspector sat in Graham's chair, his arms resting on the desk in front of him. As if it weren't Graham's anymore, just like his home and his business. The police had taken over everything, from his staff to his residents. They had sent the latter away "for their own safety," and now there was nothing left of his legacy. His castle was as empty as his heart. To be fair, he'd let them do it, had been so immersed in his own guilt and grief that he'd let it all slip through his fingers. It was his own fault.

But now they'd gone too far.

"Do you mean you're keeping Colleen locked up for no reason? Because of me? That's ridiculous! She's the one who told Olivia that—" His eyes clouded with pain. "That she should give me another chance."

DI Douglas gave him that dispassionate police-man's stare, and said nothing. Graham took a ragged breath. For some reason he felt he had to explain, to make this man understand what he himself had come to realize after it was too late.

"There was an attraction, on both sides. But it would never have worked." Graham's smile was bit-ter. "The fact is I'm rubbish at love. I loved my castle, and my residents, and I realized too late that I loved my wife. And you see what happened. So it's proba-bly for the best that Colleen and I never got that far, isn't it?" The last words were wrung out of a throat choked with emotion.

Douglas nodded, careful not to betray pity for a man obviously holding himself together by a thread. "I understand, Mr. Anderson. And the truth is we're not keeping Nurse Fitzgerald locked up for no rea-son," the inspector said, his voice soft. "She is not a person of interest in this case."

"Well, then why?"

"The fact is that Nurse Fitzgerald is helping us while we try to help you. We've believed for some time that the intended target was not Mrs. Anderson, but you, sir, and that person could very well try again. We also have reason to think that someone may have wanted Nurse Fitzgerald to take the blame for your wife's death." Graham's eyes widened. The inspector watched him for a moment and then said softly, "You yourself said she barely escaped serious injury when a door that should have been locked was not. Given the circumstances, we've set her aside for her own safety. And," he added, "she is locked in because we want the real killer to think she's a suspect. He or she may feel safe, and try to make a move. So you may expect one of my constables to be your constant companion for the foreseeable future, aye?" The inspector steepled his hands on Graham's desk. "This killer has an obvious disregard for life. He or she is willing to risk others just to get at the target, and that target was the person who normally drank your personal wine. What I'd like you to do, sir, is try to come up with any reason someone would want you dead."

Graham threw up his hands. "I have tried! I'm not in the kind of business that makes enemies. Nursing homes don't invite that sort of thing. I've racked my brain for the names of anyone I may have wronged in the past, and there's nothing! Nothing!"

"You're a wealthy man, sir. In my experience, wealthy men collect enemies. Think hard—your life could depend upon it. The killer has to be someone familiar with this castle," Douglas continued. "Someone who knows the workings of the medical facility, someone knowledgeable about drugs and poisons. Most likely someone on staff right here at Balfinnan."

"Someone on my staff wants me dead?" Graham's voice was bleak. "I never considered that. I chose my staff carefully. Most of them I knew, or my father did. Some came recommended by old friends, and some *are* old friends."

"Please go over the list again, Mr. Anderson. Maybe there's someone you don't know as much about as you thought." He picked up a copy of the employee list for Balfinnan House and handed it to Graham, who looked at it with repugnance.

"All right...Elizabeth Dunnet. Recommended by my mother's aunt. Very solid, sensible person. I like her."

Douglas sighed. "It doesn't matter whether or not you like her, sir. I'm presuming you like most of them, or they wouldn't be here. Try to look at the list objectively, and just tell me where or how you know them."

Graham shook his head, but returned to the list. "Simon Reid. Recommended by his grandfather, who knew mine. I asked for him specifically. I trust that lad with my life."

"Well, that's really what you've done with all of them, isn't it?" Douglas's voice was sardonic. "Please continue."

"Archie Fergusson is well known by the older generation around Inverness. He's an unlikely candidate, and almost never comes into the castle if he can help it. He's an old friend of one of my residents. Arabella Morton has been here since I reopened the castle. Came highly recommended as a cook, and she's a good one. But wouldn't she have had ample opportunity to poison my food years ago if she wanted to?"

Douglas said nothing, but gestured for him to go on.

"Colleen Fitzgerald." He sat back and gave the inspector a grim smile. "Well, if I were being objective, she'd be the perfect candidate. I hired her on the recommendation of a very odd character who is also acquainted with one of my residents." He eyed Douglas and cleared his throat. "I suppose you're aware of her references."

"I am. We checked into Nurse Fitzgerald's job history thoroughly. The police aren't just here for show, you know. We do occasionally do our jobs, and rather well in most cases." He puffed out a breath. "We looked into those references very carefully. Five of them: four glowing and one damning. Which seemed odd, to say the least. Closer checking into that one revealed a relationship with a doctor on staff, whose wife was the daughter of the hospital CEO...who wrote the reference." He gave Anderson another sharp look. "It seems your Nurse Fitzgerald has a rather unfortunate habit of forming attractions to married men."

Graham flushed and then returned to the list.

"Dolly Gilles. Deceased." He looked up, sadness clouding his eyes. "Now, she would have been a candidate. Knew almost everything there was to know about plants and herbs. But she was young and silly, and also a bit lazy—shirked work as often as she could. I would probably have sacked her if it wasn't for her mother. She worked as a lady's maid for my own mother. They were also friends.

"Aidan Shaw. Known him for years—we were friends in university. Hired him a few months ago to renovate the ruin on the back of the castle. He's a preservation architect, making a bit of a name for himself in the field. I was lucky to get him.

"Morag Murtaugh." He looked up for a moment, then shook his head in denial. "She looks the part of a wicked witch, that's for sure, but she's almost painfully loyal, and she's been here since the beginning, too. She was my father's housekeeper, and the most efficient woman I've ever met. I've known her the longest of any of them."

"Efficient?" Douglas broke in.

"I'd never have been able to get this place up and running without her," Graham said. "Most of the staff is afraid of her, and sometimes I'll confess I am, too. She's very fierce, has strong opinions, and is a bit intolerant. You know how they say, 'her bark is worse than her bite?' Well, I'm not sure that's quite true with Murtaugh." He looked at Douglas. "If I hadn't known her for so long, I'd have pegged her as our villain right away. But she's just too obvious unless you know her." He shrugged and went back to the list. "Flora Kemp works the night shift. Now that one... I don't know her very well, really. Only been here six months or so. But she had excellent references, and she's a good nurse. Not many are willing to take on the night shift in a haunted castle."

"Ah, yes," said Douglas. "You have a ghost here, I understand?"

"Aye, seems to stick to the upper floors. I've never seen her myself, but she's a bit of a nuisance, really. I've had some trouble keeping staff because of her. They think they see her or hear her, and out the door they go. That's why I'm so thankful for the people I have on this list." Graham looked up from the paper, frustration clouding his blue eyes. "That's the lot. There's a new aide who replaced Dolly, but she's only been here a couple of weeks. I can't believe that any of these people would want to harm me!"

"And yet," CI Douglas said as he fixed his intense hazel eyes on Graham. "It seems apparent that one of them does want to do just that."

CHAPTER 29

DO NO HARM

olleen paced the carpet in Balfinnan's great
library. The fire had gone out in the ancient
stone fireplace that dominated one end
of the room, and flickering fixtures meant to look
like gas lamps were the only source of light. Very
authentic, she thought, but also somewhat spooky.
She pulled the sleeves of her chunky sweater down
over her hands and hugged herself to keep warm.

This business of being locked up "for her own good"
was getting old. She was grateful they no longer considered her a suspect in Olivia's death, and at first it had
seemed rather relaxing to be forced to spend time in
one of the loveliest rooms in the castle, complete with
a roaring fire and endless shelves of books. Many times
she'd passed this room while on shift and wished she
could take just a few minutes to lose herself in literature.

But she'd quickly realized that Balfinan's shelves
didn't consider books by Stephen King and James

333

Patterson quality reading. If they'd only had the Outlander books, she could have spent hours rereading her favorite series.

But no...here there were books on engineering, religion, philosophy, and history, most of them written hundreds of years before her birth and all of them boring. She doubted even Finn would get excited over A Comprehensive History of Farming in Scotland from 1569 to 1822. And here was one: The Evolution of Architecture in Scotland and its Effects on Highland Culture. She grinned. Aidan might like that one.

Aidan. Despite the chill of the room, a warmth spread through her body and wrapped itself around her heart. Aidan loved her. She could still feel his lips on hers, the flame that was ignited when he pulled her into his arms and held her as if he never wanted to let her go.

Who would have thought he could kiss like that? All those months they'd spent together, laughing and talking about anything and everything—and she'd never looked at that teasing smile and wondered what else those lips could do. Never guessed at the passion that lay behind those calm grey eyes. Colleen shivered, but not from the cold. That kiss had been anything but calm!

She needed to get out of here, find Aidan, and make sure she hadn't dreamed that kiss. A moment of panic surged through her at the thought. What if she'd fallen asleep in the leather chair and dreamed the whole thing?

A smile spread over her face. Oh no, it was real. She couldn't have imagined that electricity, the smell of his aftershave, the smile on his face when she'd told him she loved him. She was a dreamer, but she wasn't *that* good.

She went to the door and tapped. No answer. Odd—the constable on duty usually answered as soon as she knocked, to make sure she was all right and see if she wanted anything. Well, she wanted something, all right; she wanted Aidan. So where were the cops when she needed them?

Frustrated, Colleen wandered back to the center of the room and looked around. Balfinnan's library felt even more like a prison now. A huge, elegant prison with books that she had absolutely no interest in even attempting to read.

She sighed and went to a shelf she hadn't tried yet. More dusty old tomes, more history. She trailed her fingers along the spines without looking, and suddenly her hand fell into a space between volumes. She looked to see a very small book that had been carelessly stuffed into a space between two larger works in a series on Scottish history. Curious, she edged it out.

It wasn't as old as some of the other books here, but it had been handled often. The spine was cracked and coming apart at the top, but the gold lettering on the front glittered in the dim light. *Balfinnan House, a Forgotten Highland Jewel.* Well, that might be a bit more interesting. Colleen thumbed through the first few pages until she found the table of contents.

Most of it looked like ancient history, but the last chapter was called "1881-1920, *the Anderson Years*." She took the book back to her chair and began to read. Not the most exciting prose, but reading about the very castle she was sitting in gave her a feeling of belonging to something important and ageless.

The Andersons had occupied Balfinnan for thirty-nine years at the turn of the century, the book said, and then abandoned it for nearly a hundred more. The pages swam as tears filled Colleen's eyes, and she closed the book and put it in her lap. Graham had been so excited to open his home again, so determined to keep it useful for generations. He was the last of his line, and now he might never have a son to inherit his home.

A knock at the library door broke into her thoughts. Thank God, the constable was back. Colleen stood up and ran to the door, determined to have her say. She was getting out of here...now.

"Please come in, officer."

The door opened. A smiling Arabella Morton stood on the threshold with a tray containing a plate of scones, a china cup, and a pot of tea.

"Hullo, lass. I thought you might be a bit bored up here all alone, so I decided to bring some scones before the police eat all of them." She rolled her eyes and grinned. Closing the door behind her, she set the tray on an ornate side table.

"Oh, thanks, Mrs. Morton. They look wonderful, but I'm not really hungry. Anyway, did the constable let you in? I want to see if he'd consider letting me out of here."

"Ach, that one? He's down in the kitchen with the others, but I'll ask him when I get back, aye? I swear I had less trouble keeping people fed when the residents were here!" She poured a cup of tea and shoved it into Colleen's hands. "You need to eat something. I'm not leaving until you take a few bites, so get busy." Her eyes fell on the book in Colleen's hand, and the teapot in hers stilled. "What's that you've got there, lass?"

Colleen looked at the book and shrugged. "It's a history of the castle. Believe it or not, there's not much interesting material to read here. This was the best I could find. The last chapter's all about the Andersons."

"It's *a pack of lies.*"

Colleen looked up, startled. Her eyes snapped to Mrs. Morton in surprise. "What?"

A shadow crossed the cook's face. She put the teapot on the tray and turned.

"That's not the way it *happened.*"

Her voice seemed different: a harsh rasp, like sandpaper scraping over unfinished wood. Unease crawled up Colleen's spine. Something was wrong with Mrs. Morton's voice—it seemed angry, full of frustration. And what was wrong with the woman's eyes? Normally a friendly brown, they now glinted with a sickly green light—even the shape seemed different. The pupils were narrow slits, pinched together under glowering brows. An odd thought gripped Colleen—*she had never seen those eyes before.*

"Mrs. Morton?"

"He thought he could bring it all back, bring the lie to life again! After everything that happened, he opened this cursed place and tried to play the hero. All the Andersons are liars and cheats, every one. They pretend to care, strut about like peacocks. But they're *frauds.*" The woman was pacing now, talking more to herself than Colleen. "I wanted to kill him back then. Tried to burn the place down around him. It belonged to the Beatons by right, but if I couldn't have it, why should he?

"He didn't know who I was when he hired me, didn't recognize the daughter of the man he'd cheated. And why would he? My miserable father deserted us after I was born, lost in his drink and self-pity. I never even knew him." The odd voice rose, became a shrill whine. "But I knew what had been done to him by Duncan! My mother told me. She begged me not to forget, to always remember that Balfinnan should have been ours!"

Colleen stood as still as she could. Who was Duncan? She had no idea what the woman was talking about, but that voice dripped with insanity. This was not the Mrs. Morton she knew.

"So I came here, and Duncan hired me because I was a good nurse. 'The best in the hospital,' he said. 'So proud to have a Beaton on my staff,' he said." The woman stopped pacing and fisted her hands at her sides. Her tight lips pursed, and the words came out in a venomous hiss. "I waited for my chance. I collected the poison and kept it safe, to use when he was alone and unwary. Sometimes it was the only thing that kept me going—that little bottle of death that would give me my vengeance."

The woman seemed to have forgotten her. If she could just edge her way to the door...

Those strange glittering eyes snapped up and locked onto Colleen's face. "But I waited too long, and allowed myself to be distracted." The hands fisted again, knuckles white. "One day *he* arrived, near death from the war. The man who could make me whole, the one I'd waited for. I never thought I'd meet someone like him, never. He needed me, and he would have loved me. HE WOULD HAVE LOVED ME!

"But then *she* came—that little conniving tart!" The voice was saturated with venom, spittle spraying into the suddenly stifling air of the library. Colleen stood frozen, unable to tear her eyes away from the hatred reflected in those strange eyes. "She stole him from me, and paraded her victory in front of everyone, like the beautiful people in this world always do. But I had the last laugh. I took back what they most prized—*life*." The voice dripped with acid. "I killed them both."

Colleen's eyes widened at the smug satisfaction in the words. *What is she talking about?*

"It was their fault that I had to give up my plan for Duncan Anderson then. The war was ending and I would be let go. I tried to burn the place down before I left, but I failed at that, too. So I stayed. The power of hate is stronger than love, and much stronger than death. I remained in the minds and bodies of my descendants, waiting for my chance to finish what I started. A hundred years I've waited, and then Duncan's spawn opened the place again and I found my opportunity. I have the proof of their treachery now—it was hidden in that book of lies you're holding. The world will learn the truth about the sainted Andersons. This one is the last of Duncan's line, and I'll see his reputation destroyed—and his life. Just like my father's life."

The figure paused, a rictus grin splitting the thin lips. "The drugs were always kept locked up, and I'm not a nurse in this form. So I studied, and learned, and made my own beautiful garden of death. I stored the berries, and I waited. I am very good at waiting."

"Then one day, there *you* were—so like her you could have been twins. And a vile slut like her, too. You thought you could step in and take what wasn't yours, just the way *she* did." The voice hissed out of thin, cracked lips as frustration twisted the plain features. "How could I know his stupid wife would drink the wine? So annoying. But maybe she did me a favor after all. No one will suspect the cook, not with a jealous girlfriend so handy. You'll be easy! Those eejit policemen already think you murdered his wife to get her out of the picture. You're taking the blame, just like I wanted. Like *she* did, a hundred years ago!"

Colleen's eyes were round with horror as she looked at the ranting thing that no longer resembled Mrs. Morton. A hundred years? Power of hate? And suddenly she knew what this thing was.

Gordon's bad ghost. The Ghruamachd.

Her eyes darted again to the door, judging her chances. The creature laughed, a horrible twisted sound, and pulled a large key from one of its many pockets.

"Did you have an idea of running, little one? I don't think so. These old doors lock from both sides—isn't that helpful?" The voice sank again to a whisper. "Oh, this'll be so much more fun now than it was then. That one didn't give me a fight at all. I really hope you do."

Strong, veined hands pulled a coil of rope from a voluminous pocket in the apron and played with it absently, slitted eyes fixed and unblinking as she moved forward. Colleen backed up until her legs hit the edge of the leather chair.

"W-why?"

The thing laughed again, a hollow, soulless sound made of ice. Fast as a snake, it lunged and pushed Colleen into the overstuffed chair.

"I told you," it said in a malignant whisper. "She stole what was mine, so I killed them both. And now you're going to complete the circle."

The rope was around Colleen's throat before she could react. Her hands went to the tightening coil and pawed at it helplessly. She stared into the demented eyes of the Ghruamachd and knew this was the end. I'm going to die! Was this what Bridget had seen in her last moment of life? Impossible pain lanced through her head and her vision began to darken. Sorrow drowned out the roaring in her ears. Oh, Aidan, I'm so sorry.

Grace.

The creature whipped its head around, and the rope loosened just a little. Colleen pulled at it with weak fingers and felt it give a little more as her eyes followed the glare of the Ghruamachd.

Across the room stood a figure made of shadow. As Colleen watched, it grew more solid and took on the form of a small woman, brilliant blue eyes blazing in a paper white face. Slowly, the Grey Lady glided forward.

"You can't hurt me," the Ghruamachd said.

The ghost kept coming, until she stood only feet away from the one who had ended her life.

"You can do nothing to me," the Ghruamachd repeated, but its voice had lost some of its certainty. The specter advanced, blue eyes fixed on her adversary.

Grace, she said again. *It is done. You will not hurt this woman.*

The ghost began to grow, shadows swirling, until she towered over the thing that stood before her.

We took an oath. An oath to heal, to do no harm. You broke that oath, Grace. You are DAMNED.

The words thundered into the cavernous library. The rope dropped away from Colleen's neck and fell to the floor, but still the ghost advanced, forcing the Ghruamachd away from its victim and across the library. A shriek of impotent rage split the air and reverberated through the room. The Grey Lady now seemed to have more substance than the creature that cowered before her, and her righteous fury bound the thing and held it rigid.

Behind them, the door opened soundlessly. Aidan and Simon, with Constable Brodie and DI Douglas in tow, stood in the doorway, transfixed by the scene in front of them. They watched in shock as Balfinnan's cook backed toward the bookshelves, her face a mask of seething madness. Her body whipped back and forth grotesquely, as if a puppet master pulled invisible strings. The awful eyes roiled in her head, their light flashing and receding as the ghost of Bridget Halloran advanced on her like an avenging angel.

You will harm no one else, Grace. Be gone!

A keening howl came from the lips of the heaving figure. The light flared in the eyes, flickered, and was gone. The cook collapsed to her knees, sobbing, her brown eyes glazed and her face blank and uncomprehending. The two policemen crossed and cuffed her unresisting hands, and the woman was half-carried from the room, her wails trailing behind her all the way down the hall.

Aidan ran to Colleen and pulled her shaking body into his arms. She lifted her face to see his and he searched her eyes. What he saw there was enough—no words were needed. They closed their eyes and rocked each other in the silence of the room.

When they turned, Simon stood alone in the doorway, watching them. A look of grim satisfaction crossed his young face.

"It's gone."

CHAPTER 30

ONLY YOUR NAME

Two kilted Highlanders stood at the doorway to Balfinnan Castle, claymores raised to form an arch. They moved back to allow Colleen to enter, accompanied by Gordon MacNabb in his wheelchair. He was resplendent in his clan tartan, and the grin on his face warmed the cool May evening and chased the clouds away.

Colleen looked down at the white lace gown that hugged her figure and flowed into a wide trumpet skirt. Her hair was pinned up in cascading curls with pearl combs, and in her hand she held a bouquet of thistle, lavender and white roses.

A bagpiper stood in the entrance hall. The notes of *Amazing Grace* poured outside to greet the bride and her escort as they entered the ancient castle. Colleen grasped Gordon's wizened hand and he looked up at her with a toothless grin.

"Ur ye ready, lass?" he asked her.

She squeezed his hand. "I am."

The piper walked ahead of them into the Grand Ballroom and stood next to the altar, which had been erected at one end of the dance floor in the center of the cavernous space. The priest had given in with grace when told that the bride and groom wanted the residents of their care facility in attendance, although the sacrament would be consecrated later in the church.

Together, she and Gordon entered the ballroom, and everyone stood to greet them. They were a blur, all these guests. Had she really met that many people in eight short months? People who were here for her, a transplanted American girl? A lump formed in her throat.

And then she saw Aidan. He stood at the altar, his eyes misty, hands clasped together in front of him. The brass buttons of his Prince Charlie jacket and vest glinted in the fairy lights that had been strung throughout the room, the gleam of which caught in his dark curls. His clan tartan fit him as if he had been born to wear the uniform of his people. He was gorgeous.

The piper put blowpipe to lips again, and the "Wedding March" resonated through the air with all its power and beauty. Colleen felt tears welling in her eyes and willed them away. It was time.

She and Gordon proceeded up the aisle to the sound of the pipes, and when they reached the front, the old man gave her hand a last squeeze. She bent and kissed his forehead, grateful for his love and support, and looked at those arrayed in front of her. Aubrey and Liz, along with the matron of honor, Kate, grinned back at her. Aubrey was already crying, of course, and even Kate's eyes were damp. Across from them stood Finn, Jack, and a solemn Simon, all dressed in kilts and formal jackets.

Her eyes again found the man standing at the altar. Aidan, looking like a Highland warrior from ages past, stepped forward. His eyes locked on hers, and the rest of the room faded away as he took her hand in his. Together, they faced the priest. In a daze, Colleen repeated the words of the ancient Celtic vows, hearing the words flow over her tongue and out into the quiet ballroom.

From this day it shall be only your name I cry out in the night, and into your eyes that I smile each morning...I will cherish and honor you through this life and into the next.

Simon, as the best man, stepped forward and gave Aidan the rings, keeping his head down and his eyes averted. It might have been that look of sheer terror on the boy's face, but suddenly Colleen wasn't nervous anymore. She gazed into the grey eyes that she had come to love so well, and knew that everything in her life had led to this magical moment. She was Mrs. Aidan Shaw now, the wife of her soulmate. She had crossed an ocean, aligned with a ghost, confronted evil, and survived. She had fought the greatest battle of all against her own heart, and she had won.

"You may now kiss the bride."

She dimly heard the priest's voice, and then Aidan was bending his head to cover her lips in a soft caress. It wasn't like their first kiss—a quick peck on Nessie's walkway—nor did it have the passion of that kiss in Balfinnan's great library, when he had staked his claim and pledged her his protection. This was a promise, an assurance that he would give her everything in his heart, forever, and it was all she'd ever wanted or needed. She returned the kiss with a promise of her own, a soft answer that told him that it would be his name alone that she would cry out in the night, for the rest of her life.

They turned to their guests, and Colleen's eyes misted as she took in the tableau spread before her. Liz, Aubrey and Kate had done wonders with the rented tables and soft lighting that threw the ancient walls into relief and turned the old ballroom into a fantasy world. The familiar drone of pipes silenced the soft hum of conversation, and the piper stepped forward. He placed the pipe into his mouth, and as the timeless melody of "The Rowan Tree" poured forth, Aidan turned to his wife.

"Are you ready, lass?"

She smiled up at him, and together they walked back down the aisle to thunderous applause. As they made their way to the center of the dance floor, the piper gave way to the band, and the huge room was filled with the lilting notes of Ed Sheeran's beautiful ballad, "Perfect."

"You are, you know," he said, his smile like a beacon as he took her hand. "Perfect."

Colleen put her head on his shoulder and closed her eyes, swaying to the music. Funny—she'd never noticed before, but he was just the right height for her. Their bodies fit together as if the heavens had ordained it. Perfect, indeed.

It was like a fairy tale, but this was real life so of course not everything was magical. Aidan wasn't much of a dancer, but neither was she. The third time she stepped on his foot she could feel his body vibrating with laughter, but he only held her closer.

This was how it should be, she thought. Holding each other, clinging to the love and the humor between them as they would for the rest of their lives. Surely nothing they would face in their future could come close to the journey they'd taken to reach this moment, but it didn't matter. Whatever might come, they'd face it together.

The music ended. Other couples made their way to the dance floor as the band took over, and Colleen took Aidan's hand.

"Let's go make our rounds," she whispered.

Graham sat among his residents at a table of honor, looking happier than he'd been in months. This was where he belonged, with the people to whom he'd dedicated his life, in the place he loved best. He gave Colleen a peck on the cheek and shook Aidan's hand. His smile might have been somewhat strained, but it was genuine. He'd be all right.

Next to him sat Morag Murtaugh, dressed in a soft mauve lace dress. Colleen stared at her in awe. Without the black dress and fierce expression she looked distinguished and serene, but there was something else. Wait—she was *smiling*. Would wonders never cease?

Colleen smiled at Detective Inspector Douglas, seated across from Graham with Aubrey's favorite policeman, Chief Inspector Alan Brown.

"This place looks a lot different than I remember," Douglas told her. "I have to admit that five months ago

I would have sworn I'd never want to see it again, but you've changed my mind. You look lovely, Mrs. Shaw."

"Thanks. And don't feel bad—I'm still avoiding the library myself." She hesitated, reluctant to bring up the name that connected them on such a happy occasion. "How is Mrs. Morton?"

"She's being treated at New Craigs Psychiatric Hospital, but the doctors aren't hopeful. Hasn't said a word since she's been there—just stares straight ahead."

"She seemed so normal," said Colleen. "So nice to me when I first came here. She had my back when Mrs. Murtaugh got nasty, and gave me tea when I was down. And all that time she was killing people."

"A document was found in Mrs. Morton's pocket when they searched her," the inspector said. "It was a signed release of the castle from a Malcolm Beaton to one Duncan Anderson, in payment of a gambling debt." Douglas sighed. "Apparently her motive was simple revenge on the Anderson family."

Nothing simple about it, Colleen thought. She felt a surge of pity. Although the inspector didn't acknowledge it, Mrs. Morton had been a victim, too. Descendent of a cursed family, she had been possessed and manipulated by her own ancestor, driven to insanity by a murderess who refused to die.

Then she thought of those who had died at the cook's hand, and the pity dissolved. Maybe it was better if the woman's mind was gone. It would be hard to live with what she had done. Colleen shook herself out of her morbid thoughts, and she and Aidan moved on.

A small crowd was gathered around Aubrey and one-month-old Ewan Coinneach Angus Cameron, who gazed around with solemn eyes at all the people fawning over him. Finn stood behind his wife, looking as if he were the only man to father a child in the history of Scotland.

Watching the baby, Jack shared a secretive smile with his wife. The look did not get past Colleen, though. She studied her friend's face and her eyes narrowed. Then her face split into a grin. "Kate!" she gasped. "Are you...?"

Her best friend widened her eyes in a look of innocence. She shrugged.

"Well, it's pretty early, but I think there's another cranky Scot in my future," she said. Jack rolled his eyes and bent to kiss his wife before pouring another whisky and downing it dramatically.

Colleen and Aidan reluctantly pulled themselves away from the celebration and worked their way over to where Angus and Nessie were seated with Alastair MacGregor, Archie Fergusson, and the Owls.

It was little surprise that conversation at that table resembled the tower of Babel, with Gladys's crisp English tones competing with the incomprehensible Scots dialect and occasional French exclamation, all hurled back and forth with reckless abandon. The aroma of Yardley's English Lavender was palpable with both of its devotees at the same table.

Colleen grinned. "Are you all having fun?" she asked.

"Och, aye, lass. It's a reit braw ceilidh yoo've pit oan." Angus nodded approvingly.

Maxine toyed with a bite of salad and stared wistfully out at the dancers.

"I was once quite a sight on the dance floor," Gladys put in from across the table. Beside her, Ronald rolled his eyes and grinned.

"Ah jist bit ye waur," muttered Old Harry. Without his newspaper, the words came through clearly.

Gladys ignored him. "I don't think I'd want to try it now, mind you, but this lovely party brings back such memories." She patted Colleen's hand.

Maxine sighed.

"Would you like to dance, Maxine?" Aidan, alert as always, held out his hand. Tears rose in the Frenchwoman's beautiful dark eyes. She placed her hand in his and the two went off to the dance floor.

"I don't think Aidan's dancing is anything Maxine is used to," Colleen murmured. "But I doubt she'll mind."

They returned after the song ended and Aidan kissed Maxine's hand as he handed her into her chair. She blushed and turned to the others.

"Our Aidan is *such* a good dancer," she announced. "I felt as if I were once again on the stage in Paris."

"I was petrified!" Aidan confessed to Colleen as they walked away. "She took the lead, and once I could have sworn she was going to lift me over her head. That woman is strong!"

"You made her happy," Colleen said. "It was worth watching your terrified face."

"Colleen!" An American accent called out. "Bring that new husband of yours over here!"

They moved to the table where her parents sat

with Liz and Flora. Two of the remaining seats were occupied by a middle-aged couple who looked somewhat familiar, although Colleen didn't think she had ever seen them before.

"These are your cousins from Dublin," her mother said. "We stopped on the way over for a visit and brought them with us. Thought you should know your family on this side of the pond. Moira's a nurse, like you."

The petite, auburn-haired woman extended her hand and smiled. "Moira Donovan," she said, her voice a musical lilt. "I'm a second cousin on your father's side."

"I'm Patrick," the man next to her added. "You're quite the beautiful bride—I see the family resemblance."

Ahh, Colleen thought. That was it. A lot of Irish people had red hair and blue eyes, but if Moira were twenty years younger, they could have passed for sisters.

"All the Hallorans seem to inherit the red hair and curls," Moira told her. She winked. "You come from good stock."

Aidan's hand stilled in Colleen's. He was staring at Moira. "Halloran?" he asked softly.

"Yes," Moira said. "My maiden name. We have lots of famous redheads in our family, and a lot of doctors and nurses. In fact, there was a nurse about a hundred years ago who worked somewhere up here in the Highlands during the Great War." She narrowed her blue eyes and thought for a moment.

"There was some sort of tragedy and she died

over here. Don't remember her name—nobody talks much about her."

Eventually, the cake was cut, the bouquet thrown, the toasts made. But Colleen's attention kept returning to what her Irish cousin had said.

"Do you think it's possible?" she asked Aidan when they found a moment to themselves.

"Would explain a lot," he said. "Why she was watching over you, why she saved you more than once." He hugged her. "And I, for one, am very grateful you have such caring relatives."

People began saying their goodbyes, and most of the residents had long since retired upstairs when Colleen made her way once again to her favorite table. Angus and Nessie were deep in conversation, heads close together, and Alastair seemed to be engaged in a friendly argument with Archie about the medicinal uses of thistle. The remaining four places were empty.

"Where did the Owls go?" Colleen asked Nessie. "They didn't leave without saying goodbye, did they?"

Nessie looked at her, her little bird eyes unblinking. "They're gone, lass," she said, her voice expressionless. "They told me to tell you how much they enjoyed your wedding, and that it was all worth it."

Colleen stared at her. She glanced at Angus, who turned to look at her with his inscrutable eyes. Her own eyes went again to the four place settings. Clean napkins folded in a floral pattern inside dry goblets, silver and plates ready for guests. Almost as though no one had ever sat there.

"But didn't they come with you?" Colleen felt a

niggling feeling of disappointment. "How did they leave? Where did they go?"

"I'm sorry, lass," Nessie said. "They said their job was done. It was time for them to go."

SCOTLAND, PRESENT DAY

Why was she still here?

The faint sound of bagpipes filtered up from the grand ballroom and into an abandoned room on the third floor. Apart from the pipes, there was no other sound. Nothing moved in the darkened corners of Balfinnan House or scurried along its passageways. Nothing living disturbed the solitude.

The Grey Lady stared at the place where a rope had once hung—the rope that ended her life. Hundreds of years? Yesterday? It didn't matter how much time had passed. Truthfully, she might have been dead before that night, though she walked among the living for a while longer.

Grace had done her a favor, she'd thought once. The vile rope had hastened her toward Alexander, toward the reunion she longed for. She and Alex were good people, had lived purposeful lives, and they would be together again—everything in her catechism told her so. Except she'd been wrong.

He was gone, and she could not follow. After a while, she thought she understood why. She had forgotten how precious life was. Wishing for death was forbidden. It was akin to suicide, and as such was a sin. It required atonement, a sacrifice. If only she knew what that could be.

For years the castle lay empty while the being that had once been Bridget Halloran waited. And then one day, life came back to Balfinnan. The castle was opened up and people walked its corridors once more. People like she had been: healers. Another Anderson sat in the office where Duncan had once held sway. Other patients lay in the beds—not injured soldiers, but those who had nearly reached the end of their lives.

Bridget found that she liked the old people, and also that she was shamed by them. Fighters, they were, women who still put makeup on faces so wrinkled that they absorbed it like sand. Men who dressed proudly in their clan tartans every morning to face another day of pain and loneliness.

They had so much courage, these people, so much pride—whereas she had none. They had suffered loss in their long lives. They had watched loved ones go before them, but they had not given in to grief as she had. They had not wished for death. And she began to see that what she had done was indeed a sin, and her fate a just penance.

She visited the old people, watched over them at night. Bridget had been created a healer and death could not steal her soul's yearning to give solace. She watched them, and when time and illness became overwhelming she stood with them at the end, touched their pallid faces gently, and helped them to go on to the place she was not permitted to enter. It seemed as though they felt her touch, though she knew it was impossible.

One day she realized that she was not alone. There was an emanation she couldn't identify, a spirit so canny that she never saw it. But she felt its wrath and its corruption, and she recognized it for what it was. Grace had returned to Balfinnan, and with her came a darkness that cloaked the halls with melancholy and unmitigated hatred.

Why? Grace had disappeared, unpunished for her crimes so many years ago. But Bridget had no illusions about the evil that had come to haunt the castle. It was pervasive and all-consuming—and this time it was not directed at her.

On a cool morning, Bridget felt something stirring in the atmosphere. Alive and vibrant, a new nurse swept into the halls of Balfinnan House and claimed them for her own. She was a healer, as Bridget had been, and her hair was the same fire-touched red. She was tiny yet strong, and compassion flowed from her very being. Bridget felt a strange kinship with her. She knew, with that extra-sensory intuition that only the dead possess, that she must keep this woman safe from Grace.

And she had done so. She had kept watch, warned, and protected the young nurse from harm. And five months ago, on a cold night in December when the wind outside howled like the hounds from hell, she had faced Grace again and defeated her.

Yet still she was here. Months passed, and she knew now that she would never leave this place.

She had done what she could, and her penance had been rejected. She was doomed to wander the halls of Balfinnan House for eternity.

"Bridie."

Pain lanced through her and she closed her eyes against the sound. Was it not enough that she be left here, never to see him again? Did she have to be taunted by the memory of his voice? Surely this was too much!

"Bridie. I'm here."

Bridget opened her eyes and found herself staring at the impossible. Alexander stood before her, his blue eyes radiating the passion she remembered so well. He stepped forward, reached out his hand...and touched her! His fingers caressed her face, trailed across lips that had felt nothing for a hundred years. She closed her eyes again and stood still, afraid to disturb the illusion. If this was more punishment, the powers had miscalculated. This tiny glimpse of heaven would sustain her for centuries to come. Tears rolled down her cheeks and she leaned into the warm hand.

"It's time, love. I've come for you."

Bridget's eyes snapped open. He was still there, smiling at her with all the love in the universe. He was real. "How—?

"You fulfilled your task, Bridie. You saved a living being from the fate that befell you after I died. I've been waiting for you."

"How are you here? Why could you not come before?"

"I wasn't allowed, darling. I wouldn't be here now, but for the Guides. I appealed to them, and they let me come with them to fetch you." His smile was radiant. "I was very persuasive."

"Guides?"

"There are those whose task it is to bridge the worlds of the living and the dead, and to help new spirits on their way. The Guides are revered in the next world, and very important. There is no passage after death unless they determine it."

"Where are they?" Bridget asked. "Why can't I see them?"

"Look." His voice was soft, reverent. "They're waiting for us."

At the end of the hall, Bridget could just make out the faint outlines of four figures standing in the gloom. Alexander took her hand and led her toward them. At the last minute, she stopped and turned to him.

"But why did they wait so long? My task was fulfilled months ago—why didn't they come then?"

He leaned down and kissed her, his lips soft on her own.

"The Guides have their reasons, Bridie. It is not for us to know why they do what they do." He took her hand again. "But I did hear them talking, and it seems they wanted to stay for a wedding."

ABOUT THE AUTHOR

M MacKinnon has always been a writer. When she was eight, she wrote a story called "Princess Zelda," a plagiarized mixture of Moses and Cinderella, and begged her mother for weeks to take it to the local library and get them to publish it. A gentle refusal to do so, while seen as a betrayal of the highest order, did not stop MacKinnon from continuing her writing. She has since learned that there are a few more steps between pencil copy and library.

M MacKinnon writes emotions. Love, hate, fear, redemption, second chances. Her writing is primarily paranormal romance with modern mystery thrown in for spice, and a little horror to stir the senses. And humor. Always humor.

MacKinnon lives in New Jersey with her husband. One month each year is spent in the Scottish Highlands, her happy place and the source of her inspiration.

Learn more about MacKinnon on her website: www.mmackinnonwriter.com.

Or, connect with her on social media:

Facebook: www.facebook.com/M-MacKinnon-539689769771150/?modal=admin_todo_tour

Twitter: www.twitter.com/MMacKinnon8

Instagram:
www.instagram.com/mmackinnon_author

If you've enjoyed The Healer's Legacy, please consider giving it some visibility by reviewing it on Amazon or Goodreads. A review doesn't have to be a long critical essay. Just a few words expressing your thoughts, which could help potential readers decide whether they would enjoy it, too.